More praise for

The Latte Rebellion

"Get ready to start your own rebellion after gulping down Sarah Stevenson's deftly written, multi-layered story about growing a voice, growing apart, and most of all, growing up girl."

—Justina Chen Headley,
author of *North of Beautiful*

The Latte Rebellion

The Latte Rebellion

Sarah Jamila Stevenson

SCHOLASTIC INC.
New York Toronto London Auckland
Sydney Mexico City New Delhi Hong Kong

ISBN 978-0-545-39827-5

12 11 10 9 8 7 6 5 4 3 2 1   11 12 13 14 15 16/0

Printed in the U.S.A.   40

First Scholastic printing, September 2011

Cover design by Lisa Novak
Cover images: napkin © iStockphoto.com/Maureen Perez;
coffee cup © Jonathan Kantor/Digital Vision/PunchStock
Interior illustrations on pages 117, 154, and 199 by Sarah Jamila Stevenson

Prologue

The jeering male voice came from somewhere behind me, waking me up from a heatstroke-induced doze.

"Hey, check it out—Asha's a towel-head."

I'm a WHAT? My neck got even warmer, and not just because it was sweltering at Ashmont Community Park.

Whoever it was, was he kidding me? Nobody used that phrase anymore unless they were hopelessly ignorant about headwear, or still carrying around a post-9/11 grudge. I knew I really should be offended.

Mostly, though, I couldn't believe what I was hearing. Even if I did have a towel on my head.

From the gasps and nervous whispers around me, I wasn't the only one in shock. I lifted a corner of terrycloth off my sweaty face—I was tanning my legs—just in time to see a furious Carey dump her cup of iced coffee all over

Roger Yee's smirking face. Light-brown latte dripped in rivulets from his now lank and soaking black hair, down his pretentious A&F T-shirt, and onto his swim trunks. The smirk dripped away with it.

One of Roger's lackeys from the Asian American Club, looking up from a nearby umbrella table, saw Roger's sorry, bedraggled self and snorted cola out of his nose, starting a ripple of laughter that drifted around the pool area and then died as people noticed the confrontation.

Roger had probably just been trying to make a stupid joke, but I didn't like his tone. It rubbed me the wrong way. And, knowing him, he'd probably said something obscene to Carey while I was snoozing away obliviously.

Now, he stood stock-still and dripping as Carey hissed, "Don't you *ever* use that word, buttmunch. I don't call *you* Fu Manchu."

"Well, you're half-Chinese," he retorted. "Anyway, I wasn't talking to you, *Wong*. I was talking to Miss Barely Asian over there." He used a corner of his shirt to wipe the coffee off his face and neck.

I sat up with a martyred sigh. I didn't want to be part of this conversation, but I was involved whether I liked it or not. "Look, *Yee*, last I checked, South Asia was definitely part of Asia. It's in the *name*. South *Asia*." I pointed to my head. "And it's not a towel. Learn some useful vocabulary words, like turban. Which nobody in my family wears, incidentally."

"Whatever," Roger said, waving a hand at me dismissively. "You're only a quarter or a half or something, anyway. And you had a *towel* on your *head,* okay?"

"What does it matter? It's still racist. And it's not like Asha insulted you," Carey pointed out. "What's your problem?"

They locked eyes for a moment, glaring at each other. Roger Yee had been our nemesis ever since he'd perpetrated the Backpack-Snatching-and-Dumping Incident of '06, which we followed rather unwisely with the Toilet Paper Revenge Caper of '07. He wasn't my favorite person, but racial epithets were stooping a bit low even for him. I mean, this was Northern California. We were supposed to be past all that.

A handful of other seniors started to drift over from around the patio like melodrama-sniffing dogs, eager for a scene. And Roger was no stranger to a good argument. He'd verbally clobbered three hapless rivals to become our student-body secretary, which made him responsible for this stupid Inter-Club Council pool party in the first place. But if it came down to it, my money was on Carey. She had that look in her eye, the ice-cold, do-not-screw-around-with-me look that she only got when she was really angry—or about to nail someone on the opposing soccer team with her cleats.

After a minute, Roger dropped his gaze and stalked off. As he brushed past Carey's lounge chair, I heard him mutter, "It was just a joke, you snooty bitch."

I bolted to my feet, the controversy-inspiring towel falling to the ground, innocuous and stripey. "You do *not* talk

3

to my friends like that," I shouted after him, but it was too late. He was gone, slamming the iron gate to the pool area with a loud clang as he left, leaving Carey glowering and redder than I'd ever seen her, and me torn between wanting to scream and wishing I'd decided to stay home.

And that's how it all started.

The Inter-Club Council annual pool party.

Unfortunately, that's not how it ended. Not by a long shot.

———

The following April:
Ashmont Unified School District Board Room

"Ladies and gentlemen." The disciplinary hearing officer cleared his throat wetly, the sound reverberating into the microphone and around the room. I didn't want to look at him, with his graying comb-over and his accusatory unibrow, so I looked down at my lap, shifting in the hard wooden chair. The murmur of voices temporarily rose, then fell. I heard a few clicks of the camera shutter from the newspaper reporter in the back row.

I'd been the one to request an open hearing—I had a right to, according to California Education Code—but I still couldn't believe how many people showed up. The room, which normally seated about fifty people, was full. Standing room only.

"Ladies and gentlemen," the presiding officer continued stiffly, "representatives of the Ashmont Board of Education, and"—I could feel him glaring in my direction—"members of the *public*, this open disciplinary hearing to consider the expulsion of Ms. Asha Jamison from University Park High School is now in session."

Exhibit A.1:
MATERIALS VIOLATING
BOARD POLICY SECTION 418.III.K

The Latte Rebellion Manifesto

If you are reading this, you are clearly sympathetic to the cause!

What cause, you ask?

The cause of brown people everywhere—

whether you have espresso-colored hair,

a perfect latte tan, or you're as light as a mocha bianca!

The world must acknowledge you!

The world will appreciate you!

Our philosophy is simple:

Promote a latte-colored world!

Forget bananas and coconuts!

Go for the seamless blend! You can't un-latte the latte!

It doesn't matter if you're only coffee on the inside.

If you're a latte at heart, you are welcome.

Iced or hot, raise your cup to the cause!

Lattes of the World, Unite!

1

Summer vacation, so far, was an epic failure. A truly monumental waste. Hot, interminable days that melted one into the next. The monotony of lying around baking in the heat broken only by the further monotony of work. Money we weren't allowed to spend (because it went straight into the college fund), earned at retail jobs we yearned to quit (because they were embarrassingly menial, excruciatingly boring, and swarming with mallrats, half of whom went to our school).

Then there was the unfortunate confrontation at the Inter-Club Council pool party.

That was what planted the seeds of the Latte Rebellion. But when I really sit down to think about it, it started a hell of a lot earlier than that.

Take this incident that happened a couple of weeks

before, at the end of junior year: Carey and I were crammed into the auditorium bathroom before graduation, touching up our hair and makeup along with the other top-ranked juniors who got to march in the Honor Guard. Kaelyn Vander Sar—who had blossomed from mildly catty to full-blown bitch on wheels after we started high school—said, "Oh, Carey, you look so *cute* in that white dress. Like a little Japanese cartoon character."

Kaelyn turned to me, blotting her shell-pink lipstick with a tissue. "And *your* dress—wow. It takes some guts to wear something like that. I guess you have to have Mexican J.Lo curves to pull it off."

I stared at her, one hand going reflexively to my hip, where I'd just tied a gauzy scarf that *I* thought was not only sassy but also accented my waist. Evidently all it did was draw attention to my butt.

The heat rose behind my cheeks, my head filling with any number of things I could tell her. *Carey is NOT Japanese. And J.Lo is not from Mexico—she's a Puerto Rican American. That is not even CLOSE to the same thing. There are these things called maps; you should look at one.* And, *am I dreaming or did you just say my butt was big?*

But in the end, I didn't say any of it. It seemed futile. Kaelyn just didn't get it. Maybe she really did think she was paying us a compliment. Or worse, she could have been deliberately trying to provoke us. We weren't exactly the best of friends, after all.

Anyway, because she had to bring up J.Lo, I obsessed about my round butt, round shoulders, and round face the whole time I was standing out there in front of the school, and Carey stood there in stony silence, convinced that being five feet tall made her a midget and pissed at *me* for not setting Kaelyn straight. It was a bad situation. But it wasn't an isolated incident, not by a long shot. It was just one of many. And they all seemed to culminate in that scene at the pool party, the summer before our senior year.

———

After Roger Yee stalked out of the party, everyone heard the squeal of tires and the growling engine as he pulled out of the parking lot in his rich-boy, tricked-out Honda. Carey and I looked at each other. She walked the few feet across to my lounge chair and sat down next to me as the small crowd dissipated, already distracted by someone else's gossip-inducing faux pas.

"Are you thinking what I'm thinking?" I said, laying my head on her shoulder. She smelled like chlorine and the vanilla-scented lotion I gave her for her birthday last year.

"Yeah," Carey grumbled. "Waste of a perfectly good latte."

"Besides that," I said, "I was thinking it's too hot out for this kind of behavior. And I was thinking I'm glad you're here. Who else would defend me by flinging refreshing beverages? Who else would care enough? I mean, *I* barely care."

"You *should* care." Carey frowned, absentmindedly finger-combing her short, light-brown hair, still damp and wavy from our dip in the pool. "It's serious. Roger shouldn't say that kind of crap. And the way he was leering at me. It was gross." She shuddered, delicately.

"I know. It was uncalled-for." I gave her an exaggerated smooch on the cheek, then leaned back. "He's an ass. It makes me want to buy a billboard and stick it up in his yard. A billboard with little pictograms: *Turban does not equal towel. U equals ass.*"

She laughed, a short bark. "Or a stone tablet carved with *Thou shalt not be a massive jerkwad.*"

"Exactly," I said. "I mean, you're the one always telling me I need to express my anger more effectively. I think we could channel our entire scholastic career's worth of annoyance at Roger into one well-placed piece of signage."

Carey sighed. "As if we could afford something like that. My parents would not be thrilled if we spent our work money on a billboard. Plus, unlike you, I have to share a college fund with my brothers. I probably need to get a second job."

"Oh, come on—I think it would be a worthwhile expenditure for such a quality human being as Roger Yee," I said, unable to hide a smile.

"He is so not worth the time and effort." She frowned at her empty cup. "Let's get refills, shall we?"

We picked up our cups and headed back to the drinks table for more iced latte, making our way past the Art Club officers, who had set up camp conveniently near the caffeine supply.

"At least the coffee here is free," I said, waving at our

friend Miranda Levin, who was VP of the Art Club. "We don't have to shell out for our latte habit."

Carey snorted. "It's the only good thing about this clique-fest, besides the pool. I mean, there's Miranda, and Shay's nice enough for a cheer clone, but look at these people. Look at Kaelyn Vander Sar."

"...Vanderslut," I fake-sneezed, trying to make her laugh.

"Asha. God. You're as bad as Roger," she said, swatting me on the arm. "Is name-calling really necessary?"

"Sorry, sorry," I said. "Please continue."

"Anyway, as I was *saying*. Check out the Queen of the Bimbocracy and her fleet of loyal toadies." She pointed surreptitiously at the bikini squad on the other side of the pool, now featuring one less fawning beefcake since Roger's departure.

"Now who's name-calling?" I set our clear plastic cups on the table and topped them both off with fresh iced coffee.

Carey smiled wryly at me. "She only wishes she had 'Mexican J.Lo curves.'"

I studied her face for a moment. "You're really bothered about this, aren't you? You know, we really *could* do something with our cash. It's our money."

"Yeah, here's an idea," Carey said, a little sarcastically. "We could print instructive T-shirts that say, *No, I am not Mexican. Neither is J.Lo. Thanks for asking.*"

"Ha ha. I can think of way better things to spend money on," I said. "We could pay for enough gas to drive to some little beach town where there are a ton of cute eligible guys who are all rich Internet millionaires. Who needs college?"

"You," Carey said. "Me. So we can get the hell out of here and away from Roger. That's what we should be spending our money on."

I reached for the pitcher of half-melted ice cubes and dropped a few more into my cup. As I watched the smooth, tan liquid rise up the sides of the glass, wishing we could just leave and forget about senior year, something clicked in my brain.

"Or," I said, "we could do something *really* fun." I stood up straighter. I'd just felt the stirrings of an idea, one I suspected might be the most brilliant plan I'd ever had in my life. Goodbye, Summer of Epic Hellish Boredom.

Hello, Latte Rebellion.

"Does your bright idea happen to involve coffee?" Carey said, as we gathered our stuff and got ready to ditch this overrated hot dog stand.

"Oh, does it ever." I couldn't help grinning from ear to ear. "Now, take this latte we've been drinking. What does 'latte' mean to you?"

Carey started laughing, and laughed all the way to the car before she was able to get a grip. "Are you listening to yourself? I mean, did you actually hear what you just said?"

"No, wait," I insisted, unlocking the car doors. "Think about it. Latte. It's two things. Coffee mixed with milk. Sometimes with cinnamon on top. Just like us. We're living, breathing lattes."

"Okay, now you've lost me," Carey said, looking at me skeptically over the top of her sunglasses.

"I'm serious," I said. "You're half-Chinese and half-European. Caucasian. Whatever. I'm half-Indian, a quarter Mexican, and a quarter Irish. We're mixed up. We're not really one or the other, ethnically. We're like *human lattes*."

"Oh, killer simile. Brav-*o*," Carey said as we pulled away from the curb and headed down the palm-tree-lined street next to the pool. "A-plus. Save that for the AP English exam."

"Perfectly blended, comes in all shades," I said, smiling mischievously.

"*Please*. No more metaphors." Carey curled up on the passenger seat, her feet under her. "Not that those ignorant mall junkies even know what a metaphor *is*."

"Yeah," I said, fervently, "and that's why I agree with you about getting the hell out of here. Beach town, Disneyland, whatever. Something. College isn't soon enough. We need a change of scenery."

"No kidding." She left a maddeningly long pause, then sighed. "So let me guess. Your ingenious plan involves a vacation."

"A post-graduation outing. If you ask me, *that's* what we need." I thumped the steering wheel for emphasis.

"Okay," Carey said. "Maybe. You might be winning me over. But the latte thing. What does that have to do with anything? Are we funding this trip with coffee sales?"

"I don't know yet. Maybe. But the latte should be like

our totem. Our good-luck charm. Our symbol of liberation." I glanced at her out of the corner of my eye.

"Who even needs a symbol?" she said, half-closing her eyes. "Let's just go somewhere with cute, brainy, ambitious college guys, please. And good food."

As we continued discussing it, it seemed only fair. We'd been working our butts off. Tutoring every Saturday all last year; Key Club, Mock Trial, and Honor Society since we were freshmen, which was why we'd been at that stupid pool party in the first place; and straight A grades, if you counted the occasional A-minus. We deserved a vacation. Something low-commitment and high-relaxation, like a cruise to Mexico, which would be downright easy to organize. Easy as pie—or a pumpkin-pie-flavored latte.

And we started to take the latte idea even further. That evening, we were lying on Carey's back patio when she asked with mock seriousness, "What does latte mean to *you*, Asha? What ... does it mean ... to *YOU*?"

I laughed and said, "It means the ultimate coffee beverage! Not just coffee, not just milk. More than the sum of its parts." I sat up in my lounge chair. "A new beverage for the future!"

"Through blending, it becomes better! Stronger!" Carey added. "More latte-licious."

"That's it," I exclaimed, suddenly not laughing anymore. "That is *genius*!"

"Um ... what's genius?" Carey was looking at me like I'd grown an ear out of my forehead.

"That's our *marketing angle*," I explained impatiently.

I was thinking too fast for the words to even make it out of my mouth. "For raising the money. The latte can be more than just a good-luck charm. It's our whole *brand*." I paused and waited for Carey to switch gears.

She shook her head, a little manically. "And we're marketing . . . what, exactly?"

"It doesn't matter. We could be selling dog collars or lip gloss or . . . *whatever*. But we could appeal to mixed-race buyers and call it—the Latte Girls, or something."

"The Latte Girls sounds so Baby-Sitters Club," Carey said, rolling her eyes. "But I see what you're saying."

"Of course you do," I said. It was so simple, it was downright brilliant. And it all fit together like it was meant to be.

Clearly, though, we had to do a bit more thinking. So far, all we had was a half-formed idea floating around in our heads about "latte as a concept" (big surprise, considering how much of it we were drinking), and how we could use that concept to raise money for our trip without relying on something totally overdone, like opening yet another coffee stand in a town full of cafés. The market for actual lattes was already saturated. Plus, who really wanted to sweat over an espresso machine all day?

That was where the really inspired part of the plan came in. Thinking of the pool-party incident and our conversation afterward, it came to me like a flash: we could sell T-shirts. Everybody liked T-shirts, especially people at our school, who seemed to buy every school- and sports-related T-shirt known to man. All we had to do was come up with a catchy design. We already had the killer market-ing idea. And we had the rest of the summer to work on the details.

———————

Enter the Latte Rebellion Master Plan. By the time school started in September, we'd written the Latte Rebellion Mani-festo and started designing a logo and website with the help of Miranda, our art guru. Carey, our tech whiz, got the site up and running on October 1st, complete with links to our virtual shop on NetPress. The logo we'd thought up was plastered across the top of the website: a coffee cup with steam forming the shape of a hammer and sickle.

Controversial, maybe, but definitely eye-catching. No doubt about it. We even came up with mysterious alter egos to mastermind the endeavor. I thought this made us appealingly enigmatic; Carey was just happy we were stay-ing relatively anonymous in case the whole plan crashed and burned.

"You really think people will come to the website? Maybe we're the only ones who think this is so brilliant and funny. As usual." Carey hitched her backpack higher on her shoulder as she looked back at one of the photo-copied posters we'd put up on the student activities bul-letin boards early this morning: *Think Latte*, with our logo and web address.

"Don't worry," I said, trying to sound reassuring. "This isn't like the time we petitioned to change the school mascot to a bagpipe player." Our current mascot was a decidedly non-politically-correct brawling Scotsman. "*That* was doomed to fail. This is a great idea. Plus... you know, it's supposed to be fun. Don't stress."

"Don't stress? Have you put *any* forethought into this?" She glared at me.

"It's going to work out fine," I told her. "Even if we only make half of what we're aiming for, we'll still be able to afford some kind of vacation." I grinned, draping one arm over her shoulders. "Don't think of it as a business, if that's what's stressing you out. Think of it as... a sociological experiment. Or a personal rebellion. A rebellion against mind-numbing boredom."

We pushed past oafish Lou Pratt, star running back for the University Park Fightin' Highlanders. As usual, he was taking up half the hallway, waving his beefy, sweaty arms all over the place, and he didn't even care. He even muttered something about "shrimpy Asians" as we walked off into the noisy crowd.

"And a rebellion against people like *that*," Carey muttered under her breath.

"No kidding." I rolled my eyes. "Anyway, all we have to do is the publicity. NetPress will print and send the shirts, and we'll reap the benefits." The light-brown T-shirt would have our logo on the front, printed in dark brown, with the words "Latte Rebellion" in fake stencil lettering. Our website URL would be on the back.

Carey said I was getting ahead of myself. "We still have the whole year to get through first," she grumbled.

"Fine, Buzzkill McGee," I said. "All I'm saying is, using NetPress is going to be great. It's like free labor. We don't have to do anything except make our cut of the profits."

"Speaking of free labor," Carey said ominously, "it took me forever to put that website together. And Miranda worked really hard, too. This had better work."

We stopped outside Mr. Martinez's room, where I had AP Calculus. "I promise it'll be worth it," I said. "Shake on it?"

We both stuck out our tongues at each other. Then we put out our hands and wiggled our fingers together like we were playing "Chopsticks" on an imaginary piano, followed by putting our hands together over our heads and doing an Indian-style back-and-forth head motion. Then I went for a high five and accidentally hit her in the head because she thought it was the part where we shake hands. We broke out in shameless hysterics, which earned us some weird looks that I valiantly tried to ignore.

We'd developed our secret handshake in sixth grade after being the only two new kids in our class, and now it was a tradition. I'd asked Carey over to my house that first week of school, and it turned out we both had protective parents, a secret and embarrassing love of old teen movies like *The Breakfast Club* and *Dazed and Confused*, and weekly cravings for pineapple pizza. We also both had a silly streak, and we spent at least a month refining our handshake. It was our first "master plan" in a way . . . but obviously not our last.

Still blushing, Carey rushed off to Physics. I walked into the math room, sat down at my desk, and pulled my homework out of my folder. While I waited for Mr. Martinez to come around and check it off in his grade book, I surreptitiously flipped to the back of my spiral notebook and took another look at the Latte Rebellion Master Plan. It was really quite simple.

Latte Rebellion Master Plan

1. Sign up for website (Carey) and put up Latte Rebellion Manifesto (Asha).
2. Design logo and T-shirt (Asha and Miranda).
3. Set up T-shirt ordering on NetPress (Carey).
4. Put up signs around school.
5. Kick the marketing up a notch.
6. Sell a ton of shirts.
7. Cancun (or Seattle, or New York City, or...), here we come!

We'd already done numbers 1 through 4. We needed to sit down and figure out how many shirts we'd need to sell in order to make it to Mexico or wherever, but the budget wouldn't be a problem. After all, I was in Calculus... as Mr. Martinez so painfully reminded me by putting a red check mark on #4 of my homework.

"Look at that one again," he said. "I think you missed a step."

Okay. So I'd have Carey double-check our budget with me.

When we first wrote the manifesto back in August, we'd been sitting at a sticky food-court table at the mall during our lunch break from Bathworks (me) and Book Planet (Carey), screaming with hilarity at the line "Lattes of the World, Unite." David Castro and his skater friends, who were sitting at the next table, kept staring at us like we'd ingested tainted Orange Julius.

Poor unsuspecting David.

A few days after putting up the Rebellion posters, we dropped four flyers in his locker, one for him and each of his pot-smoking burnout friends, slipping them in through the vents in the locker door half an hour before school started. Then we canvassed the locker areas for people we might have missed, watching who went to which lockers in which buildings, so that we could do an after-school guerrilla flyer-drop targeting the lockers of potential Sympathizers. Mostly we looked for anybody who seemed ethnically ambiguous, whether their skin was the lightest tan or the darkest brown. This made Carey nervous.

"Don't you think we're guilty of racial profiling?" She frowned at me, arms crossed, as I grabbed my French-English dictionary and closed my locker. "I mean, somebody else might want to buy the shirts. Or support the appreciation of brown people. Maybe we should just leave flyers for everyone."

"Anybody can buy the shirts," I pointed out. "The posters are up all over campus. This is just targeted marketing. You have to admit, somebody with an interest in the promotion of brown people would be a lot more likely to buy the shirt."

"*Or* people who like lattes," she added, ever practical. "I've been thinking we should really work the coffee angle."

I stopped. Carey walked a few steps before realizing I wasn't next to her.

"What?" she said.

"That is a *great* idea, Care," I said, my voice a little loud with excitement. "We should go to all the cool cafés and ask to put a flyer on their bulletin boards. This shirt would *totally* appeal to a coffeehouse crowd. Don't you think?" I linked arms with her and we continued walking down the hall to fifth-period French. "I'll be on the U-NorCal campus next Friday with my cousin Bridget for that crazy activist club she told me about," I continued. "She says it's just like Key Club, but I seriously doubt it. Anyway, I'll ask if she can put up posters there."

"Okay. I'll make it item 4-A on the Master Plan." Carey sounded happier.

"Perfect." Things were looking up. All we had to do was drive around town and put the posters up. Easy as . . . well, you know.

———

That weekend, I sat with Carey at the kitchen table, sun streaming in through my mom's stained-glass window hanging and throwing purples and greens on our budget worksheet. When I say "budget worksheet," I should point out that we were pretty low-tech—it was basically just a printed-out chart and some calculations scribbled on a piece of paper.

"So," Carey said, pointing at the spreadsheet, "once we subtract the NetPress service charge, we're making a profit of six dollars per shirt, if we keep the price at twenty." She looked up at me. "That's not a lot. How many shirts did you plan on selling?"

I frowned. We were originally hoping to make at least ten dollars a shirt, but we didn't want to charge a ton of money, either, or nobody would buy them. I thought for a minute, then scribbled down some more calculations of my own.

"Okay," I said, "according to the travel website, we can do a seven-day Mexico cruise for $400 each. A week in Seattle would be $465 each if we stay in a hostel. So . . . let's split the difference and say we need to make $1300. That'll be enough for the three of us, Miranda included."

"So at six bucks profit per shirt," Carey said, "we'd need to sell more than two hundred."

We both sat there. How could we sell two hundred shirts? Before we were faced with the actual numbers, it had sounded like such a great idea. Now it seemed impossible. Two hundred shirts—it would be like selling one to every member of the senior class. Ludicrous, to say the least. I imagined Lou Pratt in a Latte Rebellion T-shirt, his huge stomach stretching out the front, and snorted.

"It isn't *funny*," Carey complained. "This is a serious

problem." She looked down at our scratch paper, doodling an angry face with a thought balloon full of calculations.

"I know; I'm sorry. I was just..." What if she decided *not* to do this? I didn't want to do it alone. And taking our vacation alone would not only be pointless, it would be downright sad. "Well...okay. Let's make a list. An addendum to the Master Plan. Remember anything from our Econ class last year?"

"No," Carey said. "Are you kidding? Hands down, my least favorite class ever."

There was a long pause. Then the irony hit and we both started laughing hysterically, me almost giving myself a coffee noser and Carey getting hiccups.

I heard my dad in the next room mumble something cranky-sounding, and a few seconds later, my mom poked her head around the door jamb from the living room. "Everyone okay here?"

I was still coughing and laughing and she broke into a smile herself, the corners of her dark eyes crinkling as she watched us try to get ahold of ourselves.

"Your father said, 'It doesn't sound like they're studying in there,'" she said, artificially lowering her voice to imitate his Stern Dad tone.

"We're taking a study break," Carey said, grinning at me.

"We're fine," I managed to rasp, which started us laughing all over again.

"I'll take your word for it, but keep it down, okay? Dad's working on that new account with the office chair supplier. You know how he gets." My mom rolled her eyes and left us to our temporary insanity.

I was relieved she hadn't done more than peek in. It would have been way too hard to explain everything. And if my dad had decided to butt in and give us the third degree—well, then you can guarantee we wouldn't have been cruising anywhere. Our hard-earned T-shirt money would disappear without a trace into the Bank of Ashmont, never to be seen again. At least, not until we had to buy college textbooks.

By the time we recovered from our momentary lapse of reason, we were both feeling more optimistic. This was so much better than any of our schemes of the past. It blew the Toilet Paper Revenge Caper out of the water. It even beat our Take the Fight Out of the Highlander campaign. This was going to be the highlight of our senior year, and we'd have even *more* fun enjoying the "fruits of our labor," as my father would put it. Only for him, the fruit of my labor ought to have the words "Harvard," "Yale," or "Stanford" in it. Needless to say, there would be no parents on the trip.

I pulled a blank sheet of paper in front of me and started making another list.

Latte Rebellion Marketing Plan

1. Flyers in lockers of Rebellion Sympathizers: known, suspected, or potential.
2. Posters at school, in cafes, and everywhere we go.
3. Ask Bridget to put up posters at U-NorCal.
4. Send emails to everyone we know.

5. Talk up The Rebellion. Whisper about it at school. Spread gossip about The Rebellion's fabulous line of must-have clothing.

I made a quick handwritten copy of the list for Carey.

"I'll make a bunch more flyers and bring them to school on Monday," I said. "We should come up with an exhaustive list of everyone who might want a shirt. We can use last year's yearbook."

"And we should bring some flyers for Miranda so she can hand them out to the Art Club." Carey sounded a lot less stressed now, and I silently breathed a sigh of relief. I wouldn't be able to do this without her.

One thing was for sure: even *with* her, this project was going to be a lot more involved than we'd thought. But, as I reminded myself again and again, it was all about the results. Sure, the idea was pure unadulterated genius, but the best part would be when we were in an airplane together, or on a cruise ship, with one entire week of hard-earned freedom just waiting for us.

————

The following April:
Ashmont Unified School District Board Room

I was sweating, even though I had prepared for this moment. Every dull second studying *Robert's Rules of Order* for Mock Trial, all the time I spent poring over the list of charges against me and the list of rules I supposedly violated (information I had a right to, according to the ACLU and school district policy) was going to pay off, I told myself firmly.

Even though the itchy sweat under my hairline was trying to tell me differently.

"Order," the disciplinary hearing officer demanded one last time, and the crowd complied. All fifty-plus of them. Of course, that number didn't include those on the dais; the hearing panel sat behind a long, semicircular desk, slightly above the audience and directly facing *me*. I could see Vice Principal Malone standing to one side, gazing at me with an unreadable expression, and I clenched my muscles so I wouldn't fidget nervously. I stared over at the California flag in the corner of the room so I wouldn't have to look anyone in the eye.

"We will begin by reading the charges against Ms. Jamison, and then proceed to examine the evidence of her violations of school and district policy. Witness testimony will follow. After the hearing, the panel will determine whether or not to recommend expulsion to the school board." The hearing officer sighed, as if the entire proceedings bored him beyond belief. As if this was nothing but a routine disciplinary hearing. For him, maybe it was.

"Charge number one: Willfully and repeatedly violating School District Policy 418.III.K—by intentionally harassing a group of students, creating substantial disorder, and causing a hostile educational environment. This was done through the distribution of inflammatory materials on school property.

"Charge number two: Violating School District Policy 418.III.M—by repeatedly disrupting school activities and defying explicit school policy regarding unsanctioned activities.

"Charge number three: Violating School District Policy 418.III.N—by engaging in what was construed by some as a terrorist threat."

Even though I was ready for it, even though I'd known that the T-word was going to come up sooner or later, my stomach sank to the very bottom of my shoes.

This was it. My success or failure in this room today would determine whether my thus-far stellar academic life would continue on with relative normalcy . . . or whether it was well and truly over, and my lifelong career as burger flipper was about to begin.

MATERIALS VIOLATING
BOARD POLICY SECTION 418.III.K

Flyer distributed on school property. Two copies attached. Electronic mail message sent to school-wide distribution list. Two copies attached.

CALLING ALL UNIVERSITY PARK HIGH STUDENTS!

IS YOUR COMPLEXION THE COLOR OF A LATTE? A CAPPUCCINO? PERHAPS AN ESPRESSO?

HAVE PEOPLE CALLED YOU CINNAMON, CARAMEL, OLIVE... OR JUST PLAIN BROWN?

DO YOU LOVE TO DRINK COFFEE?

HELP FURTHER THE CAUSE OF BROWN PEOPLE IN AMERICA!

WWW.LATTE-REBELLION.COM

To: <undisclosed-recipients>
From: Latte Rebellion <latte@latte-rebellion.com>
Re: A Call to Arms, or All Hands on Mugs

Dear Friends,

Please read this missive carefully. We need your help.
If you got this message, you may already be playing a
key role in the Latte Rebellion. You may be a relative, a
friend, a Sympathizer, or even an Organizer.

What we need from you is simple. In order for the Latte
Rebellion to achieve its goal of spreading the word
around the English-speaking world, consuming coffee
at every turn, we must raise the necessary funds.
Towards this end we ask you to (A) buy our T-shirt, and
(B) forward this information to everyone you know and
ask them to buy a T-shirt.

Not sure you want to be a part of the Latte Rebellion?
Visit our website for more information:
www.latte-rebellion.com

Incidentally, this is also where you can purchase the
T-shirt. The Movement Thanks You!

Yours in latte-ness,
Agent Alpha and Captain Charlie

P.S. This is not a joke. We really are selling shirts.

2

Publicizing the Rebellion should have been easy. If you looked at our written plans, it *was* easy.

But thanks to my parents—and my Hindi-speaking, sari-wearing Indian grandmother, who lived several hours south of us in Bakersfield—our plans suffered a slight delay.

"I hope you finished vacuuming your room," my mother said on Monday night, rubbing a hand tiredly through her short-cropped dark hair. We were in the living room watching one of my father's favorite movies, a documentary called *Enron: The Smartest Guys in the Room.* Dad was absorbed, as usual, in the sordid white-collar drama of a huge corporation imploding; meanwhile, I was taking mental notes on what *not* to do if I was ever on the board of a multi-million-dollar company, and lamenting the fact that other people's fathers (normal ones) made their kids watch *Star Wars* or James

Bond movies, a fate I would happily endure given the choice. Not that anybody gave me one.

"I need you to work on the guest room before Nani comes tomorrow," my mom continued doggedly. "I'm giving parent-teacher conferences and won't be able to leave until four."

"Nani's coming *tomorrow*?" I stared unseeingly at the TV, frustrated. "But it's the middle of the week." My parents were very into "quality family time," so it wouldn't be easy to extricate myself in order to hang out with Carey and start our publicity blitz.

Crap, crap, crap.

"Your Nani misses you," my mother said, trying a different strategy—one involving guilt and wheedling. "She said she's looking forward to spending some time with you, helping you practice your Hindi. And she wants to teach you how to cook your favorite chicken biryani."

I groaned. My dad looked up briefly from the TV. "She really wants to teach you about your culture, Asha. I wish I'd had that at your age. Your Grandma Bee didn't even *try* to teach me Spanish." He gave an ironic laugh. "If only she'd known how useful it would be in the business world."

Useful. Har. My knowledge of Hindi would get me about as far as a five-year-old looking for a bathroom. And my parents had clearly forgotten Nani's disastrous attempt to teach me traditional dances when I was in junior high, which ended abruptly when I was trying the *dandia raas* for the umpteenth time and one of my sticks went flying and broke a vase.

Still, Nani insisted that it was in my blood. "*Arré*, it is your culture," she'd say mournfully, at least once a visit. But it wasn't that simple. Indian culture—well, it didn't feel like it was *my* culture, not any more or less than my dad's Irish and Mexican heritage. I was just me. Whatever that was.

———————

Incidentally, "whatever that was" turned out to be a more-than-apt way of describing the results of my sad attempt at chicken biryani, despite Nani hovering and issuing imperious instructions at every turn.

"*Nahi, nahi*—not like that! Let the onions get brown but don't burn them," she exclaimed, as I rushed to turn off the screeching smoke detector before we all went deaf. Meanwhile, Nani tucked the billowing, bright-magenta folds of her sari safely out of the way and rescued my slightly scorched onions, still sizzling in our biggest pot. I heaved a sigh and opened the kitchen windows to let out the smoky onion smell.

"Okay, Asha *beti*, not to worry," Nani said, rummaging in the back of the cupboard and pulling out an array of spices only my mother ever used. "It won't matter. Next step: we finish the gravy, all right?" She turned to me, an expression of concern on her plump brown face.

"Fine," I said, swallowing my pride in the face of her obvious—and understandable—fear that I'd never be able to fend for myself in the kitchen. I picked up an unlabeled jar of brown spice powder. "So, a teaspoon of cinnamon, right?"

Nani *tsk*ed. "An inch of cinnamon stick." She pointed at the jar I was holding. "That's the garam masala. Three-quarters of a teaspoon. Remember?"

I set the jar down with a thunk. This was hopeless. It didn't matter if it was my culture, it didn't matter if Nani measured everything out for me and wrote it all down in neat cursive on a sheet of scrap paper from the printer. I was not innately able to channel my Indian heritage at will, any more than I could become an Iron Chef after a handful of cooking lessons.

Yet here I was, stuck in the kitchen with a half-burnt pot of onions, an assortment of indistinguishable spices in varying shades of brown, and a grandmother attempting to hide her despair at my clear lack of culinary talent.

I really needed to get out of here.

———

"Mom," I said over dinner a few evenings later, making sure I'd finished every last grain of rice and mopped up all of my lamb korma with a piece of naan, even though I was full to bursting and did not need the extra carbs. "I have to ask you something."

She eyed my clean plate suspiciously.

"Can I go out with Carey tonight? We're supposed to go to a workshop at school on college application essays." I crossed my fingers under the kitchen table. Carey, of course, was already done with her essay. As for the workshop, I'd been planning to go, but our current project took precedence.

"College essays?" Mom glanced at Dad, who gave a quick nod. "I suppose it's fine, if you're back by nine thirty."

I let out a silent, relieved breath.

"Such a good, studious girl," Nani said, patting me on the arm and beaming.

Her familiar scent of curry powder, sandalwood soap, and mothballs wafted over me as she hugged me goodbye half an hour later. I tried not to flinch guiltily.

When I got to Carey's house, she was in the middle of cleaning jam off her brother Davey's head with a damp dishtowel.

"I'm sorry, Ash," she said, rolling her eyes. "I just need a second. My dad's in the shower and of course *this* happened. Could you just go make sure Roddy's still watching cartoons in the living room?"

"Poor you," I said, peering around the corner to where Roddy was sitting raptly in front of some anime show, watching ginormous robots bent on annihilating each other. "He's fine. He's just enjoying some wanton cartoon violence."

"Great. Now I know why he was trying to build a giant homicidal robot out of Legos." Carey sounded exhausted. With three boys under the age of twelve, the Wong household was always a few incidents short of complete chaos.

"You really do need to move away for college, don't you?" I leaned against the counter next to the sink, where Carey was washing her hands. Davey was now jam-free, sitting in his high chair and happily shoving crackers into his mouth.

"No freaking kidding. Mom is still on my case about going to U-NorCal so I can live at home. Can you believe it?" She shook her head. The University of Northern California was conveniently located here in town, but it wasn't an option for me, either. I had my eye on bigger prizes—namely Stanford, Harvard, UC Berkeley, and the über-selective Robbins College, also in Berkeley.

I hadn't mentioned it to Carey yet, but it was a recurring daydream of mine that she and I would both get into schools in Berkeley and move into an apartment together. A sibling-free, parent-free, grandmother-free, Roger-Yee-free apartment. With an ample supply of frozen enchiladas—something I actually *could* cook.

Over the burble of the dishwasher, Carey's mom shouted something about being home on time so she could finish her homework. Carey sighed.

"So," I said, "your car or mine?"

"My imaginary Lamborghini's in the shop," she said. Not for the first time, I felt relieved to be an only child—because I had my own car. It was ancient, it was slow, and it was surely not pretty—hence its nickname, the Geezer—but it was all mine. We piled in and immediately cranked open the windows to let in the cool evening air.

"What's first on our list?" I asked Carey, Keeper of the Master Plan. She shuffled a few papers.

"Um ... Mocha Loco. Tenth Street and Oak."

We drove in silence for a few minutes. The sun was

almost completely down, and the streetlights were already on. As we got close to the university campus, the sidewalks grew more clogged with students. I could smell garlic from the Italian deli wafting on the breeze, and the faint aroma of eucalyptus leaves.

"Are you nervous, Asha? You're unusually quiet," Carey said.

"Nope, not even a little. This is going to be *amazing*." I turned onto Oak and started looking for a parking spot. "I can't stop thinking about how it's going to feel to be *somewhere else* next summer . . . I mean, think about it. No parents, no school . . . just relaxing . . . shopping . . ."

". . . ogling tasty guys," Carey put in.

I grinned. "And getting them to take us out for coffee."

Yeah, we were a little obsessed.

At the last minute, a car pulled out right in front of Mocha Loco, and I swerved into the space. *Here we go,* I thought to myself as we got out of the car, making sure we had our flyers as well as pushpins and scotch tape for any contingency.

The green plastic patio tables were full of people studying. None of them paid any attention to us as we wound our way through and into the café. Inside, the tables were packed with more college students and professor types, buried in fat textbooks or having deep philosophical discussions. I felt . . . out of place. My excitement dimmed a little as we squeezed past tables and chairs, and I was convinced that I was going to bump into somebody or knock someone's coffee over with my butt. My *round* butt.

There was a two-piece band in one corner playing folk guitar ballads, and everyone was conversing at an even louder volume as a result. The hubbub of voices was giving me a headache, and I could feel nervous sweat prickling at the back of my neck.

"Now what do we do?" I stared at the throng of people and finally located a bulletin board—already crammed with flyers—on a stand next to the cash register.

"No problem; we can handle this," Carey said, grabbing one of the flyers out of my hand and marching up to the cash register. I trailed behind, not wanting to get trampled by caffeine-crazed college students.

"Here's the plan," Carey said in a stage whisper. She pulled on my wrist and I leaned toward her. "You buy a coffee from that guy. Just act normal. I'll ask him about the flyer." This was the upside of Carey's control-freakishness: she always had a Plan B. I'd seen it in action on the soccer field, as she shouted strategic maneuvers out to her teammates, but it never ceased to amaze me. I was more of an idea person, a motivator. I was no strategist.

I went up to the counter, trying to project more confidence than I was feeling. The guy behind the register was kind of cute, with dyed-black hair, dark eyes, a nice tan, and an eyebrow ring.

Make that *very* cute.

I could see a tattoo of some kind of Chinese character on his upper arm, disappearing under his T-shirt sleeve. Definitely a potential Rebellion Sympathizer. I gave Carey's arm a little squeeze and took a deep breath.

"Can I get a large iced latte, please?" It came out a lot quieter than I'd planned, more like a whispery squeak than a confident request for coffee.

"What was that?"

Carey elbowed me. I tried again.

"Um, an iced latte?" I smiled and tried to make eye contact.

"Whipped cream?" the guy asked in a bored voice. *Leonard*, his name tag read.

"No thanks, Leonard." I elbowed Carey.

"Excuse me." Carey looked up at him—he was pretty tall—and put on her cutest smile, blinking at him a little. "We were wondering if we could put a flyer for our … um … organization on your bulletin board?"

Carey has really striking hazel eyes, which was why Jonathan Burmeister wouldn't leave her alone. And before that, Kendall DeSoto, Eddie Green, and about twenty zillion others. I could see what was coming. I wasn't blind.

"Sure, go ahead," Leonard said. "It's a student organization, right? Not a corporate thing?"

"Uh—"

I nudged Carey again.

"Yes," she said stiffly.

It wasn't a lie. We were students. We were organized. Kind of.

"I'll have to have the manager take a look at it, but go ahead and put it up for now." He smiled at Carey, and handed me my latte without even looking at me. Of course.

Like I even had a chance. Let's just say that, standing next to Carey, I was not the one you'd notice first.

Carey pinned up the flyer with a stray thumbtack and then turned back toward the counter, flipping back her short hair coyly. "So what's the tattoo of?" she asked with a sly smile. "I don't read any Chinese." *And it drives her dad crazy*, I considered adding, but I refrained from doing so.

"It's the symbol for luck, combined with a horse, for year of the horse. My birth year." He leaned on the counter with one elbow, the better to show off his ink.

"Sounds pretty lucky," Carey said. "I heard horses are supposed to be intelligent and sensitive." She looked up at Leonard through slightly lowered eyelashes. "So what's your major?"

"It's my first semester, but I'm thinking about philosophy. I'm reading Kierkegaard's journals for a class, and they're really thought-provoking." Absent-mindedly, he took our two coffees from the barista and set them on the counter.

"Wow, Kierkegaard," she said, nodding. "Have you ever read—"

Ugh.

"So, this was fun. Thanks, Leonard." I grabbed my coffee and pulled on Carey's arm before I became the first person in recorded history ever to die of nausea. She simpered at him as we pushed our way out of the crowded café.

"What'd you do that for?" Carey glared at me as she yanked open the passenger-side door. "He was nice."

"We have nine more cafés to visit. We can't afford to chit-chat at every single one of them." It was sort of sickening watching her in action sometimes. Especially when you were the one who faded into the background as a result. I started the car and pulled back into traffic, narrowly missing a girl with a humongous backpack riding a bike.

"Chit-chat? Please. You sound like a schoolmarm," Carey said.

"The word 'schoolmarm' makes *you* sound like a schoolmarm."

"I seriously think you're just jealous of me. Me and Leonard."

"Now you're goading me." I sighed.

"It's my job. Some of us take our work seriously."

"That better not be a veiled reference to Calculus," I said. But I relented and smiled over at her. She laughed and poked me in the arm. We were both starting to spaz out on coffee already, with nine stops to go.

The rest of the evening went pretty much the same way; sometimes we didn't need to approach the cashier to hang our flyer and sometimes we did, but at each stop we ordered a latte. Counterproductive, maybe, since we wanted to *make* money, not spend it, but it seemed fitting. After we'd each had two coffees, we dumped the rest we bought, but it had become like a superstition to buy one so we had to do it. We kept the cups as souvenirs.

"Too bad we don't have, like, a club hideout. A secret meeting place," I said. We were getting silly by now. "We could decorate it with garlands of empty coffee cups."

"You mean like my brothers' tree house? Adorned with empty candy wrappers?"

We both laughed. "Yeah, I guess it's dumb," I said. "We don't need a hideout. After all, we're a secret Rebellion. We're already hiding in plain sight."

"We're all around you and you don't even know it," Carey intoned in a *Twilight Zone* voice.

"Exactly! Hey, maybe we should be dressing up like our alter egos."

"No offense," she said, still laughing, "but I don't want to look like the female Clark Kent."

"Not like Clark Kent. We're more like ... the Masked Mavens of Mayhem," I said in a spooky whisper.

"Out to subvert the dominant paradigm?"

I bounced a little in my seat. "You know, *that* would make a great propaganda poster. We should totally make some like that." I was inspired, envisioning our logo causing havoc (or, more likely, mild puzzlement) at places like bus shelters and U-NorCal lecture halls.

"Or at least we could make some web graphics that people could put on their own sites," Carey said, ever practical. "I'll ask Miranda about it."

"And speaking of the website, we should put up a guest book so people can tell us what they think of the shirts."

"Now you're talking," Carey said. "Hang on, let me write this down."

That's right—the tactician had had her moment of brilliance, but this was the idea-girl's turn to shine.

I grinned into the darkness of the car, the streetlights

blurring past on either side as I accelerated down Bracken Street. Energy crackled through me like a live wire. By all rights I should have been exhausted, but for the first time, I had complete confidence we were going to pull this off after all.

———————

"I don't know *where* she is," I told my cousin Bridget as I paced back and forth outside the doors of the tall, concrete Livermore Building. The edifice was imposing compared to the peeling-paint-and-dingy-stucco one-story buildings on the University Park High School campus, a contrast which didn't help my nervousness any. I took my cell phone out; no messages. "She said she'd probably come. I guess she didn't exactly commit, though." I looked at Bridget apologetically.

"No big deal, like I said." Bridget slung an arm around my shoulders. "Just give her a call and let her know we missed her, and meet me inside, okay? I'll be talking to my friend Jed. Tall. Beard. Birkenstocks." She gave me a bone-grinding one-armed hug and left, her tall, wiry frame disappearing through the glass doors.

Bridget was only a freshman at U-NorCal, but she already seemed confident enough to rule whatever room she walked into. Whereas I was a little shaky inside at the mere thought of being probably the only high school plebe in a sea of worldly college students.

I leaned against the cool concrete wall of the building

and speed-dialed Carey's number. It went straight to voice-mail, her terse "This is Carey Wong, leave me a message" hardly giving me enough time to formulate what I wanted to say.

"It's me," I said. "I'm here at U-NorCal. I, uh, guess you aren't coming to the Students for Social Justice Meeting. I thought you wanted to go, but anyway..." I frowned up at the tall sycamore tree looming over the sidewalk, the bike rack full of locked-up cycles. "I'll talk to you later, okay?"

I was confused. This should have been right up Carey's alley, what with her obsession with extracurricular activities and her quickness to point out when people were being racially insensitive—the pool-party incident was a case in point. But instead, she was nowhere to be found.

I couldn't keep waiting for her out here, though. Whether she was going to come or not, I needed this meeting. I'd dropped being a tutor at the end of last year and I was desperate for some kind of extra activity to pad out my college applications. When I called to ask Bridget for advice, she suggested ... this, assuring me it wasn't just for U-NorCal students.

Could've fooled me. If there were any other high school students here, like from Seward High or something, they blended in a lot better than I did.

I followed Bridget, easy to spot in her blue tie-dyed bandanna and paint-spattered jeans, as she strode confidently into the auditorium-sized classroom. While she stopped to talk to a dreadlocked guy in a worn-out Greenpeace T-shirt standing by the wooden lectern at the front,

I stared uncomfortably at the floor and hoped I didn't look too out of place in my dorky preppy ponytail and striped sweater.

I doubted I'd be able to contribute much to the meeting. What did I know about social justice? I should have just joined the stupid Asian American Club, except that Roger Yee was President and he probably would have drummed me right back out again for being "barely Asian."

Stupid Roger. I tried to stand up straight and look assertive, even if I didn't feel it. This was the best choice I had. And it was just for a few months. I could do this.

"Konnichiwa!" said a bright, chirpy voice. I glanced around and saw Darla, Bridget's roommate, and resisted the urge to cringe. Despite the greeting, Darla was not Japanese by any stretch of the imagination. "Random" was the most appropriate description—or, if you were being nice, eccentric. She had Japanese anime posters plastered over most of their dorm room. That wasn't too weird; what *was* weird was that she had *action figures*. Lots of them. Posed in elaborate scenarios from her favorite anime shows.

"Hi, Darla." I tried not to sound too sour.

"How's it going, hon? You applying to colleges yet?" Infuriatingly, she winked at me through her fire-engine-red-framed glasses.

"Yes," I said. I hoped my lack of conversation would send a clear hint.

"That's just *great*," she said. "You're going to *love* college. You—"

"I think we should take a seat," Bridget said dryly, showing up in the nick of time.

"Oh! Right. Here," Darla said, indicating a few desks in the front row. I groaned.

"Don't worry." Bridget patted me on the shoulder. "Nobody's going to call on you."

"Good," I mumbled, and sank down in the seat as far as possible. Next time I'd have to bring Carey with me if I wanted to survive ... if there was a next time.

"So," Bridget said, settling into the seat next to me and retying her bandanna around her wavy brown hair. "How's your T-shirt thing going?"

"Not bad." I dared a quick glance around the room. There were lots of dreadlocks, Indian prints, and black turtlenecks in attendance. "Listen ... do you think you'd be willing to put up a few posters around campus for us? We'd appreciate the contribution to our vacation fund."

"Sure. You know, your logo's very catchy. It's a fun idea. I hope you guys can manage to earn the cash—that would be great for you."

"Thanks. I owe you big-time," I said fervently. "When Carey and I are rich and famous businesswomen we'll buy you a Mercedes."

"Fab. Just what I always wanted." Bridget laughed.

"C'mon! You should feel privileged to be a part of such a stupendous idea from the ground up."

"Right," Bridget said. "Although ..." Here she paused thoughtfully. "Really, you have some good ideas in that manifesto of yours. I mean it. I think tonight's meeting might be of interest if you ever decide to … you know. Be more active about it."

"Active? Please." Carey and I fully intended to make this as easy as possible for ourselves. Additional activity wasn't really on the agenda. But with Bridget sitting there next to me, looking enthralled as the Students for Social Justice president—a guy with a scruffy ponytail—went on and on about community organizing and grassroots activism, I tried my best to listen.

Eventually, Bridget's friend with the dreadlocks went up to the front to talk about a seminar that Students for Social Justice was hosting in a couple of weeks: two guys from UC Berkeley who were planning a public health outreach program were coming here to speak about their project. It was all very noble, but I wasn't sure it related to what Carey and I were doing, despite what Bridget said. Sure, it would be nice if we managed to raise a little awareness of mixed-ethnicity people, but basically, we were selling shirts. A community health clinic made the Latte Rebellion seem like small potatoes. Small, *selfish* potatoes.

Still, I let Bridget and Darla talk me into coming to the seminar, and I promised I'd try to bring my friends— "try" being the operative word. I had no idea what Miranda would say, and Carey—well, apparently Carey had a packed schedule of her own. My parents, at least, would approve. They figured Bridget was a good influence on me, though I was pretty sure Students for Social Justice wasn't what they had in mind.

I will say one thing about the evening: It sure blew the Inter-Club Council picnic out of the water.

———————

As it happened, I had to wait until Monday to talk to Carey. Her whole family went out of town to a wedding over the weekend—her alleged reason for not answering her phone Friday night—and I had to put in some face time with the relatives.

Since Nani was still visiting, and my Nana had come up to join her for the weekend, my mom and dad threw a big dinner shindig Saturday night with all the relatives within an eighty-mile radius. I must have spent five hours washing pots and pans on Sunday, but that was painless compared to telling every single person at the party, from Mom's brother Uncle Raj to Dad's great-aunt Eva, that (a) Yes, I'm applying for colleges; (b) No, I don't know what I want to major in; (c) The official list is Robbins, Stanford, Harvard, and Berkeley; and (d) I won't hear the results until much, much later, so don't ask. Going back to school on Monday was a relief after running the interrogation gauntlet.

"These are funny," Carey said, looking over the six poster ideas I'd scribbled on the back of an old practice quiz. We came up with four more slogans together during French class, texting them to each other and giggling when elderly Mrs. Vo wasn't looking.

Latte Rebellion Official Propaganda Slogans

1. We are all around you and you don't even know it.
2. Ask not what the brown can do for you but what you can do for the brown.
3. Fear the Latte.
4. Lattes of the World, United!
5. Wanted: Rebellion Sympathizers. Must love coffee.
6. Buy our T-shirts! Please! We need money!
7. The Time is now. The color is brown.
8. It's all about the latte.
9. Forget "got milk," It's Time for the juice.
10. Ecru. Tan. Sepia. Sienna. Mocha. You.

"Yep, we are brilliant," Carey said, laughing, after she re-read our ideas aloud in the car after school.

"We *are* brilliant. It's kind of too bad we decided to remain mysterious, really. We could seriously have a million-dollar idea on our hands. Even Bridget liked it, and you know how much of a cynic she is." I drummed my fingers on the dashboard. "Speaking of which, Bridget is still on board. She said she's fine with putting up posters around the university."

"Oh, cool! You know, Leonard said he thought it was a good idea, too. He's going to love the posters."

"*Leonard?*" I nearly swerved into the adjoining lane.

"You know, Leonard from Mocha Loco."

"When did you talk to *Leonard?*" And why did she not tell me?

"Oh, I didn't talk to him. He posted to our online guest book. He said Latte Rebellion would make a great name for a café."

"He *what*?" I wasn't sure how I felt about this. Sure, he was butting in when nobody asked for his opinion, but on the other hand, maybe he'd be able to talk about it to his friends and get them to buy some shirts. I had to stay practical. "What else did he say?"

"Not much. I emailed him to tell him thanks for stopping by the website, and then he emailed me back on Saturday."

"You're emailing back and forth now?" This seemed to be happening way too quickly. And, to be honest, it wasn't entirely welcome. All I could think of, dumb as it was, was that Carey and I were like John Lennon and Paul McCartney, and Leonard was like Yoko Ono. "Isn't that a little sudden?"

"I can't help it if you're jealous," she said smugly. "He *is* cute, isn't he?"

"Yeah, so?"

"So, maybe he has a cute friend for you."

"I do *not* need Leonard's help, thank you very much." I pulled up into the Wongs' driveway but I didn't get out of the car.

"Don't say I never offered you nothin'," Carey said, poking me in the arm before getting out. I turned up my nose, pretending to be pseudo-miffed. In reality, though, I did feel a little miffed, and I pulled away from her house with a bit more mustard than was strictly necessary. Carey usually filled me in on stuff like this. What's more, she just assumed it was okay to talk to a total stranger about everything, alter egos be damned, after making a big deal out of staying low-profile. It made my head ache.

And what was all that about finding me a cute friend? I wasn't *that* much of a social outcast.

I just didn't happen to be the one to snag Leonard.

———————

Tuesday morning, I picked Carey up as usual and we drove to school in near-silence. We were both groggy and grouchy because we'd already exhausted this week's coffee fund making color copies of the propaganda posters. As I was putting my lunch in my locker and rummaging around for my copy of *Death of a Salesman* for English class, I overheard something that nearly made me drop everything.

"Oh, hey," a girl's nasally voice said, cutting across the clamor in the hallways. "I went to that Latte website thing and it was really stupid. Did you see it? Just somebody trying to sell T-shirts with some dumbass coffee logo."

"I know, and they were all on their high horse about some 'ethnicity' crap." This voice was male. "But I was thinking of buying one for my brother. He's into that kind of thing, like underground stuff."

"Yeah, whatever. What's a 'manifesto,' anyway? I didn't get it." The voices got fainter and then disappeared into the general noise of the pre-first-period hallway. I slammed my locker shut and grabbed Carey, hugging her around the shoulders and whispering frantically, "Did you hear that? Did you hear what they said?"

"I *saw* them! That was Kaelyn and Roger." Carey was not quite as excited as I was, but she couldn't keep a smile off her face. If the Bimbocracy King and Queen started talking about the site, it would be all over the school within days. And the irony of Roger helping fund our vacation— the scheme we'd come up with *because* of him and his stupid attitudinal comments—was just too delicious.

Carey and I grinned at each other, the whole Leonard thing forgotten, the need for morning caffeine completely eliminated. We were officially in business. At this rate, we might just have our first sale by the time we got home from school. And then . . . well, we'd be too busy living it up next summer to care about Roger, Kaelyn, or any of their sycophantic courtiers.

Or so I thought.

MATERIALS VIOLATING
BOARD POLICY SECTION 418.III.N

Web page describing suspected terrorist group. Two copies attached.

Who are the brains behind the Latte Rebellion?

Agent Alpha: Agent Alpha is the idea man…or rather woman…who was first inspired to form the Rebellion, in order to promote the cause of the brown people: those of us of latte skin, latte at heart, or who love to drink latte. Her agitprop skills are rivaled by none.

Captain Charlie: Captain Charlie is the tech whiz behind the Rebellion website, and Agent Alpha's right-hand woman. She is an expert at spreading the message of the Rebellion and a genius at crowd control. Fear the Captain.

Rebellion Sympathizers:

Lieutenant Bravo: Master of guerrilla marketing without whom the Rebellion uniform would not be possible. Head of the Rebellion's Propaganda Division.

3

A couple of days later we were two weeks into our marketing campaign, and we had made exactly fifty-four dollars. It was barely enough to cover our production expenses for the posters and flyers. And that was making me just a little bit concerned.

Only a little, though. A killer idea is a killer idea.

"I really thought this would happen just a teensy bit faster." I pulled my car keys out of my backpack.

"Tell me about it," Carey said. "We need a major jump in sales if this is going to work. I'd ask Leonard to help, but he already told me he's planning to buy a shirt. I don't know how much more he can do."

"Well ... I already promised Bridget a free shirt for helping us put up posters. And Darla's waiting until she gets her next paycheck, she said."

"Oh." Carey waited for me to unlock the car and slid in on the passenger side. She was frowning slightly and her voice was quiet. "We might *not* sell enough. I mean, we spent all this time, but we should at least consider—"

"It'll be fine," I said. "I mean, it's only been a couple of weeks. We might sell a hundred and ninety-one more shirts tonight, for all you know." I forced a smile and turned the key in the ignition, the Old Geezer starting up with a hacking cough.

"That's what Leonard said. He said it could happen any time and we just have to be patient. Personally, I think we should have put up more posters."

Leonard *again*. I'd just about had it with this Leonard crap. This happened every time Carey got sucked in by a new guy's gravitational field, but this was *our* project. I mean, if we'd invited him to get involved, that would have been different … and I probably would have, even if Carey hadn't batted her eyelashes at him. And now he was pulling this insufferable superior-college-student attitude, and Carey was falling for it.

"Hey, did I tell you he got one of the other baristas at Mocha Loco to order a shirt? Isn't that cool?"

Yep, Carey was definitely falling for Leonard's lines. I could tell by her babbling. It was driving me a little nuts. And, let's face it—I was a tiny bit jealous.

I was about to say something like *isn't he a little old for you?* but I suddenly felt like smacking myself in the head. The answer to our T-shirt problem was looking me right in the face, and I couldn't believe I hadn't thought of it before.

"Walking advertisements," I said, somewhat incoherently, grinning like a maniac.

"What are you talking about?" Carey looked at me like I'd grown antennae. I was starting to get used to that look.

"We should be walking advertisements for our own cause. *We* should buy shirts, is what I'm saying." I was talking loudly, excitedly. "We can wear the shirts ourselves as much as possible, around town and even out to San Francisco or something. My dad had to invest a lot when he started his store; this isn't any different."

"We've already invested enough, I think," Carey said, carefully. "I have other things going on in my life. Soccer. My SAT prep class."

"Leonard," I said, eyeballing her. With the Geezer finally warmed up, I backed out of the parking spot. "Seriously, it doesn't take time to wear a *shirt*."

"I know, but it just seems like you're letting it take over all your free time. Plus now you're going to that weird U-NorCal thing, too. Did you even *start* your history paper?"

"It is *not* taking over my free time," I scoffed. "And I did too start my history paper." I turned out of the parking lot and onto the main road, avoiding a herd of students straggling across the street to the convenience store. "Well, I've thought about a topic, anyway. I had to spend practically all Sunday night cleaning up the mess my cousins left all over the house this weekend. You know what that's like."

"Yeah," she said flatly. "Every night, at my house." Carey stared out the front window, not looking at me. "That's why I have to stay focused, Ash. You know it's the only way I'm getting out of here."

"Are you kidding? You're going to be valedictorian. Schools will be falling all over themselves to offer you scholarships," I said. "This is just another extracurricular activity to add to the list. 'Started grassroots business venture.'"

Carey snorted. "I'd hardly call fifty-four bucks net profit a business venture."

"Then I don't understand why you're so worried about the time investment. We hardly have to do anything; we already did it all. And then we get to take a vacation." I glanced at her sideways. How many pep talks was I going to have to give? I didn't know what else to say.

"I don't want to do this without you," I said finally. "It's supposed to be the three of us. Like Musketeers. The Latte Rebels." I pulled the car up at her house, set the brake, and smiled nervously at her.

She sat there silently for a moment, and then sighed. One eyebrow raised, she looked over at me and said, "If we end up on a cruise ship to Mexico, you are *so* going to owe me a margarita."

———

Nani and Nana had left over a week ago and my parents had decompressed, but my house was still a hostile environment for Rebellion Sympathizers. In other words, life went on as usual. In the evenings, my mother was busy with her red pen and spelling tests, and my dad divided his time between badgering his malingering inventory clerk over the phone and badgering me to do my homework.

Good thing he had no idea about the C I'd gotten on my last math quiz. It wasn't a big deal, just a weekly quiz, but it was mostly attributable to the time and energy I'd been spending on the Rebellion—namely, our jaunts around town putting up posters. Good thing I wasn't also juggling a job, like Carey. Not for the first time, I wondered how she was able to fit Leonard into that packed schedule.

Leonard. The more I tried not to think about him and Carey, the worse it got. I hadn't started this scheme for the hot guys, that was for sure, but that didn't mean I didn't *want* one.

Wednesday night I was supposed to go to the college essay makeup session, but instead I let myself wallow on the bed in a fit of despair, my only pathetic company a pile of balled-up tissues, half a chocolate bar I'd found on the kitchen counter, and an old, angsty Alanis Morissette CD. *I'd* talked to Leonard first. *I'd* thought he was cute, too. Carey didn't even ask me before she decided to blink those gorgeous eyes at him. Not that I'd staked a claim or anything, but this really wasn't fair. Carey, with her perfect, sporty figure, pixyish hair, and exotic-looking eyes, always attracted attention. And me…

I wiped my face on my sleeve and sat up, looking into the mirrored closet door. I avoided my own gaze, but my eyes just ended up in the places I didn't want to dwell on. My hair—long and full of split ends, the same drab, nothing brown as my dad's. Bangs that severely needed a trim. Jeans a size or two bigger than I wanted them to be. My long-sleeved gray shirt stretched awkwardly over my shoulders and boobs, but sagged around the waist that nobody seemed to notice. Apparently, "human lattes" weren't necessarily as smooth a blend as we were making them out to be.

This one wasn't, anyway.

Latte. Ha. I was no latte. I was more like a cup of Mexican hot chocolate that had been Irished up and dumped into a pot of chai. No wonder I had a bad taste in my mouth.

———

"So we're sticking with the plan," said Miranda, who was sitting with us at lunch. "Ambitious. Ballsy, even. I like it."

I smiled broadly and toasted her and Carey with my orange soda. We'd had the same classes as Miranda for years, though we hadn't spent a huge amount of time with her until she helped us with the Rebellion shirts. Still, she'd always been friendly to us. Maybe it was because we were nice to her back in eighth grade when she showed up on the first day of school, new in town, with a mouth full of braces and a big fluffy perm. Now she had ears full of piercings and burgundy cornrows.

"Well, I can't wait for my shirt to get here," Miranda

said. "Yet another thing to confuse and annoy my parents."
She grinned evilly. "I'm seriously counting the days until I
can move out."

"Try having three little brothers," Carey said. "And I
don't even *get* to move out."

"Come on," Miranda said. "You, of all people, are
bound to get a full ride somewhere."

"I don't know…" Carey stared at the irritatingly bouncy
pep rally going on in the quad for tomorrow's football game.
Kaelyn was right in the middle, of course, flipping up her
itty-bitty cheer skirt and putting on a show for the rest of
the Bimbocracy. "If I don't get any scholarships, it'll be
U-NorCal for me. I won't have much of a choice."

I put an arm around her and felt the tension in her
hunched shoulders. "Seriously. You get straight A's. You're
in Key Club. You have ample work experience and superior customer service skills. And, now you can put 'started
my own business' on the list."

"It's not a business, Asha! It's just fun and games."
Carey looked down at the table and fiddled with her half-
eaten turkey sandwich. There was a long silence. *Fun and
games?* I squinched up my face. Was that all it was?

"*Don't worry*," I finally said. "Like I told you before, all
we have to do now is make sure the flyers and posters stay
up, send a few emails, and wait for the cash to roll in." I
squeezed her shoulder, then let go.

She looked back up at me and smiled weakly. "I wouldn't
say no to extra cash, that's for sure."

"Just you wait," I told her. "Colleges will be throwing

money at you. Literally, they'll be showering you with fist-fuls of cash. You won't know what to do with it all. You'll have to start the Carey Wong Trust Fund for the Caffeine-Deprived."

"I'm totally on board with this," Miranda said, grinning.

"Golly, thanks, guys," Carey said, flicking a stray bread-crumb at me. She sounded a little more like herself again.

"Back on the topic of the Latte Rebellion," Miranda said. "If you ever want me to draw anything else for you, like cartoons of Agent Alpha and Captain Charlie, let me know. It'd be fun." She crumpled up her lunch bag and aimed it at the nearest trash can.

"You mean like a comic strip?" Carey looked at Miranda curiously. Miranda was one of the cartoonists for the school paper.

"Yeah, like *The Latte Rebellion Chronicles* or something. It'd be way better than doing those caricatures of the foot-ball team like I'm supposed to for next month's *Herald*." She rolled her eyes.

"That would be killer," Carey said. "We could put them on the website."

"Or make propaganda leaflets," I added. "Drop them all over campus."

"Yeah," Miranda said. "Something like that. Hey, have you thought about holding meetings? I bet people would come." Miranda was part South American—Ecuadorian, I thought—so I wasn't surprised she was a Sympathizer, but this was a totally new idea. We'd never talked about having meetings. It hadn't even occurred to me.

"We're not really a club," I said, exchanging a glance with Carey.

"Not yet," Miranda said. "But it would be really easy to create one. I bet Mr. Rosenquist would agree to be the teacher advisor. I can ask him if you want."

"I guess." I rolled up my Velcro lunch bag and stuffed it into my backpack. "We can think about it, anyway."

"You should. I'd totally help you set it up." Carey and I grinned, but Miranda didn't. "I'm serious—the Latte Rebellion is a great idea. There's an African American Association and an Asian American Club and a Chicano Club. There isn't really anything for people who are just...brown. Biracial. Multi-ethnic. Whatever you want to call it."

"Unless we take over the Key Club through sheer numbers alone. Bring it down from the inside," Carey said in an exaggerated whisper.

We all laughed. But Miranda had got me thinking. What if we did start a club? It would be yet another all-important line-item for our applications—"started discussion group," maybe, or "spearheaded establishment of extracurricular organization"—not to mention a major plus for any leadership scholarships.

It would be especially great for Carey. It was her dream to go to Berkeley or Stanford, and if she got a leadership scholarship...then she'd definitely be able to go. No question about it. And maybe I'd be there at Berkeley, too, or right down the road at Robbins College.

The more I thought about it, the more excited I got. No matter what Carey said about time commitments, I *had* to convince her to do this. It would be worth the negligible extra time it would take to get a group organized—I mean, what did we really need to do? Arrange a time and place, submit a charter to whoever was in charge of these things at our school, and get approval, that was all. And the payoff would be so worth it.

It would be stupid *not* to do it.

———

The following April:
Ashmont Unified School District Board Room

At the sight of Exhibit A.3—the description of our "terrorist group"—murmuring broke out all over the room, including on the dais where the panel sat. While the disciplinary hearing officer called on Principal Philips and Vice Principal Malone to recap the events that led to this charge, a few of the school board members leaned their heads together and whispered, casting sidelong glances at me and making me squirm in my seat. As if the word "terrorist" hadn't been enough to do that all on its own.

I knew I should be outraged about it. After all, I'd yelled at Roger Yee for less. But mostly, after everything that had happened, I felt numb. And I felt scared.

"We will now hear from a number of witnesses who will shed light on the circumstances prompting this disciplinary hearing," the hearing officer said when he returned to the podium. He coughed like my Old Geezer of a car when I start it on a cold morning. "I'd first like to call Ms. Carey Wong."

Now I felt nauseated.

Carey had told me that the school board had called and asked her to give testimony, but it was still a shock to see her, dressed to kill in her tailored, gray-blue linen jacket and black dress pants. I'd helped her pick out those clothes during a shopping trip last summer, but she seemed like a different person now, standing there tensely in front of the hearing panel. A person with red, puffy eyes and a clenched jaw; a person with apprehension oozing from every pore.

"Ms. Wong," the hearing officer said, "you've already told us in a separate statement about your involvement in the Latte Rebellion group. I'd like to ask you a few questions about Ms. Jamison's role in the events."

"Yes, sir," Carey said, her hands trembling at her sides. She didn't look at me.

I sucked in a sharp breath. I had no idea Carey had given them any kind of advance statement. She hadn't told me. *Why* hadn't she told me?

Had she said it was all my fault? I couldn't let myself believe that. I glanced at her parents in the audience—Dr.-Wong-the-Dad (a pediatrician) glowering in his suit and tie, Dr.-Wong-the-Mom (a professor of Asian art) looking pale and anxious—and I couldn't be sure of anything.

"My question for you, Ms. Wong, is straightforward. You were present during the planning and perpetration of the rabble-rousing." I heard someone in the audience snort with laughter. "Did Ms. Jamison knowingly violate school rules and school district policy as described in the charges against her?" He looked at her, his unibrow bushier than ever as he frowned at her.

"Knowingly?" she said, shifting her weight from foot to foot.

"Yes, knowingly," the hearing officer repeated. "Answer the question, please."

"I guess it depends on how far back you go. When we started, we didn't know it was against the rules. But later on..." There was absolute silence in the room as Carey finally turned to me and said, "I'm so sorry, Asha." Her eyes were pleading, and I knew then that she wasn't going to hold anything back.

I could hardly hear what she said next. At first I was so furious I thought I might pop a blood vessel, and I resisted the urge to clamber over the wooden table in front of me, grab her by her linen lapels, and shake her. How hard could it be to just say we didn't know we'd be breaking any rules and leave it at that? It wouldn't make any difference to her. She hadn't even gotten suspended after what happened, while my entire high school career was on the line.

The worst part of it was, she was supposed to be my best friend, my partner in—well, crime. And thinking about that just made me despondent. Why did she have to go all "I cannot tell a lie, I did chop down your cherry tree" on me? Wasn't our friendship worth more than that? As I gritted my teeth, focusing intently on not completely breaking down right here in front of the school board, the disciplinary hearing officer, and a rather sizable cross-section of my classmates and the general public (not to mention that pesky newspaper reporter), Carey said something about never intending to make trouble but getting carried away.

Carried away. "Careyed" away. I almost felt like laughing hysterically, at the same time that my eyes stung with unshed tears. On top of my fear that I wouldn't have a college career after today, now I wasn't sure I'd have a best friend, either. But I had to stay calm. It was only nine o'clock, the next coffee break wasn't for another hour, and there was still a long way to go.

Exhibit A.4:
MATERIALS VIOLATING
BOARD POLICY SECTION 418.III.K, 418.III.N

Web pages encouraging participation in possible terrorist group. Two copies attached.

Rebellion Sympathizers (added 10/31):

Commander Delta: Chief liaison to the U-NorCal undercover unit and rumored relative of Agent Alpha.

Field Officer Foxtrot: Supplier of latte and caffeinated beverages, procurer of meeting space, and consort of Captain Charlie. In short, multitalented and indispensable.

Sergeant Echo: Expert on the animated arts and assistant to Lieutenant Bravo in the Propaganda Division. Undercover operative at U-NorCal.

What can I do to help the Rebellion?

1. Buy our T-shirt. Buy many T-shirts. Buy them for your friends and family. Do they like coffee? Buy them a shirt. Do they support the cause of brown people? Definitely buy them a shirt. Makes a great Christmas, Hanukkah, Eid, or Kwanzaa gift!

2. Spread the word. Tell everyone about the Latte Rebellion cause. Send the Manifesto to anyone you think might be a Rebellion Sympathizer.

3. Promote the agenda of the Rebellion at every opportunity. The People of the Latte are all around us—all we need to do is alert them to our presence. We are the future!

4. Did we mention, buy our T-shirt?

4

"Welcome to a very special Students for Social Justice seminar!" The auditorium erupted into rowdy applause, and the club president, the short guy with the long blond ponytail who'd led the earlier meeting, made a shushing motion with his hand. I looked sideways at Bridget, ready to make a sarcastic comment under my breath, but she was staring raptly at him. I looked at him again. His hair was dull and ratty under the fluorescent lighting, and he had a big smudge of blue marker on his forearm from where he'd brushed against the dirty whiteboard behind him.

Nope, didn't see the appeal. When I glanced back at Bridget, though, I was surprised she wasn't actually drooling.

On my other side, Miranda—who'd been dragged to the meeting with almost no visible reluctance—was equally transfixed, though without the goo-goo eyes.

I sighed to myself.

"Without further delay," ponytail-guy said, "please give a warm welcome to Greg Androvich and Thad Sakai, who drove here all the way from UC Berkeley to discuss Community Outreach and Social Responsibility."

I didn't even look up. The first ten minutes were all about thank-yous and what-an-honors and names of professors I didn't know but the audience seemed to. I spent the time productively by doodling the Latte Rebellion logo in black ballpoint pen on the back of my hand.

Then, a few minutes later, a booming voice took over at the podium, eliciting a lot of enthusiastic noises from the audience. I couldn't help sneaking a peek. Greg, the first speaker, was dark-blond and lanky with little round glasses. He was talking passionately about a series of community clinics that he and Thad wanted to put together for rural and poor neighborhoods. They were modeling it after a clinic in East London.

London. I thought about that for a minute.

Big Ben. The Tower of London. Culture, nightlife, and guys with really hot accents. In short, a prime vacation destination. If our T-shirt scheme really took off…could we get as far as England?

I got a little sidetracked daydreaming about cruising down the Thames River, but when Greg yielded the floor to Thad, I started doing some rapt staring of my own. He had short, dark, spiky hair with the tips bleached, tan skin, bright blue eyes, and a quick impish grin. Carey would have called him an "über-hottie" for those eyes alone.

To be honest, I didn't hear a word he said, and after

the seminar concluded I stood there next to my seat musing alternately about the apparent superior attractiveness of college guys, and the potential cost of plane flights to England. I wasn't sure how long I stood there spacing, waiting for Bridget to finish glomming onto the Students for Social Justice ponytail guy. But I was snapped right back to reality by Miranda, who had materialized in front of me as if by magic. She was congratulating the first speaker, Greg, and Thad was standing right there next to him. Smiling. At *me*.

Miranda smirked at me knowingly. "So, what did you think? Pretty riveting stuff, right?"

"Glad you guys liked it," Greg said. He seemed to be pretty taken with Miranda; he couldn't stop looking at her waist-length braids. Thad, meanwhile, seemed to be waiting for me to say something.

"It was great," I said, a little dazed. What did *I* have to say to *him*? Apparently nothing, since I stood there like an idiot. His eyes were very, very blue.

"Thanks," Thad said, beaming. "So, do you guys go here?"

"We're just here for the seminar. We're seniors at University Park High here in town," Miranda blabbed, before I could think of something more impressive. I shot her a glare that she blithely ignored. "I'm Miranda, and this is my shy friend Asha."

"She doesn't seem so shy to me," Thad said in a friendly tone. I looked down, hiding the furious blush darkening my cheeks.

"Yeah, you just have to get to know her," Miranda said.

"Is that so?" Thad looked at me intently.

I cleared my throat and was about to change the subject when Miranda said, "Well, I have to get going. See you at school, Asha." Greg said, "It was nice meeting you guys," and both of them wandered off.

Miranda was leaving me *alone* with him. Clearly, I needed to have a serious conversation with her about subtlety and its various uses. And Bridget was still busy chatting up ponytail guy over by the whiteboard. For a second I wished Carey were here, but then, disloyally, I decided I was glad she wasn't. She'd probably just add him to her man-harem and I'd be left with no one.

"So what college do you think you'll go to?" Thad asked, looping his thumbs casually into his jeans pockets.

Of *all* the things for him to ask me.

"I'm applying to a few different ones," I said. "Berkeley ... Stanford ... Harvard. Robbins College."

"Robbins College, huh? That's in a really nice part of Berkeley, and it's got a great School of Social Welfare," he said approvingly. "Sounds like you have everything all planned out."

"Sort of." I grimaced. "I have the applications almost done, anyway."

"The all-important first step. I was pretty disorganized—it took me a year of going to community college to figure out what I wanted to do." He smiled sheepishly.

"I'm not really *that* organized," I said. I didn't elaborate, but truth was, I had no idea what I wanted to study.

Not only that, but this was the first I'd heard of the School of Social Welfare. Time to get the conversation off of me. "So, what are you studying?"

"I'm planning to double major in Economics and Public Health," Thad said. "The major advisors already said they'd accept our clinic project as an independent study."

"Wow," I said. "Sounds hard. But worthwhile."

"I don't know about 'worthwhile.'" Thad smiled. "I just think people really need this kind of thing, and Greg and I have some good ideas. We think we could manage to make a living off it."

"That's great," I managed. I didn't know what else to say. I had a ridiculous urge to babble on and tell him that I'd love to help, that maybe if I was living in Berkeley next year I could somehow be a part of it. Part of something that really had meaning.

Maybe there was something to this social justice thing after all. I know it wasn't just that Thad had the nicest smile I'd ever seen ... but that didn't hurt.

What he'd said made me think of Miranda's words last week, about people maybe being truly interested in the Latte Rebellion because it filled a need the other clubs at school didn't address. What would happen if we *gave* the Latte Rebellion some meaning, beyond just the shirts? What harm would it do? We'd still get to take our vacation (maybe even to London, I reminded myself), and we'd be doing a good deed at the same time. I bet Thad would approve.

"Well," Thad said, after we'd stood there awkwardly

for a minute. "I should round up Greg, since we have an hour's drive back."

"Okay. I should probably go too." I looked at him a little regretfully. "It was nice talking to you. Good luck with your ... clinic thing."

"Yeah, thanks ..." He hesitated. "Maybe I could give you my phone number? In case you have, you know, any questions about colleges or about Berkeley."

I felt a flutter in the pit of my stomach. "Uh, sure. That'd be great." I got my phone out, and he typed in his number. He passed the phone back to me, and before I had a chance to react, he'd taken my hand for just a moment, not quite a handshake. His hand was warm, and I felt that warmth spreading from my fingers into the rest of my body. Then he let go. I dared to take one last, quick look into those blue eyes of his before walking over to retrieve Bridget.

————

I breathed in the crisp autumn air as Bridget and I walked along one of the tree-lined pathways next to the U-NorCal political science department, where the seminar had taken place, on our way to grab a snack before I drove home. The smells of pine and eucalyptus were all around us, and people were walking here and there with backpacks. A lone jogger swerved past, the streetlights reflecting off his sneakers. It was a perfect night. Even the seminar hadn't been too bad. After all, I'd met Thad, and I'd gotten some interesting ideas for furthering the cause of the Latte Rebellion—for making it into something more than just a soulless moneymaking endeavor. A pretty successful outing overall, I had to admit.

Except that I didn't belong here, on this campus. This wasn't my element. Not yet.

"I cannot *wait* to go to college," I said, sighing. "I'm so sick of high school."

"Sorry, kid," Bridget said. "It's not over yet." She smiled over at me sympathetically.

"Yeah." And boy, was I sick of people smiling at me like that. I stared ahead into the darkness. Screw sympathy. I was ready to be done with this part of my life. I wanted, *needed*, to be doing more. To *be* more.

"Believe me, I understand," Bridget added, reaching over and giving my arm a quick squeeze. "And yes, going away to college has a distinct upside. Though I do miss my dad's four-cheese lasagna."

"Only because gourmet cuisine isn't your specialty."

"Oh, like *you* can cook." Bridget exchanged waves with a well-dressed couple passing by, a petite blonde wearing a shiny Chinese-style *cheongsam* jacket and an Asian woman in a sleek black pantsuit. "When you're all moved out, you'll learn to truly appreciate the finer qualities of the pre-prepared meal."

I felt a twinge of impatience. "Well, at Robbins the dining hall has gourmet chefs, so if I go there I won't *need* to cook." I remembered what Thad had said about the School of Social Welfare. I was embarrassed not to have heard of it, but after tonight I had to admit I was a little intrigued.

"Well, la-di-da," Bridget said, laughing.

By then we'd reached the sidewalk at the western edge of campus and crossed the street to the busy shopping district. The first café we passed was closed, and Bridget quickly vetoed all the fast food places.

"How about there?" She pointed at Mocha Loco. I glowered for a second, then checked myself. This would be a good opportunity to ask Leonard if anybody had approached him about the Rebellion sign we'd posted there, or if he knew of anyone else who wanted to buy a shirt.

It was a lot quieter inside than it was the first time I was there; there was no live music tonight, and it seemed like more people were interested in studying than talking. The lights were brighter, and the room was filled with the warm smells of brewing coffee and toasted bagels. Walking in with Bridget, who acted like she belonged there, I was a lot more relaxed.

When I saw Leonard sitting at a table near the register, I didn't even flinch. After meeting Thad, he didn't seem nearly as cute as before; in fact, his nose was a little stubby and his ears stuck out. How had I not noticed? Then I froze. Leonard wasn't alone at his table. He was clearly giving the eye, half-lidded and smirking, to someone sitting to his left.

That someone was a girl.

A girl I happened to know very, very well.

I must have gotten a strange look on my face, because

Bridget raised her eyebrows at me and then followed my gaze.

"Hey, there's Carey," she said. "Oh yeah, I wanted to tell you guys that my shirt got here today and, you know, I'm really impressed."

"Yeah," I said, and trailed off, an acid feeling in my stomach. Carey had lied to me. She'd said she had to study and catch up on all the homework she was behind on because of the Rebellion. I should have realized it was a flimsy excuse.

I stared at her hard. To be fair, she did have books and papers on her table, but her eyes were fixed on Leonard. One thin, graceful, piano-playing, perfect finger was tracing his Chinese-character tattoo.

I shifted uncomfortably. She had a right to do whatever she wanted. I couldn't stop her. I just wondered why she hadn't told me.

"Let's order something. I'll have a latte in honor of your cause," Bridget said, hustling me up to the short line at the cash register.

"But—" I said, ineffectually. I knew I would have to talk to Carey sometime, but before we even got to the counter, she looked up.

I glared at her, shooting angry vibes out of my brain like little cartoon lightning bolts. Then, the surge of anger was gone almost as soon as it had come over me, and I just felt deflated.

"Hi," I said, tiredly. "What brings you here?" I shot a pointed glance at Leonard, who had gone behind the counter to help the cashier.

"Um, hey, Asha," Carey said. At least she had the decency to look embarrassed. "Ben is having a slumber party with two of his friends tonight and they're watching zombie movies. Hard to study calculus when you can hear guts being ripped out and strewn across the post-apocalyptic landscape."

"Okay," I said. Ben was the oldest of her brothers, age eleven. It was a pretty good excuse, but ... I was still annoyed. Not to mention that it was a known fact that cute guys were not an effective study aid.

"I hope you're getting a lot done." I looked at her nearly blank math homework.

"Yeah," she said, blushing harder. "Kind of. Hey, how was your seminar thing?"

"It kicked ass," Bridget said, putting one arm around my shoulders. "Asha managed to lure in the poor, unsuspecting, and very hot speaker while hardly saying a word." She grinned and I cringed. "Thad, wasn't it? He took one look at you and he was toast with a side of jelly."

"Right." This was stupid. Why was Carey sneaking around to see Leonard? This was supposed to be all about us, about getting away next summer, not about roping in men like it was a cattle drive. But if we did form a club, like Miranda had suggested ... maybe it would keep us focused, and keep idiotic stuff like this from getting in the way.

There was a brief, awkward silence.

"Well," I said stiffly. "We were just grabbing a snack before going home." I tried to smile bravely.

"Okay," Carey said, fiddling with her pencil. "Talk to you later?"

"Sure. I'll call you tomorrow." Just to get the Leonard scoop, if nothing else. *If* she was even going to tell me. I sighed and put my hand out, palm up with my fingers split in a Mr. Spock "V"—the first stage of our secret handshake. For a minute she just looked at it, twiddling her pencil awkwardly. Finally she put her own hand out in a "V," palm down. I looked at our hands there together, hers a pale creamy brown, mine a little darker and more olive-colored, and felt a little sad.

I stepped up to the counter with Bridget.

"So what do you ladies want?" Leonard sounded bored, as usual. He didn't even really look at us.

"How's it going, *Leonard,*" I said. "Thanks again for letting us put up our poster."

"Oh," he said, finally making eye contact. "That's right, you're the Latte girl. Carey's friend. Yeah, a lot of people saw the poster."

"Cool," I said, trying to sound like I didn't care. "Can we get two lattes? Bridget, what else do you want?"

"I'll have a cinnamon raisin bagel with cream cheese. What are you getting?"

"I'm not really hungry," I said.

"Is everything okay?" Bridget asked quietly, in my ear, as Leonard left to retrieve our order. "What's up with you and Carey?"

I sighed. Maybe this was one of those problems where, if you just ignored it, it would go away. "Nothing. Just ... I'll tell you later." Leonard came back with two clear-glass coffee mugs and a plate holding Bridget's bagel. I was about to put a couple of quarters in the tip jar when I noticed another jar next to it. Taped to it was a slip of paper that said "Rebellion Collection," with a crude pen drawing of our logo. Next to it was a stack of our flyers.

"What is *this?*" I pointed at it, incredulous.

"Oh, Carey and I thought of that," Leonard said. "We thought it'd be a good way to get a few extra donations for the cause."

"Oh *really*. Well, thanks, but I think we'll be okay with the T-shirts." I crossed my arms and glared at him.

"Hey, don't knock this idea so soon. You might need the Rebellion Collection to pay for overhead costs, if you don't sell enough shirts."

Bridget laughed. "Unbeliever! You wouldn't be saying that if you'd *seen* the shirt."

"Believe me, I already ordered mine. I can't wait," Leonard said dryly.

I'm sure you can't, I thought. *I'm sure you can't wait to get into Carey's pants. If you think she's going to fall all over you just because you said you'd help with the Rebellion, then you're in for a surprise.*

Then again, judging from Carey's intense interest in his tattoo, maybe Leonard was the one who needed to watch out. And maybe I'd just have to let Carey chew him up, spit him out, and get over him.

———

"This shirt is *amazing*," Miranda said, reverently. "It's really cool."

"The v-neck looks good on you," I said, packing away the remains of my lunch and wadding up the paper bag.

"Thanks." She beamed and turned around in a circle to show it off.

"The Latte Rebellion thanks *you*," I said with a satisfied smile. "We wouldn't even have the shirts without you. And you're helping us augment our London fund."

Miranda had been enthusiastic, earlier, when I told her about my idea to try to make it as far as London, but she'd been just about delirious when I agreed to maybe form a club after all.

"This is so perfect," she'd said, jumping up from our table in the quad and pacing back and forth behind me, her long braids swinging. "Our school *needs* this, if we ever want to move past these dated, static racial categories. I mean, if you order a latte, it's not just going to be a latte. It's going to be a soy milk half-caf, or a double with no foam, or a single with a shot of vanilla and a sprinkle of cocoa. Tons of ingredients, tons of options."

I thought *I'd* had the monopoly on goofy coffee metaphors, but when combined with the jargon about "static racial categories," Miranda had reached new heights of absurdity. Absurdity so classic it would go straight onto the Rebellion website.

"I'm half-caf, double strong," I said, flexing my biceps Arnold-style and grinning.

"That doesn't even make sense," Carey said. "Those cancel each other out."

"Come on, guys, I'm serious. With the Latte Rebellion, you can be whoever you want to be, because we're all mixed up." Miranda sat back down next to me, but I could tell she was still fidgety. "Even the *President* can't disagree with that."

"Yeah, yeah." I was still smiling, but when we tried to get Carey to be more enthused about the idea of a club, it didn't go quite as well. I told her about Thad and Greg's presentation, and she accepted the London proposal without comment, but as I expected, she was hesitant to add anything new to her schedule. Plus, things were still a little tense between us since our run-in at the café with Leonard. Every time I promised myself I'd talk to her about it, I always ended up convincing myself it would be better to just let it go.

It was easier, and less awkward, to talk about the Rebellion instead, even if she wasn't on board yet with the new plan.

"I know it sounds like more work to hold meetings," I said to her in the car after school, trying to sound reasonable. "But you have to admit it would be another college application bonus. 'Launched extracurricular group' sounds pretty good, right?"

"I guess so," Carey said. "But do you really want to add *that* to everything else we're doing? You've already got that other new club."

"Maybe." I thought about it. "But that's Bridget's thing.

The Latte Rebellion is *our* thing. And it isn't really a bad idea. It could be entertaining to see where this goes. And it's perfect for all your leadership scholarships." I didn't add that it was perfect for *my* college applications, too, which needed some padding to separate them from all the other honors kids with the same AP classes and club activities as everyone else.

"Um, hello, our anonymity? I only agreed because you said we'd only be doing publicity, and then the shirts would basically print themselves." Carey's voice was tired. "I'm not interested in being a spokesperson for anything."

"Seriously, we can put bags over our heads for all I care," I said quickly. "But it'll still be worth it. At least our college applications will be memorable." Having a chaotic mess of different cultural backgrounds—that wouldn't really help me, especially when I ended up having to check the "other" ethnicity box. Having a personal statement topic that instantly showed exactly how different I was—*that* would be huge. "It's prime essay material," I concluded. "You could totally use that."

Carey snorted. "Like you've got entirely altruistic motives."

"Okay, maybe not. But what I do have is an idea for a club that could really be worthwhile. Not to mention it would liven up the next few months." I took one hand off the steering wheel and flicked her arm playfully. "Where's your sense of adventure?"

"My sense of *adventure*? I'm saving the 'adventures' for when we've actually got the money earned and graduation is over. Right now I'm just a teensy bit more concerned with actually getting my applications finished," she said, looking at me meaningfully.

"Come *on,* you sound like my mom." I was annoyed, again, that she was being so resistant. Maybe she *was* feeling guilty about spending all her free time with Leonard.

"You don't have to be mean about it," Carey said, and stared out the side window. I could feel one of her icy silences coming on—she could give the cold shoulder like nobody else. Sophomore year, Chris Naysmith had been idiotic enough to ask her for an Oriental massage and she was still not talking to him. I'd gotten the silent treatment a few times myself, because stupid things did tend to come out of my mouth. She always forgave *me*, though.

"Come on, I didn't mean it that way."

More silence. Then she heaved a martyred sigh.

"We wouldn't have to make that big a deal out of it," I said, relieved. "Miranda and I will make all the arrangements. I just don't want you to be mad. I want to do this together."

"We can *talk* about it," she agreed, sounding sulky. "I need time to ... entertain the notion."

"It isn't a *notion*. It could help us sell more T-shirts if people actually want to join a club. And maybe we can do something meaningful while we're at it, instead of just being greedmongers."

"'Greedmongers' isn't a word. And you never complained about being greedy before," Carey pointed out.

"Yeah." I laughed edgily. "But Miranda's right—it

could actually work. A club for people who are just ... generally brown. Not one particular race. Not one particular nationality. People besides us might really be interested in something like this." I realized I had unintentionally echoed what Thad had said about his clinic project.

"You're right about that," she said ominously.

"What do you mean?" I looked at her out of the corner of my eye as I turned onto her street. She was still staring out the side window, drawing squiggles in the condensation on the glass with one finger.

"Have you even looked at the guest book on the website?"

"Not since you first put it up. Why?"

"Well ... it's interesting. One person was all 'you go, girls' and that kind of thing. I think it was Miranda's friend Ayesha. And then someone else was like 'people like you need to go back where you came from.' Can you believe that?"

"Wow," I said, my voice coming out in a squeak. I hit the brakes jerkily and pulled up to the curb in front of Carey's house, reeling. Who would say something so blatantly offensive and ignorant? It felt even worse than what Roger had said. At least he wasn't afraid to own up to his dumb comments. This could have been anyone. It was the *Internet*, for cripes sake. I felt a little sick. "Why didn't you mention this before? That's crazy."

"No kidding," Carey said, opening the car door. "You need to take a look, then tell me if you want to form a club."

I blinked, not sure why my eyes were suddenly stinging. I couldn't tell if I was shocked, affronted, or enraged—or some unholy combination of the three.

"Carey, if there are still psychos out there who think brown people should 'go back to where we came from,' then we really *should* form a club. Maybe the Latte Rebellion is sorely needed. Maybe we have real work to do."

Carey snorted and got out of the car. "Sorely needed? *Now* who sounds crazy?"

I didn't care how it sounded, though. I knew this was the right thing to do. I mean, seriously. *Go back where you came from*? If people were actually spewing that garbage *now*, in the twenty-first century, there was zero doubt in my mind that something had to be done. As Carey herself liked to say before getting on the soccer field, the best defense was a good offense.

"Hi, Mr. Rosenquist," I said a little shyly, shaking his hand as Miranda and I arrived outside the Student Council office. I'd never had him as a teacher, but he was famous around school for being younger than most of the other teachers—in his late twenties—and for doing a lot of unconventional projects in his psychology classes. Miranda said he'd be interested in the Latte Rebellion club, and she was right about that.

"Asha, right? Call me Chris. Ms. Allison speaks very highly of you." He grinned. Ms. Allison was my English teacher this year, and as far as I could tell, she hated her job, so her liking me was news to me. "I'm flattered you've asked me to help with your club. It sounds very avant-garde."

I wondered what, exactly, Miranda had told him about it. "Well, we're glad you're willing to be our advisor," I said nervously. "Thank you."

"Not a problem, not a problem." With a flourish, he pulled our neatly rolled-up paperwork out of the pocket of his leather jacket. "My John Hancock's already at the bottom. Let me know when you want to start holding meetings."

"We'll keep you posted," Miranda said.

"Can hardly wait." Mr. Rosenquist gave a little wave and strode off toward the teachers' lounge.

We opened the door to the Student Council office, where we were meeting with a representative from the Inter-Club Council and one of the ICC teacher advisors to get the Latte Rebellion approved as an official student organization. But as soon as I saw who was sitting behind the round table in the cramped, institutional-green-painted room, I felt my stomach drop to the bottom of my lucky tennis shoes.

Wouldn't you know it. Our Inter-Club Council representative was Roger Yee. He was sitting there smirking with unrestrained glee, and I knew immediately that this wasn't going to go well. And Vice Principal Malone, sitting next to him, was just plain scary. Ms. Allison may not have liked her job, but Mr. Malone didn't seem to like *students*.

"Have a seat," Mr. Malone said impassively. I handed

over our paperwork and Miranda and I both slid into our chairs without a word, exchanging a meaningful glance.

"Let's see here..." Roger drawled out each word with obvious enjoyment. He shook his head, his trendy, shaggy haircut immobile with hair gel. "The Inter-Club Council has reviewed your proposal for a new organization—for mixed-race students, isn't that right? Interesting, interesting...but we are *so* sorry to report that your proposal has been declined." He pursed his lips in mock regret, looking right at me.

"But Mr. Malone," I said, feeling anger start to rise, "we meet all the requirements. Mr. Rosenquist said he'd be the teacher advisor."

"I'm sorry," Mr. Malone said, sounding completely uninterested in the proceedings, "but that's what the ICC recommended. I read their report and I found it convincing. They just aren't sure your idea has the staying power to be viable, and there are already a huge number of ethnic clubs on campus."

Yeah, I thought, glaring at Roger. Like the Asian American Club. Well, he could have his club full of flunkies and yes-men. I, for one, was *not* going to be yet another groupie of the Bimbocracy. I stood up.

"Asha, hang on," Miranda said. "Roger, Mr. Malone, you know we have a good case here for this club. We've met the requirement of six registered members from the student body. I don't see why you'd just reject our proposal out of hand."

"Oh, we considered it carefully," Roger said, flipping

his pen around his fingers in a most annoying and show-offy fashion. "We just feel that your purpose is a little too *vague* to demonstrably benefit the University Park High community."

Roger, I was starting to see, was as full of crap as an overflowing toilet, and about as delightful to be around. I'd be willing to bet he hadn't even *read* our proposal. I pushed in my chair and grabbed our paperwork out of Roger's hands. Miranda stood up, too.

"Fine," I said through gritted teeth. I tried valiantly to think of a clever parting shot, but I couldn't. Instead, I forced out a quick "Thank you for your time" and headed for the door, Miranda right behind me.

This was clearly unfair. Just as clearly, something had to be done. And I knew exactly what I wanted to do.

Online communications among possible terrorist group members, from Latte Rebellion website bulletin board. Two copies attached.

Posted: October 20, 10:15 p.m.
By: SepiaRose
I think it's great that you guys are doing this! It's been a long time since we've seen any progress in getting equal representation for people of color in our society. Keep up the good work! There's sympathy for the cause everywhere! Great T-shirt—I can't wait to get mine.

Posted: October 21, 7:15 a.m.
By: Sk8orDie95
I know who you are and your stoopid idea is lame. Why dont you geek chicks get down off your high horse. Go Fightin Highlanders!!!!

5

The first general meeting of the unapproved, unofficial Latte Rebellion was held on Halloween night at Mocha Loco. Carey, Miranda, and I were all wearing our T-shirts, along with brown paper bags on our heads that we'd cut down to size, with jack-o-lantern holes cut out for our eyes and mouths—partly for fun, since it was Halloween; partly because it matched the shirts; and partly because none of us wanted to become gossip fodder at school. Plus it let us keep our aura of mystery, let us be our alter egos tonight.

It was 7:45, fifteen minutes before the meeting was supposed to start. Nobody was here yet that we were aware of, except for Leonard, who was working behind the register.

"Is everything ready?" Carey fiddled nervously with the ballpoint pen she'd been using to write up our meeting agenda. Convincing her to come—and take minutes—had been a lengthy process involving several consecutive days of whining, a substantial chocolate bribe, and repeated reassurances of our total anonymity.

"I think we're set." To be honest, I was just as nervous as she was. Maybe more so, since I was supposed to do most of the talking.

"You'll do great," Miranda said, rocking back and forth in her rickety wooden chair. "This is going to be amazing! When's your cousin supposed to get here?"

"Any time now." I grimaced behind my paper bag. "And if she brings her roommate, that means an official head count of … seven." I drank a sip of the latte I'd already ordered to get myself amped up for the meeting.

"Oh, I don't know," Miranda said. "Judging from the comments on your website, at least a few people from U-NorCal are coming."

"Yeah. I saw that too." Carey sounded even more edgy at the prospect of college students coming, even though she'd had no problem with inviting Leonard. Leonard, who we'd had to add to the list of Sympathizers on the website, and who threw off our alphabetical order of aliases by insisting on skipping Echo and going straight to Foxtrot. Pretentious, interfering friendship-wrecker.

"I don't know if U people are going to want to come to a high school thing," I said. "Just the thought gives me performance anxiety."

"Are you kidding? Having college students come to your meeting is great," Miranda said. "You could drum up some serious interest. And hey, you don't want to run the Rebellion for the rest of your life, right? This way you can kind of … fish around a little for someone to take over." She straightened her paper bag. "A successor, if you will."

"A successor?" I'd just figured that eventually our scheme would run its course, we'd have our money, and that would be it. The End. I was still getting used to the idea of this being an actual *group*, let alone finding someone to take it over after we were done, or had started college, or whatever.

"*I* think finding a successor is a great idea," Carey said, her mask rustling a little as she shifted position in the hard wooden chair. "I'm already feeling burned out just from preparing this meeting. And we have that calculus test on Monday."

"Ugh, *don't* remind me." To distract myself, I looked at the agenda again, written in Carey's tiny, crabbed, perfectly neat writing. I was going to start off with the introductions and manifesto, Carey was in charge of pushing T-shirts, and we'd all three contribute to the Q and A session. I hoped Bridget would help, too.

As if on cue, the door opened, letting in a swirl of crisp air and a few stray leaves along with Bridget and Darla. Bridget was wearing her Rebellion T-shirt, and I laughed when I saw what she was wearing along with it—a black fedora, ripped black jeans, and dark glasses.

"Hey, if it isn't the whole wrecking crew," she said, putting a half-empty bag of Halloween candy on the table.

"What's this?" I stared at the candy with mock incredulity. "We can't buy an airline ticket with fun size M&Ms."

"Har har. It's so you can feed your constituents something. Everyone likes free food." Bridget sat down at the small round table next to us.

"You three look so *cute!* I can't wait to get my shirt, you guys," Darla said before making a mad dash for the coffee counter. The Rebellion shirt would be a decided improvement, since she was currently wearing a baby tee with Sailor Moon's sickeningly cute bug-eyed face on it.

"So what's in store for tonight?" Bridget asked, putting her hot pink Chuck Taylors up on the chair next to her. I pushed the agenda over toward her and she ran one finger down the list, scanning it quickly.

"Lookin' good," she said. "What's your plan for the discussion session?"

"Well," Miranda said—this was her brainchild—"we were going to ask if anybody had anything to say about the ideals of the Latte Rebellion ... any thoughts about what to do at our next meeting. What we should do in the future to encourage appreciation of brown people and mixed ethnicity. That kind of thing."

"That should be interesting," Bridget said, a little too neutrally.

"What do you mean?" I looked at her sharply.

"Nothing, really; just that there are people already talking about it. I know this ... uh ... outspoken girl from my English class is coming, and she was pretty fired up about it." Bridget reached for the bag of M&Ms and took out a packet.

I didn't want to think about it. "Thanks for spreading the word, I guess."

"No problem. Still coming to Students for Social Justice tomorrow?" She glanced at me, then Miranda.

"After this?" I thought about it. "Maybe not. I might see how this plays out first."

"Or you might spend all evening on the phone with *Thad*," Miranda teased.

I looked away, embarrassed. I still hadn't called him, and wasn't sure if I would. I wouldn't know what to say.

Bridget chatted with us for a couple more minutes, and I nervously downed most of my large coffee. By the time it was nearly empty, I felt jittery and anxious to get started. I glanced around. A few of the tables near us were already occupied. I recognized a handful of people from school, including David Castro and one of his skater friends, Matt Lee. Matt was wearing one of our shirts. So was Maria McNally, a junior who was a notorious overachiever and one of the charter members of our failed school club. I'd always thought she was part Latina, but I couldn't be certain—and I was the last person to insist someone might be Mexican. Maria had a notepad and mechanical pencil out, ready to take notes, and she'd brought a group of three other juniors.

I felt butterflies in the pit of my stomach; this was already so much more of a big deal than we'd originally planned. But Roger hadn't given us much of a choice.

By the time I called the meeting to order—banging my empty latte mug on the table to get everyone's attention—there were about twenty people in our corner of the café, where we'd set several chairs and tables apart and put up a Latte Rebellion poster behind the "head table." People had been staring sideways at the three of us in paper bags and whispering to each other. Now was the moment of truth.

I swallowed hard.

"Welcome to the first general meeting of the Latte Rebellion." My voice sounded reedy and shaky, but there was scattered applause and a few sarcastic whoops. "Before we begin, you may be asking yourselves why we're wearing these paper bags over our heads."

"Yeah," a couple of people shouted.

"Take it off! Take it *all* off," said David Castro, turning to Matt Lee and laughing.

"Order ... order!" I banged the latte glass again, feeling like I was in a TV courtroom drama. "We are wearing these paper bags because the Rebellion is not about individuality. It is about our power as a group, as a movement; about the power of our ideas. We don't want our identities, our appearance, distracting from the cause."

The meeting area was silent, and all I could hear was the random clinking of coffee cups and rustling of papers. Everyone was looking at me. I could even feel Carey's and Miranda's stares from behind their brown paper bags. I took a deep breath, armpit sweat trickling down my sides, and rushed on.

"Having said that, I would like to introduce the key

members and Sympathizers of the Rebellion. Some have chosen to remain anonymous, while others choose to show their faces. Yet all are equally important to the movement." I ran through the list, pointing out Agent Alpha, Captain Charlie, Lieutenant Bravo, Commander Delta, and even Field Officer Foxtrot, who gave a cocky wave from behind the coffee bar.

I then solemnly read through the manifesto. When I got to the part that said "The world must acknowledge you! The world will appreciate you," people started muttering "yeah!" and "right on!" And when I recited the concluding mantra—"Lattes of the world, unite!"—the whole group actually cheered and clapped. Not like they would for, say, a band, or even a pep rally, but still, it was amazing. Carey and I had written it sort of as a joke. But here were people—a few white, a few black, but mostly every shade of brown—sitting in a café, listening to everything I was saying and *not laughing*.

This was a novel experience. But also... really, really cool. I felt a slow and quiet satisfaction spreading through me. And if it hadn't been for our club proposal getting summarily rejected, this might never have happened.

When we opened up the floor for the Q and A and discussion, of course somebody had to ask "Who *are* you guys, really?"

"If you don't already know," Miranda said solemnly, "we can't tell you." A few people laughed at that. The girl who asked the question got up and left soon afterward, looking bored, but we still had a bigger group of people than I'd ever expected.

There were a few other comments, and then a girl got up and asked—demanded, really—to read a poem. Carey, Miranda, and I looked at each other. Bridget glanced at me meaningfully; evidently this was the loudmouth from her class.

The girl, who had short, spiky black hair and what could only be described as a pierced face, pulled a piece of paper out of her pocket and cleared her throat.

> *"For decades upon decades*
> *We have been oppressed*
> *Suppressed*
> *Re-PRESSED into their MOLD!*
> *No longer! A new age has begun*
> *In which nothing is black or white*
> *But like coffee with milk*
> *Latte."*

She paused for breath, and I chose that moment to jump in before anybody else decided to get up and leave.

"That was … an unexpected addition to our evening," I said. "Thank you, um …"

"Radha," she said, looking up, surprised. "I have four more stanzas if you want to hear them."

I was too appalled to speak. There was a brief silence, and then Maria McNally stepped in, waving a hand to get our attention.

"We should read a stanza per meeting," she said. "Maybe to wind things down at the end." There was unanimous, possibly ironic, applause. I looked at Maria gratefully and she gave me a tight smile.

"Tonight was just an introduction to the Rebellion," Miranda added. "But we should have a plan for our next meeting. What do people want to talk about?" Carey pulled out her pen and sat with it poised over her spiral notebook. The room was suddenly filled with enthusiastic shouts, the awkward poetry moment forgotten.

"The accomplishments of brown people!"

"How to start a dialogue about mixed ethnicity!"

"Where to meet hot chicks!" That one was David Castro, not surprisingly. Still, I was thrilled to the core that *we'd* done this. That we'd created a group people actually wanted to be involved in, that meant something to them—something more than just a new T-shirt.

For the first time in my life, maybe, I was doing something meaningful and important. And maybe this was where I belonged: where people appreciated me for being mixed up. It didn't matter if they couldn't see my face. I was one of them, and we were the Latte Rebellion.

———

When I walked through the front gate of University Park High School the following Monday, I screeched to a halt right next to the first bank of freshman lockers. Something was very weird. Sure, the same groups of kids were milling around the locker area and loitering outside various class-room buildings and smoking cigarettes just off school property. But the first thing I noticed was that there was a lot more coffee than usual. People were holding paper cups with cup warmers around them, draining the last dregs before throwing them away, or pouring hot liquid out of thermoses into the little screw-top cups. Even the campus security guard had a Styrofoam cup in his hand.

Of course, it could have just been discount-coffee day at the convenience store down the street, and it *was* a cold November morning.

But it didn't seem like coincidence after I saw the number of people who were wearing Latte Rebellion T-shirts. *Our* T-shirts. I hadn't had a chance to check on how many we'd sold by now, but it seemed like every tenth person was wearing one. I counted at least five on the way to my first-period history class alone.

Was the Rebellion really so... popular? Friday night at the meeting, it felt serious but it felt *underground,* like we were an indie band that only a handful of people knew about. I mean, when I wore my T-shirt to the grocery store with my mom earlier that night, all I got were some strange looks and a free sample from the coffee counter.

Then I thought again about the twenty-some-odd people who'd been staring at me in my paper bag mask, most of them earnest and enthusiastic. There was Miranda, who really thought we could accomplish something. Radha, who wrote a *poem.* To be honest, it felt good to be the center of attention. For my *ideas* to be the center of attention, instead of my Mexican J.Lo curves or my unfortunately placed towel.

At lunch, I took another look to see who exactly was wearing the shirts. Matt Lee was wearing his again, rumpled as though he'd slept in it. Ayesha Jones was wearing one. Rosanna Nasser, who was on the volleyball team. A rumored gang member named Quentin Rodriguez. One of the varsity cheerleaders, Shay Saintmarie. I couldn't help feeling a little twinge of pride every time I saw one.

Later that day, I was rummaging in my locker for a missing assignment when I heard Shay say something to Kaelyn that really got my attention. I ducked down a little, hoping they would continue ignoring me.

"…Amber left right after they introduced everyone," Shay said a little breathlessly, "but Stephanie stayed and said it was all weird and hush-hush, like the people leading the meeting didn't want anyone to see their faces. Isn't that crazy? Like a James Bond movie." She flipped her relaxed dark hair, perfectly contained by a shimmery gold headband, back over one shoulder.

Kaelyn snorted. "Whatever. It's just another stupid club. Who cares?"

My cheeks burned, but I kept rustling papers in my locker even though I'd already found my physics worksheet.

"They're supposed to be planning something *really* major, like, I don't know, maybe a party, but it's still under wraps; at least that's what I heard. *I* think it's cool."

"Well, I happen to think the cheer car wash is pretty

major," Kaelyn said acidly. "But you still haven't told me whether you think *that's* cool." I couldn't see her face from where I was hiding, but her tone was pure venom.

"Oh, come *on*, Kay-Kay. Seriously. You think I'd forget about that? I already made signs." I heard a locker door slam shut, and from the corner of my eye I could see Shay put her arm around Kaelyn's stiff shoulders as they walked off. I straightened up and stretched my neck, unable to keep a gleeful smile off my face. They'd been talking about *us*. We, the Rebellion, were literally the talk of the school.

On Wednesday, Ms. Allison came up to me after class as I was stuffing my English notes into my binder.

"Asha, may I speak to you for a moment?" She leaned on the desk next to mine, which had already been vacated, and let out a heavy sigh.

"Sure, I guess," I said, putting my notebook into my backpack. Ms. Allison smoothed her navy blue skirt and tucked a lock of graying-blond hair back into her bun. I could see sweat stains under the armpits of her white blouse. She stared at a spot somewhere above my head.

"I see you're wearing one of those Latte Rebellion T-shirts that are so popular these days."

"Yeah, they're cute, huh?" I smiled and hoped I sounded noncommittal. Why was she asking *me*? I mean, I was the only one left in the room, but still.

"They're certainly unique," she said. "Is it one of these new brand names?"

"Uh ..." I thought frantically. "I guess so." I really didn't want any teachers prying into this. Plus, there was the fact that we weren't supposed to exist in the first place, thanks to Roger.

"I hadn't really pegged you as someone who cared much about fads." She glanced at me sharply.

I swallowed. "It was a gift."

"Well, some of the teachers and administrators have noticed that an awful lot of students are wearing these shirts. We were worrying that it has some sort of... significance."

"Um... I heard someone say it was some kind of... an advocacy group." I couldn't believe I pulled that one out of my butt.

"Advocacy group." Ms. Allison sounded skeptical. "Mrs. Eastman and I visited the website after school yesterday, and she thought it looked like a childish joke. I'm not so sure about that. We thought we might bring it up with Vice Principal Malone, since he's advising the Student Council this year."

"I'm pretty sure it isn't anything to worry about," I told her, trying to sound like it didn't mean anything to me.

But the truth was, I was shaken. The last thing we needed was for Mr. Malone to start snooping around. If he made the connection—if he realized it was us—we'd get called into the office to explain ourselves. He might end up telling my parents, and on pain of lecture I'd have to spill everything, down to our underlying fundraising scheme. And then my parents would probably laugh, ho-ho-ho, what a cute idea, you little scamps, and promptly confiscate our earnings and put them squarely into the college fund, never to be seen again—which would totally defeat the purpose of having done it in the first place. No way was that an option. No way in hell.

We'd just have to stay anonymous, swear our charter members to secrecy, and hope nobody spilled the beans until our vacation money was safely squirreled away—or better yet, safely spent.

———

I reported the incident to Carey and Miranda later that night. We were sitting around Carey's kitchen table, ostensibly studying and keeping an eye on her brothers while Dr.-Mr. Wong and Dr.-Mrs. Wong were at a dinner party.

"What did you get for number eight?" Carey put her finger down on the page to hold her place while she took a long gulp of hot chocolate.

"Plus or minus radical five," I said. "And so then Ms. Allison said she hoped not to see any 'trouble' started by the sudden popularity of this 'Rebellion business.'" I laughed, edgily.

"That's not right," Carey said.

"Well, I *know*," I said. "It's just a bunch of shirts."

"And the most insidious social movement known to humankind, mwahahaha," Miranda intoned. It was supposed to be funny, but I was kind of freaking out.

"No, I mean the math problem." Carey pointed at my homework. "I think you forgot to—"

"Forget the math problem," I said, pushing my notebook aside. "This is serious! What if the school administrators make the connection? Malone already knows Miranda and I proposed a club that was refused a charter."

"This *assignment* is serious," Carey insisted. "You can't afford to get another C on a quiz."

I shrugged and glanced at her sideways. "It was just one quiz. Mr. Martinez drops the lowest quiz grade." Whereas, getting called into the vice principal's office would result in a call to our parents, if we got into enough hot water. And then, bye-bye vacation.

"Dropping the lowest quiz grade is not the point. The point is ... the point is, I am so not ready to think about getting into trouble for this. So. Not. Ready." Carey stared determinedly at her math book.

"It's not like we're meeting on campus or anything. They can't do anything to us. And they won't find out who we are." Miranda sounded a lot more confident than I felt. I was starting to be really glad she was on our side. We needed a cheerleader—and I didn't mean Kaelyn.

"That's true. There aren't any identifying characteristics on the website. We even signed up for that private domain thingy." I calmed down a little and managed to finish another calculus problem. "Which is a good thing. My parents would freak if they knew we were doing this."

"Are you kidding?" Miranda put her pencil down. "Parents love this stuff. Even my mom was excited. 'I'm so glad you're involved in something worthwhile and socially responsible instead of doodling cartoons all the time,'" she mimicked, in a nasal voice with a slight Hispanic accent.

"Well, I'm not going to tell mine." I knew what they'd say, and it would have five different kinds of "no way" in it. Students for Social Justice was okay, but I cringed at the idea of them finding out about the Latte Rebellion, and me having to explain why I wanted to keep doing it after the club proposal was shot down. They might support the ideas, but they would not be okay with me "wasting" money, or wasting time on what they'd consider a futile endeavor.

"Don't tell my parents either," Carey said. "Oh, and for god's sake, don't tell them about Leonard. I'm supposed to be at your house tomorrow night, studying."

"You're eighteen, Care; they can't do anything." Her parents, like mine, were protective, but surely they were used to the constant stream of would-be suitors by now. I didn't see why *I* had to be her convenient excuse to see Mr. Snoogums. "Since when are you going out with Leonard?"

"Yes, dish, please." Miranda put her chin in her hand and focused her attention on Carey.

"We're not *going out*," Carey said unconvincingly. She couldn't suppress a tiny, self-satisfied smile.

"The hell you aren't," Miranda said, laughing. "Look at your face!"

"We're just going to a comedy show at the University Theatre. And dinner first," Carey added in an undertone.

"Going out to dinner!" I practically squealed. "Why didn't you tell me *before*?"

"Because I knew you'd screech," she said. "You know, I felt bad … after running into you that time."

"Why did you feel *bad*? You can go out with whoever you want. You don't have to tag along to my boring crap." Even if that "boring crap"—i.e., Students for Social Justice—led directly to more inspiring ideas for the club, more popularity for the Rebellion, and, of course, more T-shirt sales. I took a sip of hot chocolate and tried to look like I didn't care, even though my hands were trembling a little. "Knock yourself out."

"Gee, thanks," Carey said, sarcastically.

"Simmer down, kids!" Miranda said. "Why don't we finish this problem set?"

I let myself be distracted, but the truth was, it really got to me. It wasn't the fact that Carey was going out with Leonard the Tattooed Lamewad so much as my growing suspicion that Carey was losing interest in the Latte Rebellion, in the scheme we'd had so much fun hatching together. The suspicion, which I realized had been burgeoning inside my head for a while, that she wasn't as interested as I was in seeing it through.

She hadn't wanted to turn the Latte Rebellion into a club in the first place, after all. I knew she was more worried about getting a scholarship, about finally getting out on her own without three brothers hanging off her like monkeys. But this—clubs, activities, socially worthwhile endeavors—this could only *help* her get a scholarship, if she'd just put in the time. Time we would spend hanging out together, as an added bonus.

Instead, I felt like I was seeing her less than ever.

———

That night, although I kept thinking about Carey, I finally worked up the nerve to call Thad. I had no idea what I was going to say to him; I didn't really have any questions about colleges, since I knew where I was going to apply and the deadlines weren't for another month or more. But I felt like he'd asked me to call, like he might wonder why I hadn't. And it wasn't a chance I wanted to pass up.

So I dialed. After a couple of rings, he picked up.

"Hi, this is Asha, from the U-NorCal seminar," I said in a rush, half-afraid he wouldn't remember me.

"Oh hey, I was hoping I'd hear from you," he said. "Thanks for helping me wind down after my trained monkey speech."

"No problem. I specialize in inane, non-challenging conversation." I squeezed my eyes closed and smiled so hard my cheeks ached.

We exchanged a few pleasantries, but my mind kept wandering back to Carey. I found myself asking Thad whether he and Greg had ever had any disagreements when they were figuring out their clinic plan.

"Not really," he said. "We went back and forth for a while on which model we were going to use, and then I got kinda p.o.'d at him last week because he slacked off and did this slam poetry thing he's into, but nothing major." I could hear him smiling. "Why?"

"Oh," I said. "I started this ... thing ... at school with a friend of mine. And I'm not sure she really wants to be involved now. I thought she was into it, but ..." I cringed at how stupid I sounded, suddenly unsure I wanted to tell him about our ideas. What if he thought they were juvenile, amateurish? I pictured myself trying to explain the Latte Rebellion to him, and everything coming out all wrong.

But he might be interested, too, said a quiet voice inside my head, which I quickly smushed right back down. Come on, I told myself. He knows nothing about you. You just met this guy, you talked to him for a total of ten minutes, and you think he even gives a crap? He doesn't want to hear about your little problems.

In the end, caution—or was it fear?—won.

"I guess we just had different expectations of the project," I finally said.

"Sorry to hear that," Thad said, and because he didn't ask for more information, I didn't elaborate.

It was my dad who asked for information, once I'd said goodbye and flipped my phone shut.

"Who were you talking to? What's this about a clinic project?" He leaned too casually on the door frame. I'd left my door open, and clearly he'd been eavesdropping.

"It's just this . . . guy I met at that club meeting I went to with Bridget," I told him. "He's working on a community clinic project." I smiled a little, thinking about Thad, but my smile turned to a grimace when I thought about how utterly non-smooth I'd been on the phone.

"A guy?" My dad shifted and peered at me as if he suspected I wasn't telling him the whole story.

"*Yes,* Dad, a *guy.* Jeez, do you have to interrogate me about everyone I talk to?"

"Asha, please. I'm just asking a question. I'm trying to

take an interest in your life." He sighed and straightened up. "I know you've been busy with school, so I'm glad you had a chance to do something with Bridget. I just don't want you to get distracted."

"When was the last time I got distracted?" I was now extra glad my parents didn't know about the Latte Rebellion. "I'll be fine. Remember, you gave me that speech about time management when I started high school. I won't let guys distract me." I fidgeted on the bed, then added under my breath, "Like any guys are ever interested in me anyway."

"Let's not start that," Dad said with an exasperated sigh. I didn't want to start down that road either—that way lay madness and melancholy—but Dad *really* hated it.

"Just … keep your eyes on the prize, kiddo, and don't blow it," he said shortly, and left. I shut the door after him and flopped back on the bed. Relieved, yes, but to be totally honest, I was still thinking about Thad. Awkward phone call or not … something about him made my innards fluttery and my brain gooey. Or maybe it was the other way around.

Either way, I realized that I didn't really have the grounds to accuse Carey of anything Leonard-related when I was just as clearly guilty of letting myself get—as my dad would put it—sidetracked. Unfortunately, this was not one of those realizations that made me feel like a weight had been lifted from my shoulders.

———

I adjusted the paper bag on my head; my forehead was sweating and I hoped it wouldn't soak through. A month to the day after the first Latte Rebellion meeting, we were holding the second official meeting, back at Mocha Loco with its increasingly familiar burnt-coffee smell. It was just like before—a couple of our posters hanging on the wall behind the table where we were sitting, the three of us sipping our lattes and waiting to get started under the watchful gaze of our cartoon alter egos.

Only this time, every seat in the café was turned toward us.

There had to be at least fifty people crammed into that small, brightly lit room. *Fifty.* My stomach flip-flopped a little. Carey was shifting nervously in the chair next to me and even Miranda seemed fidgety. She'd wrapped her long cornrow braids up into a bun so they wouldn't show underneath her paper bag—we were all a little extra paranoid that someone at school would find out who we were, ever since Ms. Allison's weird conversation with me. It seemed like every time somebody wore a Latte Rebellion shirt at school, the teachers would give them sidelong looks and have furtive, whispered conversations with each other at lunchtime or between classes.

I wondered what would happen if someone recognized our voices and decided to say something. Or if word got back to Mr. Malone. Would we get a warning, a black mark? Something that would screw up our academic records? None of us needed that.

I stood up and the room went eerily silent. I gulped my latte and set it down on the glass table with a decisive clunk, and then set my note cards aside. Miranda and Carey looked at me in surprise.

"Due to the potential threat faced by Agent Alpha—myself—Captain Charlie, and Lieutenant Bravo, by outside forces hostile to our cause, who might fear us as instigators..." I cleared my throat and continued in a scratchier voice, in the hopes of disguising it a little. "In order to preserve our anonymity, today's meeting will be conducted by Sergeant Echo and Field Officer Foxtrot." I bowed, handed Darla my note cards, and took my seat. I would talk to the core crew of Sympathizers about this later so they didn't think I was going rogue, but for now I felt some of the pressure ease. This was, after all, supposed to be a group effort.

There was a pause, and then the room erupted in noise. Applause, some of it, but the surprising—and somewhat disturbing—part was the shouts of support: "Keep it real, sister!" "Fight the power!" "Right on, you do what you have to do!" "The Latte's got your back!" I exchanged glances with Carey and Miranda, and I could see Bridget sitting in one corner looking mildly startled, which for her was the equivalent of utter amazement.

Of course, the Tattooed Lamewad looked perfectly calm, even happy to lead the meeting. But he was the main reason Carey had even agreed to be here, so it was hard to be too much of a hater.

"Okay, people." Leonard stood up and leaned on the coffee counter. "Let's get into what the Latte Rebellion should be doing to promote the cause in our manifesto. Think globally, act locally, right? Let's take suggestions." He waved a hand in the direction of his audience. Carey uncapped her pen, ready to take notes, looking raptly at Leonard—as raptly as you could look at someone when you had a paper bag over your head.

The ideas started off pretty dull. Bake sales. Car washes. Candy grams during homeroom, with coffee-flavored candy. Then, one person suggested painting a mural of prominent mixed-race and just generally brown people, like Keanu Reeves and President Obama, on the wall of the University Student Union.

It wasn't a bad thought, but was it really feasible? It wasn't like Carey, Miranda, or I had any time to actually do any of it. And what if we ended up doing something that would *drain* the vacation fund? I whispered this to Darla, who was sitting at our table, and she nodded vigorously like a little bobble-head.

"Does anyone have ideas that *won't* deplete our limited finances in five seconds?" Darla grinned impishly. The room went quiet, and you could practically hear all the mental gears grinding. Considering Darla's obsession with action figures, I was floored by her skills with an unruly crowd.

"We could bring in a guest speaker," Ayesha Jones said suddenly. "Hold a public seminar." She was in student government and debate club, so I wasn't surprised she suggested it. What did surprise me was the flurry of shouted approval, enthusiasm, and ideas that came next. It seemed like everybody was into it. Even Carey couldn't think of a downside. After all, with a guest speaker, neither of us would have to do the talking.

"Maybe you should call it a rally. It sounds more upbeat," Bridget said. Another cheer went around the room, then people actually quieted down and got organized. Darla wrote down suggestions for speakers and locations in a ridiculously tiny notebook that had a Transformer on the cover. Then, she and Leonard came up with a step-by-step to-do list and delegated so efficiently that even my dad would have been impressed.

I had to hand it to Leonard: he was good at getting people organized. Darla, meanwhile, was amazing at drumming up support and excitement. I was in awe. And, frankly, I was kind of jealous, wishing just a little that I hadn't given up control of the meeting. It was probably better this way, though, having Agent Alpha sort of fade into mythological status. I could get more done behind the scenes, especially if I didn't have to hide my head under a bag, I told myself. But I still felt torn.

When I looked back at the entire situation so far, it was crazy; surreal. I never thought so many people would notice or care about the Latte Rebellion, not really. I just thought people would buy our shirts because they thought the design was cool, and then basically we'd take the money and run and no one would remember much about it. After the shirts ended up at the bottoms of people's closets, the website would live on as one of those strange artifacts of some passing fad that nobody understands anymore, like the Peanut Butter Jelly dancing banana website.

I didn't know exactly what was going to happen now, but clearly, that was not it.

The following April:
Ashmont Unified School District Board Room

Carey went back to her seat, her head bowed and not meeting my eyes. Nothing else that happened today could possibly be any worse. Even if the disciplinary hearing board decided to expel me, I wouldn't feel as raw or as torn apart as I did thinking about Carey, about how our friendship was never going to be the same, because she'd obviously placed me at the bottom of her priority list.

Then, my guts twisted again as the hearing officer called for Miranda.

"Ms. Levin, please speak loudly and clearly so that all the panelists can hear you."

"No problem," Miranda said grimly, standing rigidly in front of him. She was an inch or two taller than he was, which created the impression that she was the one asking the questions. Her long braids were tied up tightly into a bun and she was wearing wire-framed glasses I'd never seen before. Knowing Miranda, they were just for show, but they made her look a few years older.

"Now, Ms. Levin," the hearing officer croaked, "I understand that you, too, were heavily involved in this

'Rebellion.' I'd like to hear your impression of the events, and how you happened to get drawn into Ms. Jamison's ill-advised disruptions of the educational environment."

"Gladly." Miranda took a few index cards out of her pocket and I could hear a collective sigh go around the disciplinary hearing panel. "I'll keep this brief. Asha and Carey might not have known it when they first conceived of the Latte Rebellion, but this was a cause worth investing time into, an opportunity to inform and educate, and a set of ideals worth fighting for. It was *not* a 'terrorist threat.' Not at all." She met the hearing officer's gaze levelly and fearlessly.

"Are you denying that Ms. Jamison's actions caused a disruption during school hours?" He looked at her skeptically.

"Ms. Jamison did what needed to be done," Miranda said, and there was a sharp intake of breath from someone in the audience. I could feel my dad glaring at me from the seat to my right, and I bristled. He'd been acting as if I should have just ignored everything that happened, as if it didn't matter what was important to me. "And no, I don't think what she did caused the disruption. We all know what happened, and witnesses will tell you that Asha was not the instigator. As for what she *did* do ..."

My muscles tightened, but I couldn't look away from Miranda.

"All Asha did was enable our voices to be heard. Voices that don't always *get* heard," Miranda said. Her voice was shaking a little, but still calm. "The Latte Rebellion wouldn't have gotten as big as it did if it hadn't been needed. Sir, do you realize there are people out there who still think that to be proud of being mixed-ethnicity is somehow un-American? Somebody left a comment on our website saying that if we're not happy with the way things are, we ought to go back where we came from." She let out a short bark of a laugh, but I could hear surprised murmurs from elsewhere in the audience. I glanced quickly at my parents, and saw that my mother—*my* mother—was enthralled, watching Miranda as if she'd never seen her before.

"I don't know about you," Miranda continued, looking now at each member of the panel in turn, "but if we can open even a few eyes to reality, and have people appreciate us for who we are, then all of this was worth it. *All* of it."

The hearing officer seemed shocked into silence, along with the rest of the room. As for me, a little of the weight I'd been carrying all morning had been lifted, and I finally felt hope for the first time that day.

Then my father leaned toward me and said, quietly, in my ear, "If this is the type of trouble your friends at school are getting you into, then maybe taking you out of there would be a blessing in disguise." My mother nodded.

I sucked in an angry breath, so outraged that I wanted to scream at him, but I kept my mouth clamped shut. I didn't trust myself to say anything coherent. Plus I'd probably get booked by the school board for creating another "disturbance."

If my parents weren't on my side, then no matter what Miranda said, I wasn't sure I had much hope. The whole disciplinary hearing panel could vote me back into school—hell, they could throw me a parade and shower me with confetti out on the football field—but if my father wanted to pull me out anyway, it didn't make any difference. None of this did.

Exhibit A.6:
MATERIALS VIOLATING
BOARD POLICY SECTION 418.III.K

Inflammatory materials distributed on school property.
Two copies attached.

6

The turnout at our December 10th rally-planning meeting was even bigger than before. People were leaning against the tan-painted walls of Mocha Loco or finding space between the crowded tables to sit on the floor. Carey, Miranda, and I sat at a table up front with David Castro and pretended to be normal audience members, letting Leonard and Darla handle the heavy lifting.

Not speaking up was a bit harder than I'd thought; you should have heard the applause when they announced we were close to meeting our T-shirt sales goal.

I gleefully relived this scene more than a couple times over the rest of the week. And at this particular moment, recalling the raucous cheering and yells of support was helping me get through a decidedly less euphoric situation.

"Asha, come here and stir this dal, please, or the lentils will stick to the bottom of the pot. Quickly—*jaldi, jaldi!*" my Nani said impatiently. She bustled to the other side of our kitchen and checked on the apple-filled pastries Grandma Bee had placed on a cookie sheet in the oven.

"Blanca, these are turning brown," Nani said, shooting a look across the kitchen at my dad's mom, who was pulling a plate of deviled eggs out of the fridge.

Unlike the Sympathizers at the planning meeting, this was a crowd I dearly wished I could have avoided. Putting both sides of my family in the same house for a multiple-holiday Diwali-Christmas Festival of Insanity was too much to handle. Never mind that Diwali was long past and Christmas wasn't here yet. With both grandmothers fighting for control of the kitchen prior to our annual mid-December dual-family blowout, there were clashing aromas competing for dominance, flour was everywhere, and there was a constant tug-of-war over the spice rack. As a kid I'd loved the excitement—and, of course, the presents. Now I kind of wished we were atheists.

"They shouldn't be done yet, Geeta," Grandma Bee insisted, her voice cutting across the household noise as Nani made as if to remove the pastries from the oven. "You must have overheated the oven when you were baking your, ah, chicken casserole. And *please* call me Bee. You know nobody's called me Blanca in years."

"Only if you'll call it biryani," Nani muttered peevishly under her breath.

"*¡Ave María Purísima!*" Grandma Bee said, sighing. This was one of the rare occasions when she got so exasperated she resorted to Spanish. The rest of the time, it was strictly English Only. She even got uncomfortable when Nani spoke Hindi.

My fourteen-year-old cousin Christopher cowered at the kitchen table where he was tossing a fruit salad, and I hunched over the gigantic pot of dal on the stovetop and hoped I could make a quick escape. I'd rather be backstage. Or, preferably, not even in the building.

At the Latte Rebellion meeting I'd been officially backstage, sitting quietly at our table and trying not to attract too much attention as the first-ever lecture and rally were meticulously planned out. There was a short list of three potential speakers, and Maria McNally volunteered to hold an under-the-radar meeting at our high school to get the word out. We—Agent Alpha, Captain Charlie, and Lieutenant Bravo—had been put in charge of making propaganda-comic-style rally flyers, using Miranda's genius artistic talent.

Weeks ago, Miranda had sketched out three superhero characters with paper bags over their heads and the Latte Rebellion logo on their spandex bodysuits. All three were mild-mannered and respectable young women by day, but were ready to throw on their Latte Rebellion outfits and jet out the door if they heard that a brown person somewhere was being oppressed. When we told Miranda how amazing her drawings were, she did a little happy dance because her list of prospective colleges included some prestigious art schools. None of us had heard anything from colleges yet, though, except for a few kids who did Early Decision.

If Robbins College had had an Early Decision option, I totally would have gone for it. I kept thinking about that School of Social Welfare and about Thad, right down the road at UC Berkeley. But I had to wait around like all the rest of the peasantry.

Christopher dropped the fruit salad spoon on the floor, somehow managing to send squishy bits of banana, orange, apple, and kiwi everywhere. In fear of the raging grandmas, he began to apologize pathetically. I winced and tried to ignore the sudden flood of solicitous, reassuring babble that ensued as both Nani and Grandma Blanca swooped in with paper towels.

It seemed fitting, somehow, that the thing to bring the bickering matriarchs of my family together would be a fruit salad. Not the weeks of meticulously planning out the big meal via emails back and forth, making sure to include favorite dishes from both the Indian-American side and the Mexican-Irish-American side of the family. Not the menu that included both biryani and Spanish-style rice, in addition to the mixed nuts, deviled eggs, and roasted turkey breast.

Nope, it was the plain old cobbled-together culturally neutral fruit salad. An out-of-control riot of flavors and colors tossed willy-nilly into a bowl (and, thanks to Christopher, partially onto the floor).

Yeah, that was my family, all right. A real riot. And I was caught up in it with no way out.

Truthfully, though, I was a little relieved to stay close to home and stop worrying about the Rebellion for a couple of days. There was a lot of pressure now that it *was* a club, and it was exhausting to have to keep track of it all—the meetings, the guest speaker—*and* make sure that our vacation was still possible. Every week, I transferred whatever money we'd made out of the online payment system and into the bank account I'd opened for our travel fund. It was something Carey had volunteered to do, but somehow I'd ended up doing this, too. Not only that, but most of our college applications were due at the end of December, and I had to scramble to get those finished in what little spare time I had left.

By the time the wrecking crew that was my extended family cleared out of the house and I felt like my Winter Break had officially started, all I had the energy to do was flop on the bed, ready to hibernate. Which was basically what I did: sleeping till ten every morning, watching daytime TV until the afternoon, and trying to go out as often as possible in the evenings so as to avoid my parents' obsession with cable news shows.

The Wednesday after the family blowout event, I came inside after a long, chilly day of Christmas shopping with Miranda and Carey and found both of my parents sitting at the kitchen table, looking up at me *very* somberly. Dad was chewing absently on the end of a pen, which he only did when he was mega-stressed. He had his reading glasses on like he'd been working.

"What happened?" I asked. When they didn't answer

right away, I dropped into one of the cushioned wooden chairs. It had to be bad. I thought about the constant barrage of reports about the weak economy lately—the ones my parents kept watching ad nauseam—and started to get a horrible feeling. "Is everything okay?"

"Oh, Asha," my mother said, shaking her head and looking down at a piece of paper in front of her. I leaned over to peer at it and felt the bottom drop out of my stomach. My semester report card. And it clearly wasn't up to par.

"You went through my *mail*?" I said, stalling.

"Don't avoid the subject," my dad said, his voice flat. "We're talking about your report card, not your personal mail. A report card that is not, by any stretch of the imagination, up to your usual standards." He looked at me, and I squirmed in my seat.

"It's only one semester," I began desperately. "I have a lot of time to bring up my grades. Nobody looks at midterm results. It's just been … senioritis," I concluded, clenching my hands in my lap and hoping I sounded convincing. But I was in deep Titicaca.

In the long silence that followed, a bird tweeted cheerfully in the purple-leafed plum tree outside the kitchen window, as if to mock me.

"If this is 'senioritis,' then maybe you need some treatment," my dad finally said, thick eyebrows drawn down in an ominous frown. I knew he wasn't trying to be funny. "Right here it says you got a B-minus in Calculus. A B-minus! That's almost a C." I avoided his hard gaze. "Last quarter you got an A-minus in math. I don't understand it.

And your other grades … History, B; Biology, B-plus … what happened, Asha?"

"I got an A in English," I pointed out. My voice trembled, but I tried to keep composure. It couldn't be *that* bad. I'd done fine on my SATs and on my first quarter report card. This one set of grades didn't really matter.

"Look at these comments, though," my mother said, quietly but with worry in her voice. She slid a finger down the computer printout. "'Student shows aptitude for this subject but does not put full effort into class assignments.' You got that comment from three of your teachers! You've been spending all this time 'studying' with your friends, but maybe we need to rethink that arrangement."

They'd said nearly the same thing back in eighth grade, the time Carey and I let Kaelyn (yes, *that* Kaelyn) convince us to ditch school and go to the mall—they weren't sure my friends were a good influence, I'd behaved irresponsibly, I'd allowed peer pressure to get the better of me … the list of my faults went on and on. They were just *so disappointed*. My mother had said she felt responsible, and I knew she was afraid she'd made some critical mistake in raising me and this was the beginning of the end. She had the same look on her face now as she did then.

I bowed my head, cheeks flaming. "I guess we haven't been studying very efficiently." What could I say? There was nothing *to* say, unless I wanted to confess everything. Which I didn't.

"We're just concerned for you," my dad said, his voice softening. "I realize it's hard to keep going at the same pace when high school is almost over, but if you don't maintain your effort, it *will* hurt your chances of getting into college. Your final grades matter, you know that. We just want you to get the success you deserve, honey, but you have to put the work into it."

My dad segued into his favorite soliloquy about how he was a self-made man whose parents never went to college and never could have gotten as far as he did in life if he hadn't worked hard every second of every day, blah blah blah. And my grandparents—on both sides—had worked so hard fighting against prejudice and ignorance. They would be so disappointed if they knew what had happened.

I tried not to roll my eyes. If my grandparents *really* knew what I'd been doing, with the Latte Rebellion ... I wasn't so sure they'd be disappointed.

I sighed and fiddled with the empty envelope stamped with the school letterhead. Part of me wanted to tell my parents everything, about how we'd had this bright idea about raising enough money to take a vacation next summer without having to waste valuable study time on anything so prosaic as a regular *job*. But I couldn't. If I tried to explain, it would come out sounding all wrong. Just like every other time I tried to explain myself to them, it would end up being my fault anyway.

Dad's lecture went on and on, the point essentially being that if I started hanging out with "troublemakers" and slacking off, I would ruin my life, eliminate any chances of going to college, and end up in a dead-end food service job for the rest of my life. Going into food service was the worst thing imaginable to my parents.

Meanwhile, my mother kept nervously wringing her hands and talking about how they wanted me to have every opportunity and that was why they wanted to nip whatever it was in the bud and put me back on the path to good study habits. I nodded and said "yes, Dad" and "no, Mom" at the right spots, trying not to scream from frustration.

Still, there was the mocking little voice in my head that kept insisting I should have listened to Carey. She'd kept telling me I needed to spend more time on Calculus, and I hadn't wanted to hear it. Who would? But now I was paying the price.

It wasn't the grades that bothered me so much; I knew I could bring them back up. It was the fact that, from this point on, I would be under major parental surveillance, which effectively put the kibosh on any Rebellion involvement. And that was exactly what happened. I couldn't be alone in any room of the house for even half an hour before one of my parents came in—ostensibly to check if I needed a snack, or to rummage in a kitchen drawer, or to turn the living-room TV to some depressing program about bad stuff going on in the world that I couldn't do anything about.

Despite that, I still managed to get away every so often to see Carey. It *was* Winter Break, after all. As long as I took textbooks with me—and presented neatly finished home-work afterward—even my dad didn't complain.

The final Friday of vacation, we had a mini New Year's

Eve party at Miranda's house. Besides Carey and I, Leonard, Bridget, and Darla were there, sitting around in the cozy living room, drinking sodas and eating chips, and reminiscing about how the Latte Rebellion used to be such a small-time operation. Now it was more about working for a cause and following it through, do or die.

Even though I missed the old days, I couldn't help feeling a little excited about that.

"Hey," Leonard said. "I have to show you something." He asked Miranda if he could use her computer to go online. We all crowded around the back of the office chair in the corner of her parents' living room and watched as he surfed to the social networking site FriendSpot, easily the most popular website around school. He typed "Latte Rebellion" into the search box.

The page that came up made my jaw drop, and I heard Carey gasp. Someone had set up a FriendSpot address for the Latte Rebellion, with our manifesto reprinted and a link to the website we'd originally set up; even one of Miranda's comics was gracing the top of the page.

"Did *you* do this?" I frowned at Leonard. I wouldn't put it past him to try to bask in our reflected glory.

"Hey, it wasn't me," he said. "I thought you guys set it up. I was just going to show you the comments page." He clicked a link, and a page loaded. A really *long* page. There were over a hundred comments, 99% of which were from people we didn't know.

"They just … took our stuff," Carey said, sounding shell-shocked.

"They probably think they're 'promoting the cause,'" Bridget said, rolling her eyes.

"This is nuts," I mumbled, feeling a little short of breath. I knew I wasn't in control anymore, and I wasn't sure if I was terrified...or excited.

"I think it's kind of cool," Darla said. "Flattering. Your T-shirt sales are going to go through the roof now. And this means more people will come to our rally." She paused, looking serious. "*You guys* did this. You should be proud. Obviously there was a need there, an interest. Maybe it's meant to happen this way."

"Yeah," Miranda said, holding up a celebratory can of soda in an impromptu toast. "If we make enough, Asha, you'll make it to London no problem. I might even visit my sister in New York when the NYU semester lets out. Can you imagine?"

A small spontaneous cheer went around the room, though I couldn't help noticing Carey was still put out about something—probably having her web copy swiped. But even that didn't bother me. I was shocked, but I was *proud*. We hadn't meant for this to happen, but we'd done it. And we *were* going to reap the rewards. All the way to the airport.

———

About a week later, I was sitting at the kitchen table under the watchful sidelong gaze of my dad, who was putting away clean dishes from the dishwasher. I had my English notes open in front of me, along with my copy of *The*

Stranger and a library book on existentialism. I was putting a sincere effort into doing a good job on this paper even though English was always pretty easy for me. My only problem seemed to be...attention span. Senioritis. Major distraction. Whatever you wanted to call it.

To be truthful, the problem had a name, and that name was the Latte Rebellion. And the problem had a second name (kind of like Oscar Mayer). That second name was Thad, he of the hypnotic blue eyes and mesmerizing phone voice.

I shook my head and put pen to paper again. *Philosophical implications of the narrator's killing the Arab stranger on a beach. Reflections of Sartre's personal beliefs. How this work is still relevant today.* I was busy narrowing down the ideas I'd brainstormed when my cell phone bleeped from the counter, jarring me out of my concentration. I was halfway out of my seat when my dad said, "I'll get it. You keep working."

"It's *my phone*," I said loudly, but he ignored me. I heaved a martyred sigh and looked back down at my notes, bristling. If it was Thad, I was going to be so peeved. Not to mention mortified.

"Hello?...Oh, hello, Caren. How's the studying coming along?...Good, good..." Normally my dad cracked me up when he was trying to be ultraserious, like when he called Carey by her full name, Caren, or when he'd tried to get me to write a business plan for my lemonade stand in fourth grade. It wasn't so cute this time.

"Oh, Asha's just working on her English paper....Yes,

that's the one. . . . Oh . . . I guess it's all right. She can take a little break . . . Bye now."

I had to admit, I was surprised. I thought I'd be chained to the kitchen table for the rest of the night and then sent promptly to bed like a five-year-old. Instead, my dad handed me my phone and a chocolate-chip granola bar and said I could take a fifteen-minute break. Maybe he was trying to bribe me into being a better student.

I carried the phone into the home office, which was empty and private.

"Hey, Carey," I said. "You called just in time. I was about to go crazy thinking about the futility and ennui of it all. I thought I might drive to the beach and maybe find somebody to take out my ennui on."

"And do what—bore them to death?" Carey laughed, but then abruptly stopped and her voice got serious. "Hey, listen. I have to tell you something. But first you have to sit down. Are you sitting?"

"I'm sitting," I said. "I've *been* sitting. All I do these days is sit and study."

"That's good," she said, sounding surprised. "I'm glad, Ash. You know, you could still be a salutatorian if you—"

"I know, I know." I sighed, doodling coffee cups on my mom's phone message pad. "So what were you going to tell me that was so shocking and appalling?"

"Oh! Right. You know how Leonard showed us that knock-off FriendSpot page?"

"Uh-huh."

"Well," Carey continued breathlessly, "I went online a

few minutes ago to check *our* website, and the guest book was full of comments like 'Don't stop now, guys!' and 'Fight the power' and that kind of thing. And so I go to NetPress to check on our T-shirt orders, and listen to *this*. In the past week, our income has...well..." She swallowed, audibly. "We've made three thousand dollars."

There was a long pause.

"Asha. I know you heard me."

"I heard you." I could hardly get my brain around it, though. My hand was busy scribbling down the calculations but my conscious mind was saying *does not compute*. "This is incredible! Where are these orders *coming* from?"

"That's the crazy part," Carey said. "Some of them are coming from Berkeley, and San Francisco, and Los Angeles...even from, like, Texas and New Jersey. Everywhere."

I swallowed, hard. I didn't know what to think. People must have been passing the word over email, and it must have spread like wildfire.

"Are you thinking what I'm thinking?" Carey said.

"I think so." I was slowly coming to a realization. An absolutely amazing, mind-boggling realization that made me drop my pen and clutch the phone with both hands, that made me feel like hyperventilating. It wasn't just that we'd hit the big time, that people at school and even at U-NorCal were buying our shirts and wanting to spread our ideas. It wasn't really about the Rebellion at all. It was about something infinitely more important—Carey and me.

Almost in a whisper, I said, "We did it. We're going to London."

MATERIALS VIOLATING
BOARD POLICY SECTION 418.III.K, 418.III.N

"Copycat" web page encouraging participation in possible terrorist group. Author unknown. Two copies attached.

Attention Latte Rebellion Sympathizers!

Latte Rebellion T-shirts are now available for a limited time only from www.FearTheLatte.com! Available in original brown-on-tan classic design! Also in brown-on-light-blue, orange-on-yellow, and tan-on-white!

If you're thinking about buying that T-shirt, we've got an offer you can't refuse! For a mere two extra dollars, get our complete *Latte Rebellion Propaganda Kit!!* Includes T-shirt and a supply of ten posters, ten comic books, and twenty flyers—get the Rebellion started for yourself and spread the word!

And don't forget to come to the first official Rebellion Rally in Berkeley, California, on February 15th! A Sensational Seminar that's open to the public! Bring your favorite rant for the after-hours poetry slam!

7

My excitement at selling five hundred shirts kept me floating all week. It was so much more than we'd expected to sell when we first started. Oh, we'd *hoped* we were going to sell all two hundred, but we figured that even if we didn't quite make our monetary goal, we could at least spend a weekend at a hot springs or something. But in this new scenario, Carey and Miranda and I would be patting each other on the back and grinning all way to the bank. All the way to London, in fact, where we would proceed to party like rock stars with hot British guys while touring the Tower of London and Big Ben and so forth.

But it was only January. Graduation, and the end of June, was a long way away. Our college applications were in, but we still had midterms, physics labs, another English paper, and AP tests to go, and I had to "get back on track," as my dad put it, so that I wouldn't slip too far in the class rankings.

And so that I would be deserving of any potential vacation time next summer. Studying in the living room one night, I'd let slip the vague idea of going somewhere with Carey after we graduated. I hadn't mentioned London, but still, Dad's reaction was noticeably tepid.

Not that I expected anything else. He shrugged off my enthusiasm and said we'd talk about it after I got my act together.

"Honestly, Dad, I am not off track," I insisted, glaring down at my AP History study guide. Sometimes I thought all he cared about was that stupid little numerical rank—which was still in single digits, by the way. That, and the number of A's and whether there were pluses or minuses attached to them. "I don't need another lecture," I said under my breath.

"I'll believe that when I see some improvement in your performance." Dad turned briefly away from the TV and glowered at me. I sat on my hands, resisting the urge to slam my book shut and fling it across the living room. "Don't think you can get lazy just because things have been easy for you up until now. If you think it's going to be this easy in college, you're in for a rude awakening."

"I won't have so many 'distractions' in college," I muttered, parroting one of his favorite lines from a classic lecture about how higher education was going to be the greatest personal enrichment experience of my entire sad lifetime. Not that I didn't believe him, but still. I'd heard this all before. It was a golden oldie on the *Dad's Greatest Hits* album—one that he dragged out every time I got a substandard grade, like a B-plus.

He leaned forward to grab the remote control from the heavy oak coffee table and turned the volume down considerably. "You know, you'd probably get more studying done if you weren't in the room with the TV."

My mom should have been the one to be OCD about grades—Carey liked to call it "Asian Parent Syndrome." Instead, for me, it was my good old Mexican-Irish-American dad. Much to his dismay, I wasn't a workaholic like either of my parents. At least, not in ways that meant anything to either of them. He was always telling me about how "today's teenagers have a sense of entitlement" and "you'd better work hard now if you want to get ahead later." It was cliché city. Carey and I used to laugh about it, mimicking our dads getting all worked up; that is, until she lost her sense of humor at some point in the last few months. It was amazing how things could change so quickly.

Despite London seeming so far away, the next couple of weeks went by in a blur. I spent most school nights studying at home, except for a few trips out of the house with Carey and Miranda. Saturdays I went to an AP prep course and Sunday was reserved for "family time." This meant lunch of takeout Chinese food followed by a walk around the neighborhood, a DVD on the living-room couch with low-fat popcorn, and some kind of sit-down Sunday dinner. If my mom was cooking, that meant chicken korma, mildly spicy on its bed of basmati rice, or some sort of vegetable curry with a salad. If my dad was cooking, it meant turkey burgers or spaghetti.

It might not sound too bad, but after three weeks of this schedule, I was going stir-crazy. I could barely pay attention in class, and I yawned through every lunchtime club meeting—the sporadic, unofficial Latte Rebellion school meetings that Maria McNally had started leading after the rally idea caught on. I was about to throw in the towel, forget about the Rebellion and everything else, drop out of school, and work at McDonald's for the rest of my life. At least then I'd have financial independence.

When the time came for the next Rebellion rally planning meeting at Mocha Loco, I called Bridget. I really wanted her to come with me, because Carey had soccer practice and Miranda was sick with the flu.

"Bridget, the services of Commander Delta are urgently needed," I said as soon as she picked up the phone.

"Now? I have an essay in Poli Sci due next Friday. Ten pages. And an art history paper due the Monday after that. Commander Delta is officially on administrative leave."

"Seriously, Bridge. Someone has to go to this meeting with me. I'm too nervous to do it by myself." And I was. I wouldn't be there in my official Agent Alpha capacity, but I couldn't picture being there without *someone* to back me up.

"I'm sorry, but I have to tell you, this semester is really killing me."

"It's just for a couple of hours," I said, a little desperately.

"Asha, it isn't really the time commitment, it's ..."

There was a strange hesitation in Bridget's voice that I wasn't used to hearing. "Okay, listen. Wednesday I wore a Latte Rebellion shirt to my Poli Sci class, and as I was walking out at the end of the lecture, this guy actually *grabbed* my shirt and said something stupid like 'Hey, I thought that Latte thing was all full of race radicals.' And then this other guy got in his face about it and they started yelling about who has the right to say what, or whatever, and I just...I couldn't deal with it. I got the hell out of there."

I was completely dumbstruck. When I'd first worn the shirt around town, nobody seemed to have any idea what the Latte Rebellion was. And now this?

"I know it has nothing to do with *your* project. It's just all these other wanna-bes and...zealots who are taking it a little too far. It gives me a bad feeling, you know?"

"But nothing's going to *happen*," I said. "It's just people who don't know anything about the Rebellion who are overreacting."

"I don't know," Bridget said. "There are tons of news stories where even peaceful protesters get pepper-sprayed by the cops. Or worse. It's easy for things to get out of hand, is all I'm saying. It's great that so many people are interested, and I'm glad your idea was successful, but...don't you think it's gotten enough of a life of its own that you can, I don't know, let it go a little?"

This was one of the longest speeches I'd ever heard Bridget make, and it left me feeling hopeless and desperate. We couldn't be losing one of our core Sympathizers.

"You have to come, Bridget," I tried again. "I told my

parents I'd be out with you. I promise you won't have to commit to anything."

"I'm serious," Bridget said. "I'm sorry, but I just can't do it. It was fun while it lasted, but I have my classes to worry about, and believe me, they are *something* to worry about this semester. I thought last semester was hard."

"Aaargh! I can't believe this," I screeched, panicking. I hung up the phone. Sure, we had the money for our summer vacation, but we also had a rally to oversee, a high school student body just prickling with gossip about the mysterious origins of the Latte Rebellion and its exciting upcoming events, and a whole lot of random people throughout the country apparently sympathetic to the cause.

Maybe Bridget was right. This was out of control.

———

I was depressed for about a week after Bridget told me she had to abdicate her duties as Commander Delta. But I went to the meeting anyway, just to keep tabs on the planning process for the Latte Rebellion Rally and Poetry Slam. It was only two weeks away. Miranda and I were in the process of making and distributing propaganda materials, and, along with Carey, the three of us had final say over the program of events for the evening. The other people on the planning committee could not stop bickering, but since I was at the meeting alone and incognito, I couldn't voice a strong opinion. On top of all that, I was still barely pulling a B in calculus, and I got docked half a letter grade on my

English essay for turning it in a day late. That meant I had to spend more time studying than ever, thanks to my parents' Homework Boot Camp. I was completely and utterly swamped.

So I really wasn't prepared for what happened next.

I was sitting at the computer in my parents' home office, taking a much-needed study break to check email. I had my hair wound into a bun with a pencil sticking out of it and was wearing sweat pants and a baggy T-shirt. Sipping from a cup of hot chocolate, I logged into my account, hoping for something besides spam about penis problems. And boy, did I get it.

In my inbox, forwarded from our Latte Rebellion website, was a new message. An advertisement, to be specific—for Latte Rebellion T-shirts.

I blinked. I was getting a really weird feeling about this.

I sucked in a breath and looked closer. The message was from somebody calling themselves rebellion@fearthelatte .com. And the shirts! They looked exactly like the ones we were selling on NetPress, only you could buy them in different colors—ugly ones—and they were charging five bucks more apiece. Not only that, these people were advertising something called a Propaganda Kit—which I *knew* for a fact had nothing to do with either Miranda or Darla, as the two official Ministers of Propaganda—with copies of all our posters, comics, and flyers. When I went to the official Latte Rebellion site, I saw the same ad in our guest book, and on the social networking page, too.

I went to the FearTheLatte website. It was virtually identical to ours.

At first, I was furious. We'd worked so hard coming up with our ideas, our shirts, designing our website, everything, and here was someone copying them ... to make a buck? To look cool? I didn't know. I felt sick to my stomach and pushed my hot chocolate to one side. I guess the page was supposed to be an homage, but it was just weird. They were still referring to Agent Alpha and Captain Charlie and Lieutenant Bravo as these great initiators of the Latte Rebellion, but obviously they had no idea who we were. I wasn't even sure they knew we were real *people*, let alone high school students who set it all up on a lark. We had attained some kind of mythical status. At least our alter egos had.

I sent emails to Carey, Miranda, Darla, and Leonard, entitled *Emergency Rebellion Meeting! R.S.V.P. A.S.A.P.!* Obviously, something had to be done. Didn't it?

———————

A couple of evenings later, we were all sitting around Miranda's kitchen table, the scuffed Formica surface covered in textbooks, notebooks, and a spilled stack of extra Latte Rebellion flyers. Ostensibly I'd gone there to review for our physics test the next day. The excuse had gotten me out of the house on condition that I come home with evidence I'd actually accomplished something, so I had a physics worksheet on the table in front of me that I resolved to tackle the minute we finished discussing this new dilemma.

"Guys. We all know this was not exactly what we set out to do when we started the Latte Rebellion." I spoke in a hushed, serious tone, calmly reciting what I'd been planning to say, but I couldn't help raising my voice slightly as I continued.

"But people came on board and really supported us, so we thought we'd try to see it through, even after we accomplished our original mission and sold enough T-shirts. It was a setback when Bridget said she couldn't do this anymore, but we weathered it.

"It's been a wild ride, and I'm glad you were all here with me. But ... I just don't have a clue what to do about *this*. Do you?" I drummed my fingers on the table, feeling fidgety and anxious.

"Not even an inkling," Miranda said, smiling. I knew she was enjoying watching things unfold, no matter how crazy they were getting. I loved her for it, but I was envious of how calm she was. Darla sat back in her chair with an enigmatic smile, blinking at us owlishly through her red-framed glasses. Carey, meanwhile, looked nervous as hell. Leonard put an arm around her and I felt the familiar twinge of irritation.

"You know," he said, in his infuriatingly calm way, "this is the kind of thing that happens when you come up with an idea that's ... bigger than you are. Clearly there were tons of people looking for something just like this. Don't think of it as a *bad* thing." He smiled down at Carey, who still looked like she was about to throw up.

"Well, I did a little research online," Darla said, leaning forward conspiratorially, "and I found out that this copycat website is registered to someone named Eric Segal in Cedar Rapids, Iowa. Maybe we should try to get in touch with him. Ask him to take it down."

"I don't know," I said. "Why would he want to take it down? There's obviously a demand for shirts, and with the amount he's charging, he's not going to want to stop selling."

"Or he could be sincere," Darla added hopefully.

Carey rolled her eyes. "Who cares if he's sincere? The point is, he flat-out stole practically our entire site. But personally, I don't have time to worry about it." She sounded pretty mad, like she didn't want to be here, even with Leonard playing with her hair and making me want to vomit.

I opened my mouth to reassure her, but Tattoo Boy beat me to it.

"No worries, babe," he said. "If you need to step back a little, you do what you need to do."

"Whoa, whoa, *whoa*." I put down my can of cola. "It's not like this is a full-time job here." I exchanged a meaningful glance with Carey. "We're trying to figure out how to keep it under control."

"Unless you *want* it to be out of control," Miranda said. I looked up at her in surprise.

"What I mean is, you want the ideas to spread around as much as possible, and we've done that," Miranda said earnestly. "Knowledge is power, right? It's all pretty cool. I take it as a compliment that people want to copy us."

"*I'm* just glad nobody knows who we are," Carey said, glaring down at her empty coffee cup.

"There *is* a certain power, a mystery, in anonymity," Leonard agreed. "It's almost as though the Rebellion has grown more powerful *because* its leaders remain anonymous and claim only the credit for founding the movement."

I resisted the urge to mimic his pompous blathering.

"You say, 'grown more powerful'; I say, 'ballooned out of control,'" Carey muttered. I looked up at her and smiled worriedly. I was freaked by how pessimistic she sounded.

By the end of the night, we decided that Leonard, Darla, and the other U-NorCal students would take over the key speaking roles for the Rebellion more or less permanently. Maria McNally would stay in charge of the informal meetings at our school. I would still work on the rally, making a last appearance as Agent Alpha in order to introduce the guest speaker, a UC Berkeley professor. We'd take enough money out of the T-shirt account to cover our travel plans, and the rest would be kept under tight control, for legitimate Rebellion activities only: the rally speaker's honorarium, for instance. What I'd do after that, I wasn't sure.

But as we went back to our physics homework, worksheets dutifully lined up in front of us, I kept shifting in my seat, jiggling my legs, tapping my foot. I was having trouble keeping still—not because of caffeine, for once, but because I felt a tiny, inexorable stirring of anticipation about what might happen next. Call me crazy.

———

Over the next few days, though, I was lulled into a sense of…if not security, then relative calm. I didn't have another meeting with the rally planning committee until next week, and my parents had finally let up enough to stop answering my phone for me. Which was good: the real bright spot of the week was talking to Thad again. This time, *he* called *me*.

There were a few minutes of awkward small talk again, while I cringed and tried not to sound like the humongous dork that I am, but then I took a deep breath and finally told him a little about myself…and, very vaguely, about the Rebellion.

"So, w—they're putting on this rally over in your neck of the woods pretty soon," I said ultra-casually. "I thought I might go. Oh, and I heard there's a poetry slam, in case your friend is interested."

"Oh yeah," Thad said. "Greg told me about that. One of my professors is the guest speaker, so if I go I might get extra credit. But I was going to go anyway. You'll be there?" He sounded hopeful. "I don't want to be stuck all bored at a table while Greg is doing his thing."

"Sure. I, uh, might be a little late," I added, remembering that I was supposed to make an Agent Alpha cameo.

"No worries," he said. There was a pause, and I fidgeted uncomfortably on my bed, wondering what to say.

"So…I didn't have a chance to tell you, but Carey and I were planning to visit London after we graduate. We have this whole vacation plan and everything."

"Oh man," Thad said enviously. "I wish I could go

with you guys. I'd love to go check out the clinic in East London and see what they're doing in person."

"Yeah?" My stomach felt fluttery and nervous.

"You'll have a great time," Thad said. "I wish I'd been able to travel after high school. I probably would have realized a little sooner what I wanted to do with my life."

"I'm not expecting *that* to happen," I said. "But it'll be a nice change of pace. Plus I've always wanted to go to a real pub."

"You should! You should live it up—go dancing, or clubbing, or whatever it is you like to do." He chuckled. "So what *is* it you like to do, besides going to social justice meetings and poetry slams?"

I laughed, then told him just enough to be intriguingly mysterious. Not enough to hint at my secret identity. I hoped.

I also learned a few things about Thad. His favorite food was sushi, but he didn't eat any terrestrial mammals. He loved comedy movies, the dumber the better. He had two younger sisters, who still lived with his parents in Utah. When they were little they'd lived in a small town where being mixed-race was unusual, so they got stared at a lot.

"I can totally relate," I said.

"I bet you can." I could hear the smile in his voice, and it really made me anxious to see him again. But after that phone call, it was back to the boot camp routine for me: get up, go to school, come home, study, eat dinner, study some more, go to bed. Lather, rinse, repeat.

I started to count the days until school let out, and

until Spring Break. Not that I'd be doing anything interesting. No Florida beaches; the closest approximation for Carey and me would be driving into San Francisco to Ocean Beach and freezing our butts off by a bonfire with the popular kids, sharing toasted marshmallows with Roger and Kaelyn. Ha. Not likely.

The weird part was, we were popular too, now, in a way. Not that people knew who we were exactly, but they knew we were involved with the Latte Rebellion. A few kids at school, like David Castro, had seen us putting up posters and slipping flyers into lockers. But the majority of people had no idea we were the instigators, and we had no intention of telling them.

Three days before the rally, right after the final planning meeting, I called Carey to fill her in on the details and double-check on our plan for the evening.

"I forgot to tell you, we've got the Berkeley Poetry Slam champion emceeing our poetry slam—you can't tell me that isn't cool. And the guest speaker wrote *Uncut, Undried: The Complexity of Race in America.*"

"You haven't even read it," Carey accused me, correctly. "What do you care? And don't you have a makeup history test to study for?"

"It's the day before, genius." I frowned and switched the phone to my other ear. "Anyway, aren't you coming? You said you'd watch me make my introductory remarks."

There was an uncomfortable silence at the other end of the phone line. I couldn't even hear Carey breathing for a second, and then I heard her let out a long sigh.

"Asha, I don't think I'm going to make it. I have soccer practice again."

"What are you talking about? We were going to leave the rally before the poetry slam and have dinner in San Francisco. That was the plan."

"Yeah … but, listen. I think I'm going to have to back out of all this." Her voice sounded funny—pinched and small.

"What do you mean 'all this'? The rally? That's okay— the planning's already done." I didn't like the sound of what Carey had just said. A horrible sinking feeling crawled through my stomach.

"Not just the rally, Ash. I mean all of it. I'm still behind on homework, my parents are going on a business trip for a week and I have to watch my brothers, and then after that I have to work extra shifts at Book Planet if I want to make up the income I'll lose while my parents are away … This is just a really tough time for me."

I could hear the longing in her voice—she couldn't wait to quit this. I thought back over everything she'd said over the past months, all her worries about what was going to happen, all her doubts and misgivings, and suddenly it seemed all too clear.

"You've wanted to back out for a long time, haven't you?" I accused her. But I didn't have to ask, because a sick certainty had settled into my chest. And now even Leonard's enthusiasm for the Rebellion wasn't enough to keep her involved anymore. She'd made up her mind.

"No, I—"

"You've just been waiting for the chance to quit! I can't believe you." I was fuming, almost incoherent. I paced angrily across my bedroom, kicking a stray green sandal under the bed in the process. "After everything we did, all our plans—and the rally's in two days! This isn't fair," I said loudly. I knew I was being dramatic, but I didn't care. She was deserting me.

I felt like I'd been kicked.

"Hey, who's not being fair? I worked hard on that website," she retorted. "I put just as much into this as you did. And we got what we wanted! What more do you want from me?"

"What do I *want* from you? It's not about that." I was stunned. "You know that as well as I do. Anyway, you're the one who said people should care about this kind of thing. And now they do! We're finally accomplishing what we talked about."

"Asha, this isn't what I signed up for. I don't know what you thought we were planning when we first talked about it, but ... I just don't *know*."

"What does it matter what we first planned? I thought we were doing something worthwhile," I said. In a quieter voice, I added, "I thought we were having fun."

There was a long silence. I felt tears running down my face and dripping over the phone receiver. Finally Carey spoke.

"Well, it hasn't been that fun for me."

What do you mean, it hasn't been fun? I wanted to yell at her. *This was one of the most outrageous things we've ever done. Didn't we laugh our butts off making up the manifesto? Didn't you meet Leonard because of the Rebellion? And what about all the people who come to our meetings, who believe in the Rebellion and want us to succeed? How can* you *mean anything you just said?*

Instead, I just took a deep, shaky breath and hung up the phone.

The following April:
Ashmont Unified School District Board Room

"Ms. Jamison," the disciplinary hearing officer said loudly, startling me out of my depressing visions of finishing out the school year at St. Elizabeth's—or worse, at continuation school. "In light of what Ms. Levin has just shared with us, I need to ask you to clarify a few of the facts here." He sounded tired and croakier than ever.

I sat up straight on the hard wooden chair. This could be it for me. What I said right now might be the deciding factor, and all I could think about was whether my dad might insist on pulling me out of school anyway. I couldn't focus; I cleaned my glasses but it didn't help. And now the hearing officer was already talking and I'd missed the first part of what he'd said.

"...honestly expect us to believe that you didn't have any idea you were engaging in a potentially inflammatory activity?" He peered at me over the top of his spectacles. I swallowed past a lump in my throat.

"We—I didn't *know*," I said, lamely. The hearing panel uniformly glared at me, and I started to get a little annoyed. "We thought it would be fun. We didn't think it would get so out of hand. I mean, we're high school kids, not scheming counterrevolutionaries." I glared back at them, one by one. "We're honor students. Soccer players. Aspiring artists. We started a business, and we tried to start a legitimate campus club. When we were thwarted, we took our club off campus. Then somebody—*not us*—decided to take our ideas a little too far. And then ... well, you know what happened next. You know who was responsible for that, too."

"I am aware of the other individuals involved, but we're talking about you, Ms. Jamison, and *your* role in the situation, particularly the events of April 18th."

I could feel my dad's eyes boring into the side of my head, and I gritted my teeth before continuing. I hadn't expected to be put on the spot right away. I was supposed to get a closing statement, a real chance to get my side of the story out. Not ... this.

"Maybe I should have realized that some people might take our ideas the wrong way," I said finally. "But I don't have a say over what other people think, just like I don't have a say over what they do. I can only take responsibility for what *I've* done." I felt like I'd just said the cheesiest teen-movie line in the world, but the sad truth was that I really meant it. And because of that, everything about the situation suddenly seemed absurd, far away, like it was happening to someone else. Some of the tension dribbled out of me. I looked steadily back at the hearing officer, no longer quite so terrified.

Then I glanced at my dad and his unreadable expression, and the nervousness crept in again. His face was carefully blank. I had no idea what that meant for me.

"Interesting food for thought," the hearing officer said dryly. "On that note, I'd like to call a brief recess. There is a water cooler in the outside hallway, and restrooms are located around the corner. All panel members and witnesses should return in fifteen minutes." He took off his glasses and rubbed his forehead as the room exploded into noise. Half of the hearing panel got up and quickly exited the room through a back door. I wished I could escape, too, but my mother put her hand on my shoulder as if reading my mind.

"Asha, you're doing fine," she said, reassuringly, but I could see worry lines creasing the center of her forehead. "If I were in your shoes, I—"

"Asha! Oh, my God. I had no idea it was going to be like this. I mean, this is *crazy*. But you're doing so *awesome*." It was Shay Saintmarie. She wriggled her slender cheerleader frame into the row behind me and gave me a breathless hug.

"Thanks," I said, a little taken aback.

"You really are," she said again, and smiled. "We're all behind you. Well, mostly." She glanced at the back of the room and I followed her gaze. Of course. Kaelyn. "Anyway, I better go to the little girls' room while I still can, but I just wanted to tell you that we've got your back."

"Okay," I said, confused. Who was "we"? And why would Kaelyn even bother to come? But before I could try to figure it out, Miranda was standing where Shay had been a moment ago, grinning from ear to ear. My parents looked from one girl to the other, flabbergasted.

"Girl, you have got this in the *bag*. I am so proud of you." Then she sobered. "I'm sorry about Carey, though."

"Yeah, that was ... really tough." My eyes felt a little watery just thinking about it. I smiled weakly. "I'm glad you're here."

"You think I would miss this?" Miranda said incredulously. "Hell, no. Though I'm going to need some caffeine if I want to get through the rest of it. Want me to get you a coffee or something?"

"Maybe a soda," I said. Coffee was the last thing I wanted.

Miranda smiled sympathetically and hurried out the main doors. My dad took the opportunity to put one arm around my shoulders and steer me over toward a quieter corner of the room, my mom bringing up the rear.

"What you don't need is for people to be distracting you right now," he said testily. "Don't they have any respect for your situation? You're literally on trial. They should be giving you some space." He looked around, everywhere but at me, frowning.

"Daniel," my mom said, warningly. "This isn't easy for Asha. Let her friends support her."

My dad crossed his arms and leaned against the wall. His dark hair, which had been neatly slicked back when we left the house this morning, was disheveled and falling into his face as if he'd been the one on trial. "If they're really your friends, they should have kept you out of this mess in the first place," he mumbled.

"Dad, that's not fair. There wasn't anything they could have done," I said. I was starting to wonder what kind of trouble *he'd* gotten into at my age. But I didn't ask. Today wasn't about him, and it wasn't about whatever might have happened thirty years ago.

In fact, inside I was smiling a tiny victorious smile. If he was angry at other people, or resentful about some mysterious event in his past, then he *wasn't* angry at me. At least, not entirely. And maybe, by the time this was over, I'd have a chance of convincing him that I'd done what I thought was the right thing. That I hadn't been irresponsible deliberately, just to flout everything he'd ever tried to teach me about the real world, about being a "sensible young woman focused on my academic future." He might still be irritated with me, and he might not agree, but if he came out of it realizing not everything was my fault, I'd at least have that small victory. I'd know he didn't think I'd failed.

Even if I was expelled.

Inflammatory materials distributed on school property. Two copies attached.

THE LATTE REBELLION WANTS YOU!

*Are you brown of skin,
tan of complexion,
or enamored of coffee?*

Then come to the
First Official Latte Rebellion Rally
and Poetry Slam!

February 15th, 7 p.m.
At the Java Maven in Berkeley!

Keynote Speaker:
Dr. Adina Malik, Professor of American Cultures
at UC Berkeley
Faces and Races: The Browning of America

Also Featuring:
Diva ArchMinority, Bay Area Poetry Slam Champion
and
The Pinoy Paladin, Berkeley Poetry Slam Team

Be There or Be Caffeine-Deficient!

8

The next day was a blur. I spent most of the time trying to put on a brave front, trying not to think about what Carey had said to me over the phone, trying not to think about the fact that we'd yelled at each other and I'd hung up on her. She took the bus to school; I drove there alone. We avoided each other's eyes during passing periods and gave each other the silent treatment during classes. Carey would be leaning forward attentively and taking copious notes, and I'd be across the room in my assigned seat, painfully conscious of her ignoring me. I'm not afraid to admit that it sucked big-time.

At lunch, Carey was conspicuously absent.

"You just missed her. She said she was going to the library to do research for that history paper," Miranda said, eyebrows raised. "She seemed stressed out; is everything okay?"

I pressed my lips together. Obviously Carey hadn't mentioned our argument, and I was torn about whether to confide in Miranda or make excuses. Miranda was looking at me, but not expectantly, just curiously. Her wide eyes were rimmed with black eyeliner, setting off her braided hair, which she had dyed black over the weekend.

"You know, your hair looks good like that," I said.

"You're avoiding the question," she said. "I know something's up. You're doing that grimacing thing."

I felt my face crumple, and I blinked back tears that suddenly threatened to flood out over my cheeks and onto my lunch. I took a few deep breaths to try to suck the tears back in by sheer willpower. "Carey and I had a minor disagreement regarding the future of the Rebellion."

"Way to be detached." Miranda put her hand on my arm. "What really happened?"

I leaned my head back, staring out the window at the wispy gray clouds as if I could just fly away and start fresh somewhere far from here, without all this baggage, without the stupid Rebellion, even without Carey.

"Nothing. Everything," I said, shakily. "She said she couldn't be part of the Rebellion anymore."

"She did?" Miranda looked stunned. "So ... what did you say?"

"Well, there's nothing I can do to stop her. But I told her it wasn't fair, and that I thought we were having fun doing this together. And she said it *wasn't* that fun for her. That's when I hung up."

"You hung up, huh?" Miranda gave a cynical smile. "Well . . . I can understand why you'd be kinda pissed."

"I know!" I sniffled a little. "It was like we were kids again, just throwing ourselves into some random project. Like when we started our own magazine in seventh grade."

"I can totally see the two of you doing that."

"It was called *Fast Times at Ashmont Junior High*." A few tears sneaked out and I stifled an angry sob, my chest aching. I wanted to take all the copies I had of *Fast Times* and throw them right in Carey's face. I wanted her to remember what it was like, what *this* was supposed to be like.

Miranda squeezed my arm.

"I wish I'd known you guys in junior high," she said, clearly trying to distract me. "Thank God we left Nebraska. I mean, *you* guys remember. I showed up freshman year all skinny, with those braces and that hideous perm. And my brother's hand-me-down flannels."

"It seems so far away." I wiped away a stray tear. "I mean, look at you now." With her traffic-stopping braids and model's tall frame, I could hardly even picture what she'd been like before.

"*And* the kids in Nebraska all thought I was Asian, so they'd chant 'ching chang chong' at me like I was some kind of idiot." Miranda smiled that twist of a smile again.

"Well, your eyes are kind of almond-shaped," I said. And then I couldn't help it; a small grin sneaked onto my face.

"What?"

"Sorry...I know it's not funny." I paused. "The thing is, when Carey and I were in elementary school, people used to insist we were Mexican."

"But neither of you looks even remotely Hispanic in any way," Miranda said.

"Of course not." I rolled my eyes. "But people see what they want to see."

"Because you're brown and they can't tell what you are." Miranda picked at her cheese sandwich. "You know, this is why the Latte Rebellion is a *good* thing. It'll open people's eyes. I mean, it's not like we just automatically identify with whichever group we look the most like."

"Yeah." I nodded. "Not to mention, ethnicity isn't anybody's whole story anyway." Thank God. I didn't need anybody trying to figure out who I was based on being mixed up, though "mixed up" wasn't a bad description.

"Maybe," Miranda continued, "what people said to you in elementary school made this inevitable."

"Huh. Maybe," I said. It did make sense. Maybe Carey and I *did* do this for a reason, even if it was subconscious.

"That's what'll be so great about the rally," Miranda added, perking up a bit. "It'll raise awareness, and the poetry slam will bring in even more people. I'm looking forward to it." She paused, then asked, "Are you even going to go, since...?"

"Of course," I said, a little sourly. "I promised to give the introduction. Paper bag and all." Then something occurred to me. Carey wasn't going, but that didn't mean I had to mope around just because she'd decided to blow me off. I was free to do whatever I wanted now.

"Actually, I think I *will* stay for the poetry slam after all. I might as well, since…" We sat there without speaking for a few minutes, eating potato chips. I shook my head a little at the thought of going to the rally without Carey. We'd been inseparable since sixth grade, but that was a long time ago. Maybe we needed a break. It was an uncomfortable thought, one that made me feel like the ground was sliding away underneath me, like I was freefalling down a hillside without any clue where I would end up.

"I'm glad you're going," Miranda said. She patted my arm again. "We'll have fun."

I relaxed a little despite myself, and managed to wrestle my thoughts to a more positive place. There were other Latte Rebels in the sea. Or in the coffee pot, maybe. And at the rally, I'd be meeting lots of them.

On Saturday around five, I fired up the Geezer and headed for Miranda's house. I was fidgety with excitement, despite the collapse of my original plans with Carey. After all the afternoons spent plastering rally posters around town and driving into Oakland, Berkeley, and San Francisco to poster the college campuses there, and all the meetings where I had to sit there feeling like a fool with a paper bag over my head, today would be Agent Alpha's biggest moment yet.

Not only that, Thad would be there to witness it. Even

if I was keeping my secret identity under wraps, just knowing he was going to be in the audience made my stomach a little fluttery, and not in a bad way.

I pulled up to Miranda's house, a small, tidy bungalow in an older neighborhood full of tall, winter-bare trees. She was already waiting outside on the porch and slid gracefully into the car, putting her crocheted black bag at her feet.

"I cannot *believe* today is finally here," she said. We grinned at each other. She'd helped me put up all the posters, along with Darla, and of course it was her artwork gracing most of them. "Gun it, Jeeves."

I obliged and peeled out of her driveway with a slight screech of tires, which set us off giggling. Most of the way there, we yelled along with the lyrics of really stupid disco songs on her MP3 player as the farm fields and green shrubby hills rolled past in the orange light of the setting sun. We passed through a few smaller towns before finally reaching the more densely built-up areas and increased car traffic that signaled the outskirts of the San Francisco Bay Area. The last ten minutes of the drive, we turned off the music. I rehearsed my introductory remarks, and we speculated on what the speaker was going to talk about and whether either of us would ever have the guts to go onstage at a poetry slam (no for me; maybe for Miranda).

When we got there, I parked the car in a busy garage in downtown Berkeley, and we walked to the café along streets crowded with vendors, cars, bicycles, loiterers, shoppers, and, of course, students. I was starting to get really nervous now, and we stepped into a florist's shop next to the Java Maven so I could put on my paper bag face. Miranda was going to be a regular, inconspicuous audience member. Lucky her.

"I'm not sure I can do this," I said. "I seriously might throw up."

"Think of it as a rehearsal for your graduation speech," Miranda said, smiling gently.

"Oh, sure." But at least then—*if* I got to speak—I'd do it as myself. I wouldn't have to represent for the whole Rebellion. I looked at my feet. "God, my stomach hurts."

"You'll be great. They all love you already. Agent Alpha is a legend. You could go up there and do the chicken dance and they'd go nuts."

I tried to smile as I pulled the paper bag over my head. My stomach was still going crazy when we slipped through the door into the Java Maven's main room. *Special event today,* the sign on the door said, scotch-taped to a poster for the Latte Rebellion Rally. I gulped and strode toward the scarred wooden podium at the front of the room.

———

It's just like the Latte Rebellion meetings at Mocha Loco, I told myself. *No big deal.*

Except for all the people.

Stark fluorescent lighting flooded the room and illuminated at least a hundred, maybe a hundred and fifty, coffee-guzzling onlookers with expectant faces—sitting at little round tables, piled onto extra chairs, and lining the walls at the back of the large rectangular space. Most of them were wearing Rebellion T-shirts, both the original and the illicit versions. The baristas looked frazzled but pleased at the continuing stream of customers, and people were chattering happily and loudly.

That is, until the door closed behind me and people turned to see who it was. When they saw my trademark paper-bag mask and Latte Rebellion T-shirt (original, of course), the room slowly went quiet. The wave of silence started from the tables nearest the door and spread gradually inward, heads swiveling and conversations abruptly ending. It was exactly like one of my recurring nightmares, where I have to give an oral report in class but I'm missing a critical item of clothing, like my pants.

At least this time, I actually *was* wearing pants.

Miranda slid quietly past me—as we'd agreed, she was pretending not to know me while I was in Agent Alpha drag—and took up a standing position halfway back, next to a window. I tried not to look at all the staring faces as I choked down my nervousness and walked to the front of the room.

It was so packed that I didn't have a hope of seeing Thad, if he was even here. I hadn't realized it until that moment, but I was counting on him being there to give me an extra boost of moral support, even if he didn't know he was doing it. Even if he didn't know I was Agent Alpha.

As I got closer I could see Leonard, conspicuous in his tan Rebellion shirt and black pinstriped pants. He motioned me to a seat marked with a paper sign reading "Reserved for Rebellion Staff." He was going to introduce me, and then I'd make a thankfully short speech to open the evening's events.

In the seat next to me was an intense-looking woman with rich dark-brown skin, short salt-and-pepper hair, and elaborate dangly earrings. She was carrying a sheaf of note cards and a pile of brochures advertising *Uncut, Undried: The Complexity of Race in America*. Clearly this was Dr. Adina Malik, the keynote speaker. She cast her sharp gaze on me when I sat down, and one side of her mouth quirked upward in a smile as she took in my paper bag head.

"I take it you're one of the founders of this little grass-roots movement," she said.

"Yes, I'm, uh …" I swallowed. Did I want to blow my cover, even for the keynote speaker? This wasn't a joke any-more—Dr. Malik was taking it seriously. So it didn't feel quite right to introduce myself as Agent Alpha.

Are you scared? said a taunting little voice inside me.

It wasn't like I'd see her again. People were talking now, and nobody was in our immediate radius to overhear, which I confirmed with a furtive glance around us.

"I'm Asha," I finally said, in a near-whisper, feeling like my stomach was going to drop out of the bottom of my shoes. "Thank you for coming to speak." I hoped my voice didn't sound too distinctive.

"Why, you're very welcome," she said, smiling slightly. "It's not every day that I get to be in on the ground floor of a unique group like this. You know, your ideas are really quite interesting."

"Thanks; we've enjoyed the experience." I didn't know what else to say.

"I'm sure you have enjoyed it," she said. "I'm sure you have. Oh, to be young again and on the fighting front..." She fanned out her note cards, looking wistful. I had no idea what she was talking about. All I knew was, Leonard was going up to the podium to do his thing and I was up next.

"Attention Rebellion Sympathizers," he said, pulling the microphone closer. His voice boomed out with a squeal of feedback and the room quickly went silent again. There were clinks of coffee cups and the rustling of papers, but nobody spoke.

"Thank you all so much for coming," Leonard continued. I was still amazed he could get people to listen to him so intently. "We have an exciting event in store for you all tonight, starting with our keynote speaker Dr. Adina Malik, and ending with a world-class poetry slam."

Now everybody clapped and whistled.

"But first, my friends and fellow latte lovers, we have a very special introduction in store for you. Please join me in welcoming the mastermind of the mixed-race movement, today's voice for the Rebellion of the future, our own Agent Alpha!"

This time, the applause was deafening. The room rang with whoops; people stomped their feet and clinked their spoons against their cups. I got up and the noise made me dizzy. I clutched at the podium as if it were a walker and I was an old lady with a broken hip.

Gradually the room quieted down. I pulled the microphone down a little and cleared my throat, the sound echoing around the room embarrassingly loudly. Everyone was staring at me, waiting. Then I glanced at Miranda standing by the window and blinked in surprise: there was Thad, standing just a few feet away, both of them smiling encouragingly. Of course, Thad couldn't know it was me, but even so, the fog in my brain dissipated somewhat. It was replaced by a tiny stirring of anticipation, just enough to prod me into action. I wanted *him* to be impressed by my speech, even if nobody else was.

I reached into my back jeans pocket and got out the folded piece of paper that passed for a speech.

"Greetings, Rebellion Organizers, Sympathizers, and Friends," I began, in what I hoped was a strident and impressive voice. I took a deep breath to continue, but was interrupted by applause. I felt like I was in a movie. Or—did I dare even hope?—like I was standing in front of the senior class giving a graduation speech as salutatorian. Unfortunately, thinking about graduation speeches reminded me of Carey—and the fact that she should have been here, and wasn't. It was just Miranda, and me, and here I was with a paper bag on my head. Not to mention sweat running down the back of my neck.

"Thank you," I said. "We appreciate your support." I looked down at my notes. *We have an exciting evening planned, blah blah friggin' blah.* Good lord. Rehearsal for graduation, my ass. This was most definitely not high school; far from it, in fact. But I'd prepared a litany of stock phrases and meaningless clichés worthy of a ninth-grade class president—and not a very creative one at that.

I frowned. I folded up my note paper again and took a deep breath.

"Friends, it has been over five months since the inception of the Latte Rebellion; since I, Agent Alpha, along with Lieutenant Bravo and Captain Charlie, first outlined the basic tenets and put them on the web so the world could understand our point of view—a point of view that is often ignored, or subject to inaccurate and ignorant assumptions."

The room was nearly silent, listening. I couldn't bring myself to look out, not even at Miranda, who knew exactly how little I'd been thinking about justice and equality when we'd first come up with the Rebellion.

While earlier I'd been sick and tired of the paper bag hat, now, just like at that first meeting, I was kind of glad for it.

Are you that scared? said the little voice inside me again. Yes. Yes, I was. But it wasn't going to keep me from saying what I knew I needed to say. What I *wanted* to say.

"The world must acknowledge us," I said forcefully, quoting from our manifesto. "The world will appreciate us. And we have done a lot that's worthy of appreciation. We are artists and activists, businesspeople and leaders. Students who want to create a better world. We," I concluded vehemently, "are latte."

I had to pause for several whoops and whistles, and

shouts of "Respect the Latte!" But, slowly, the noise of the room finally drowned out that annoying little voice in my head and I found myself grinning under my bag, finally feeling the excitement that had the audience buzzing.

"Tonight's spokesperson for latte ideals, our keynote speaker, is Dr. Adina Malik, a professor in the American Cultures department right here at UC Berkeley. Dr. Malik is an expert in the very causes that the Latte Rebellion holds dear. She is the author of *Uncut, Undried: The Complexity of Race in America*, and has spoken on the subject of mixed race and multiculturalism at colleges and seminars across the country." I paused. This felt … kind of good. I was almost done, and I had managed not to make a fool of myself. Just like at that first Mocha Loco meeting, everyone was listening to me, and not only that, they were smiling, nodding, clapping. Even Thad. I was a little dizzy again, but this time it wasn't from nervousness. It was much more like exhilaration.

"One of the ideas the Latte Rebellion posed early on was 'ask not what the brown can do for you, but what you can do for the brown.' Dr. Malik will now enlighten you with her response to that question, with her ideas on what you can do for the brown, in her speech on *Faces and Races: The Browning of America*. Please welcome Dr. Malik."

As the crowd clapped enthusiastically and Dr. Malik gathered her notes and came up to the podium, I slipped to the back of the room and out the door, according to plan. I walked to the bookstore a block away, trying to ignore the weird looks I was getting for having a paper bag over my head, and rushed into the tiny one-person bathroom, back-pack in hand, locking the door behind me.

I thought I'd feel relieved to get my speech over with, and I was—but I was also riding high on an unfamiliar, thrilling surge of energy. I crumpled up the paper bag and shoved it into the garbage, feeling a smile spread over my face at the thought of being myself again. I pulled a sweat-shirt on over my Latte Rebellion T-shirt and took my hair out of its ponytail. I even changed my shoes from the vin-tage brown Doc Martens I'd been wearing to a pair of black tennis shoes, in case anyone had memorized my wardrobe.

With my shoes safely stashed in my backpack, I wiped the sweat off my face and neck with a wet paper towel, touched up my lip gloss and headed back to the café. I loitered outside until a couple of people wandered by and decided to go in, and then I followed them so I wouldn't attract as much attention. Once I was in, I slipped around them to get over to where Miranda and Thad were stand-ing. I felt like a secret agent. A real one, that is.

Dr. Malik was talking about identity and living on the borderlands of multiple cultures. Miranda was totally entranced, so all I did was nudge her to let her know I was there. She caught my eye for a second and smiled.

Thad, on the other hand, grinned widely when he saw me, and before I could worry about whether I should shake his hand or what, he pulled me into a quick hug that left me feeling warm all over again. Okay, more than warm.

"Glad you could make it," he said, smiling slyly at me. Had he guessed my role? Recognized my voice? I tensed a little. What if he had? If so, he didn't bring it up. "I was looking forward to seeing you again."

Now I was *really* blushing hard.

"It's nice to see you, too," I whispered.

"Can I buy you a coffee?" He put a hand on my arm just for a second, but long enough for me to wish he'd just leave it there and forget about buying the coffee.

"You don't have to," I said.

"*Shhhh*," someone behind me said.

"I practically insist. I'm getting myself another one anyway. Save my spot?"

"Sure." I stared after him as he sauntered toward the counter. He wasn't wearing a Rebellion shirt; just a black T-shirt over a long-sleeved gray shirt, and jeans. Jeans that looked mighty nice. I glanced at Miranda, who gave me a wink and a knowing smile. I narrowed my eyes at her, and she grinned and turned back toward the keynote speaker. It was obvious Miranda had said something to Thad about me while I was out of the room—something that prompted that public display of affection. I just wasn't sure what, and maybe I didn't want to know.

"Thanks," I said, as Thad returned with two paper cups—lattes, of course. He smiled again but didn't say anything more, just turned his attention to Dr. Malik, who seemed to be reaching some sort of crescendo because her voice had gotten very loud, breathy, and excited.

"Clearly, brothers and sisters, if we have learned anything from the past hundred years, or even the past ten— it is that we have a calling. *We*, as the population of the future, the future of the human gene pool! It is *we*"—this was punctuated with an emphatic thump on the podium— "*we* who must bring this message to those unwilling or unable to be here today. Let us leave here tonight full of energy, full of passion, full of camaraderie as we go forth with linked arms into the future!"

The room exploded. People got up from their chairs, some of them standing on their seats, and the air was filled with whistles, whoops, and resounding applause. The walls reverberated with it. I clapped more sedately, as did Miranda and Thad. When I glanced at him, he gave me an ironic smile. Again, I wondered if he'd guessed who I was.

When the cheering and chaos died down a bit, people started to mill around during the twenty-minute break before the poetry slam started. Leonard, Darla, and a few more of the college-aged Latte Rebellion people were standing near the podium with Dr. Malik, congratulating her and shaking her hand. There was now an unbelievable crowd at the coffee counter, and some people had retreated outside to loiter on the sidewalk or have a smoke, talking excitedly.

"Unbelievable, huh?" Miranda linked arms with me, grinning widely.

"Yeah." Unbelievable was right. *Surreal* was even more like it, maybe. "Um, what did *you* think of the speech?" I asked Thad.

"Interesting stuff," he said. "I'm in Dr. Malik's *Mixed Race in America* class, so I'm used to her rhetorical style."

"Oh," I said, feeling self-conscious all of a sudden. I

might have *sounded* like I knew what I was talking about up at the podium, but now that I was unmasked and unprotected, and talking to Thad face to face, I felt like I didn't have anything to say. And I wouldn't know about rhetorical style if it came up and pinched me on the butt.

"So, did either of you sign up for the poetry slam?" he asked casually, after an awkward pause.

"Nope," Miranda said. "Maybe next time."

"Speak for yourself," I told her. "Maybe *never* is more like it."

"I didn't either," Thad said, "but Greg's going to be in the first round. You guys remember him, right?" He gestured at the front of the room, where some of the slam participants had gathered. "At least that speech turned out pretty okay. I'll get my extra credit, anyway. And I knew you'd be coming, so ..."

I ducked my head self-consciously, embarrassed but pleased. "But you look like you're, um, mixed-race. Or ..."

"Yeah, I guess I am. A little of this, a little of that." He smiled.

I laughed. "I know the feeling." I felt something release inside me, and I relaxed for the first time all evening.

Thad grinned at me, his eyes meeting mine. "Are you two going to at least stay for the slam? If you stick around, you'll get to experience the poetic stylings of Greg 'the Rhyme Schemer' Androvich."

"Definitely," Miranda said. "I love that striped hat he's wearing. Very geek chic." We all laughed. "Seriously. I would wear that."

"I'd believe it," I said, glad the attention was off me for a minute so I could think straight. "That would so go with your black-and-white striped socks."

"Sure, if I wanted to look like an escaped parolee."

"Nah, I think it'd be more 'Cat in the Hat,'" Thad insisted. "That's better, isn't it?"

"Um…" Miranda and I looked at each other, and I tried not to crack up.

"Okay, so how exactly does a poetry slam work? I've never been to one," I said. "Should we, like, sit up front or something?" I hoped not. Maybe Thad was a big poetry fan, though.

"Not unless you want to," he said. "I'm not into the whole audience judging thing. I'm really just staying for Greggo. He wants to get onto the Berkeley Slam Team, but he just started performing this year. With competition like The Pinoy Paladin, it's tough to get a spot." Thad nodded at a short, dark-haired, bushy-browed guy in a black leather jacket and backwards baseball cap standing off to one side, looking over a battered piece of paper.

"Well," said Miranda, "should we just stay here?"

"Sure. Then we can be close to the door if we need to take off. I'm supposed to be back by eleven." I hunched my shoulders, embarrassed. But before I could try to save face, Leonard went up to the microphone again and boomed an announcement out into the room.

"Attention, ladies and gentlemen! Quiet, please." He tapped the mike, and an annoying crackly thud echoed out into the ruckus. Miranda, Thad, and I slid into the nearest available chairs. "Thank you, people. Without further ado, it is my privilege to present you with the emcee of the first annual Latte Rebellion Poetry Slam, Ms. Diva ArchMinority!"

The room erupted into applause yet again as an attention-grabbing figure made her way to the podium. She was wearing a low-cut, spangly red dress and black go-go boots, and had her hair piled into an elaborate up-do that was probably a wig. She was wearing black, elbow-length, fishnet gloves with the fingers cut off and glamour-girl makeup.

But Miranda and I grabbed each other and screamed along with the crowd, laughing to ourselves because that figure was unmistakable.

Diva ArchMinority was none other than Bridget's roommate, she of the myriad anime action figures: Darla.

Exhibit A.9:
MATERIALS VIOLATING
BOARD POLICY SECTION 418.III.N

Online communications among possible terrorist group members, from another Latte Rebellion website, reported to the School Board on 3/31. Two copies attached.

Posted: February 15, 8:02 p.m.
By: UncleSam
i cant believe there are people who buy into ur dumb club. theres just no way theres so many of u people out there. wake up!!!!!! this is a total fraud not a movement. maybe like a bowel movement. haha anyways u probly all are terrorists and want the world to be ruled by the middle east and mexico and orientals. go find ur own country if u dont like this one.

Posted: February 16, 10:36 a.m.
By: DramaRaja
It's people like *you*, UncleSam, who make it necessary for groups like ours to form. This is a free country and everybody has a voice—unfortunately that includes you! Latte Rebels, we need to do something about this kind of inflammatory rhetoric before it turns into hate crime. We need to get our voices heard!!

Posted: February 16, 11:07 a.m.
By: ThinLizzie85
Right on DramaRaja!!! You tell 'em. We're all behind you!

Posted: February 16, 2:30 p.m.
By: ChineseDragon
Hell yeah! This means war!

9

I rubbed my temples, trying to ignore the shrill-voiced girl yelling into the microphone about injustice and single motherhood. After Darla had showed up looking like a Japanese pop star crossed with Bugs Bunny in drag, we had endured over an hour of ranting, raving, and rhyming. Greg had already had his moment to shine, but he was being upstaged by all the people who seemed to spout one-liner after one-liner, making the crowd hoot and holler.

Miranda had watched his entire performance with her chin cupped in one hand, her expression rapt and considering. I had a bizarre vision of a double date with the four of us, Greg in his stupid hat and me in my paper bag mask, and shuddered.

Miranda glanced at me. She jerked her head toward the door and raised her eyebrows questioningly. I nodded, relieved. Poetry slams were *not* for me, I decided. It was just too much noise and bluster, completely different from when we were busy creating the website or going to planning meetings; at least then there was a tangible product. And it didn't give me a splitting headache.

I put on my sweater, glancing at Thad regretfully. He saw that Miranda and I were getting ready to leave and put his hand up to his ear in a gesture I couldn't for the life of me interpret. Was this some kind of Berkeley-style good-bye wave? An activist "fight the power" thing? Should I do the same thing in return—put my fist to my ear?

Miranda poked me and pulled her phone out of her pocket, waving it in front of my face. *God, I'm such a dork.* I smiled weakly and nodded. I wanted, really badly, to lean back in and return the hug Thad had given me when I first walked in, but a girl with a bullring-pierced nose and red knitted snood had already honed in on our seats. Plus, to be honest, I didn't know if any attempts at flirting would be successful, since it was something I was frustratingly incompetent at. Or maybe he was just thinking of me as, say, a little sister—horrors! So I settled for a wave—a regular one—and what I hoped was a sultry smile. I'd have to find out later, over the phone, if it had had the intended effect.

———

The following Tuesday night, I called Carey. It had been one of the weirdest weeks of my life, and not just because of the rally (surreal as it was to see Darla in something other than an anime T-shirt).

The only other time Carey and I had been angry at each other for this long was in eighth grade, when we both had a crush on Roy Anderson and I decided to do something about it by asking him to the Halloween dance. She was so mad, I got the ice-queen treatment for eight days straight.

But on the night of the dance, Roy tried to freak-dance with me, called me a bitch when I wouldn't, and then proceeded to swap spit all evening with the school's most notorious slut. Carey saw the whole thing and, needless to say, both our crushes ended that night. We both vowed—over root beer floats at the Denny's across the street, after leaving the dance early—never to let anything (or anybody) so stupid come between us again.

And I was thinking about our vow when I called, silly as it was. Just like then, I didn't want to be fighting with her. I wanted us to be part of the Rebellion together, but failing that, I wanted to at least put an end to the silent treatment. I really missed Carey. In all the sappiest, most sentimental friendship-movie ways imaginable, I missed her.

"Hello?" She picked up the phone, sounding distracted. I heard her put one hand over the receiver and hiss, "Roddy, I'm *on the phone*. Go sit at the table and read your book, *please*."

"Hey, it's me," I said, flopping back onto the bed.

"Oh."

I couldn't quite tell what that "oh" meant. It could have been "oh" as in "oh, it's you; what the hell do you want?" Or it might have been "oh" as in "oh, I'm surprised you called, yet also profoundly overjoyed." I swallowed, my throat dry, and turned onto my side, pulling my knees up to my chest.

"'Oh'?" I said. "Is that it?"

"What did you *want* me to say?" she said, tiredly.

"I don't know," I said, clenching my jaw. "You know, you could have called me."

"*You* could have called *me*," she pointed out, logically.

"Look, I'm sorry I hung up on you," I said. "I was just … mad because I didn't want you to quit, that's all. This is stupid. All of it's stupid," I said in a rush.

She was quiet for a minute. "I know you don't think it's stupid. You don't have to say that on my account."

I sighed and stretched my legs back out. "Look, I know you're busy and you have a lot of extra crap dumped on you. I'm sorry I tried to make you keep going. I just thought … especially with Leonard involved, you might want to …"

"Oh, *Leonard,*" she said. "I barely had time to talk to him this week. But he visited a few days ago to bring me coffee when I was studying."

"That's … nice," I said. Strangely, I meant it.

"Yeah, but I told him I couldn't do anything more with the Rebellion."

I blinked. I hadn't expected that. I'd expected her to give him some kind of noncommittal answer, to try to string him along. And here she was being *honest* with him. "Was he mad?"

"I don't think so. He seemed okay. It's kind of hard to know what he's thinking, you know?"

I laughed stiffly. "No kidding."

"Anyway, he wanted me to come to the rally too, but I had soccer practice and work. He said fine, and we talked on Sunday. He told me how everything went. He said you gave a good speech." I heard Carey put her hand over the mouthpiece again. "*Not now!* Just a minute." One of her brothers was whining shrilly.

"Sounds like you have your hands full," I said. I couldn't exactly argue with her excuses, but I felt a little forlorn. And I couldn't help wondering whether she was being as honest with me as she was with Leonard. "I guess I'll let you go."

"Okay. Sorry," she said. "My brothers are going crazy. They got into Mom's Valentine candy."

"Oh," I said. "Well, I guess I should do homework, anyway. Okay if I call you later to check calculus answers?"

"Sure," she said neutrally. I didn't know what she was thinking, and it was a strange, unfamiliar, uncomfortable feeling. "Talk to you later."

"Bye." I flipped my phone shut and tossed it toward the foot of the bed. I felt tears start and wiped them away, frustrated. My conversation with Carey wasn't exactly what I'd been hoping for. I'd pictured us laughing like normal by the end of the call, after I'd updated her on the rally and Thad, and then we'd be saying goodbye with promises to sit together at lunch again and study for our physics test on Friday. Instead, it had been awkward and weird, and I wasn't even sure anything had been resolved.

I was at the kitchen table doing French homework when my mother came in from the living room and handed me the home phone. It was about a week and a half after the rally, but the ongoing tedium of my life made it seem like months had gone by. I glanced up, wondering if it was Thad, and if so, why he hadn't just called my cell. Or maybe it was Carey, who had thawed a little since our last phone conversation.

"Nani wants to talk to you," Mom said. "I told her about that boy you met. The one from UC Berkeley."

I groaned. "*Why* did you have to tell her? Nothing's even going on with him." Not yet, anyway.

"Just talk to her." My mother patted me on the shoulder and smiled wryly. "She's curious. She wants to know what's going on in your life. You remind her of herself at your age."

God, how could that even be? I apprehensively brought the phone to my ear and said, "Nani?"

"Hullo *beti*, I don't want to interrupt your studies for too long, but I wanted to tell you something. Your mother was telling me how ... busy you've been."

Oh, no. Cue the "why haven't you called?" guilt trip, or worse, the nosy interrogation about Thad and the inevitable questions about whether there were any "handsome college-bound Indian boys" at school that I could be lusting after instead. I fielded that question at least once a month, and my answer was the same—why do they have to be Indian?

Couldn't they just be cute and college-bound? What did their ethnicity matter? Just because I was Indian—half, at that—did not mean I was destined to marry Anil Prakash, who wore wire-rimmed glasses, plaid shirts, and tan slacks to school every day and could barely talk to a girl without stammering. Or Bhabu "Bob" Kumar, who was a meathead baseball jock. Honestly.

I braced myself for what was no doubt coming, clenching my fingers around the phone receiver.

"I'm very proud of you, Asha, but I have to admit I'm a little worried about you. You're always so busy. Too busy to talk to your old Nani, eh?" Her voice was soft with concern.

Oh no, here it comes.

"I know you're nearly eighteen now, but you're still a girl to me. And…I want you to remember while you're still young that life isn't all about work. You're doing very, very well." I heard her sigh heavily. "Please just be sure to take a break every now and then. Call your friends. See a film."

I did a double-take. This wasn't what I'd been expecting. Not at all.

"It worries me when I talk to your mother and all she tells me is how much you've been studying and studying and studying. I know your parents push you a bit, especially your father, but don't forget to stop and take a breath, okay, dear?"

"Um…yes?" I said, a little dazedly.

"And Asha *beti*, truly, you can always call me. It doesn't have to be a holiday. I would be thrilled to hear all about your adventures with your friends. When I was young, I just adored walking with my girlfriends through the shops downtown, eating hot fried snacks from the vendors and holding the beautiful saris up to our faces … I'll never forget those days. They're as valuable to me as the time I spent in the teachers' college."

Nani went on in that vein for a few minutes. By the time we hung up, I'd hardly said a word.

She was right. I'd never spent much time thinking about how hard my parents pushed me. It was just a fact of life. Carey dealt with the same thing, though she put a lot more pressure on herself than I did. But what I couldn't tell Nani was that the Rebellion was giving me that outlet, that feeling that there was more to my life than manic test prep and petty competition for grades.

I could hardly get my mind around the fact that, of all people, it was my elderly Nani who didn't seem to mind that I wanted my life to be about more than just a perfect report card, the perfect college, and the perfect list of achievements.

At least there was *somebody* in my life who wasn't telling me I needed to buckle down and get serious.

———————

A couple of weeks afterward, I was sitting in the living room after dinner with my parents, half-watching TV while catching up on reading for most of my classes. I was in a pretty good mood, since I'd just gotten off the phone with Thad.

Unfortunately, the news show my parents were watching was all sordid and depressing, and I was aching to change the channel to mindless entertainment like Celebrity Dance-Off. But no such luck.

"... report that the gunman, who has taken five international students hostage, is Raymond Gretch, also a student at the college," chirped the news reporter.

"Horrible," my mother said. My dad *hmph*ed in agreement. I tried to block it out and focus on *Invisible Man*.

"Though it isn't known whether Gretch is personally acquainted with the hostages, a search of his Blue Sky, Indiana, apartment turned up printouts of several of the students' schedules, copies of class assignments, and other evidence that Gretch had been following them around the Blue Sky College campus, including flyers for the Model United Nations and an organization called the Latte Rebellion, advertised as a club for students of mixed race."

My head jerked up involuntarily, and in a second I was just as glued to the TV as my parents were, hardly able to believe what I was hearing. The newscaster continued rattling off speculations about the gunman, but didn't mention anything more about the Latte Rebellion. Still, I was in shock. We'd made the news! Sure, it was bad news, but the bad stuff wasn't about *us*. And now we were practically a household name. I didn't know what to think, but it felt like the bottom had dropped out of my stomach.

Then my mother said, "This Latte Rebellion nonsense again. Asha, I'm not sure you should be wearing that shirt. They sound ... extreme."

"Troublemakers, Lalita," my dad grunted, and turned the sound up on the television. "Kids acting up."

"It's just a club," I said, suddenly worried. What else had they heard? Had I missed something? "Didn't I tell you about it? I went to that...uh...lecture on the weekend and it seemed fine. They had a Berkeley professor."

"Berkeley professor." My mom looked thoughtful for a minute. "Still, Asha, these so-called 'movements' can get out of hand. When extremist fringe groups start to form..."

"Mom, believe me, the Rebellion is just a club to promote acceptance of mixed ethnicity. It is not an 'extremist group.'" I looked up from my English notebook. "Trust me on this one."

She narrowed her eyes at me. "Trust you because you've heard things? Or because you're involved?" *Uh-oh.* I didn't answer and tried to appear riveted to my homework. She continued. "Either way, I'd prefer you stayed away from this type of controversy. Even if the views of the club aren't dangerous, that doesn't mean some people won't overreact."

"Mom, you're being overprotective!" I slammed my book shut melodramatically. "I'm not one of your elementary school students."

"Asha, please don't talk to your mother in that tone of voice." My dad looked up from the TV briefly.

I wasn't in the mood for a fight, so I opened my book again with a sigh.

It was already March. Just a few short months until graduation, London...and freedom. I just had to dig my heels in, grit my teeth, and hold on. Of course, my teeth would probably be gritted all the way down to nubs by then.

At least all the time I'd been spending catching up on studying was paying off. I got an A-minus on a major calculus test I'd been stressing about for weeks, and soon after that, I got an A-plus on an English essay. My parents were overjoyed ... which made me feel just a tiny bit less guilty that I'd fibbed about the Rebellion. Fortunately for me and my grades, the Rebellion itself had been pretty quiet except for email updates, though I was sure that would change now that we'd been mentioned on national television.

I'd been floating along through life as if everything was just peachy. Then I came crashing down to earth like a lead balloon.

It started with an unexpected B on a physics lab. It was a huge lab that had taken weeks to complete, and I was aggravated because the B was due to the slackers in my group rather than anything *I* hadn't done. Still, the teacher gave me a disappointed head-shake when she handed back my lab notes, as though I'd been responsible for keeping the three jokers in line and had failed miserably.

Then, at lunch, I made a cameo appearance at the Latte Rebellion club meeting. Miranda went with me this time, and to my surprise, she stood up and cleared her throat to make an announcement.

"Guys, I have really big news. Have you been to the Rebellion websites lately?" Miranda looked around Mrs. Carville's history classroom, where the meeting (allegedly a meeting of the International Club, of which Maria McNally was conveniently secretary) was being held. Of about thirty people there, only a few nodded knowingly. "Well, the news is, *we are a nationwide phenomenon.*"

There were gasps, and then David Castro asked, "What does *that* mean? Do we get to have, like, a reality TV show?" A few people laughed. I just sat there, motionless, clutching my pen.

Miranda gave him a wry smile. "No, I mean that there are no fewer than *fifty-two* chapters of the Latte Rebellion at high schools nationwide, and about a hundred at colleges and universities. People, this is *huge. We* are huge."

"And," she added dramatically, "as you may know, the Latte Rebellion has officially been mentioned on national television."

Now that was something I *did* know. There was a burst of noise, and everybody chattered at each other in amazement, lunches forgotten.

"—the hostage thing—"

"—think it's bad press? Like guilt by association, if—"

"—nothing to do with—"

"—said the guy was mixed-race, too, like one of the hostages, but—"

"—I'm tellin' you, our own TV show."

"Guys! Quiet down, everybody," Maria McNally said, in a voice that made me wonder if she'd been a kindergarten teacher in a former life. She pushed her retro-chic granny glasses back onto the bridge of her nose and clicked her mechanical pencil, glancing briefly at me.

"We should decide what we want to do," she continued, "in terms of damage control. Maybe we should suggest to Sergeant Echo and Field Officer Foxtrot that the website have links to all the different chapters. And we should make a statement on the front page about having no connection to the hostage situation. Faris, take notes." She poked him in the arm. Faris was her annoying little freshman flunky, though she insisted they were dating.

People were nodding and grinning excitedly. As for me, I was ... well, a bit giddy. Kalamazoo? Savannah? Bozeman, Montana? And Blue Sky, Indiana, where the standoff had taken place. I had barely heard of some of these places, but evidently they had enough Sympathizers to constitute a chapter of the Rebellion.

Then something a little unpleasant occurred to me.

"I don't mean to be a buzzkill, but if we post anything on the website, isn't there a possibility that it'll just connect us with the hostage thing in people's minds? What if people misinterpret it and start protesting against us or something?"

"Oh, I'm a very clear writer. It won't be misinterpreted." Maria gave me a small, tense smile and Faris nodded approvingly, floppy blond hair falling over one eye. "I'll give Sergeant Echo the text we want posted. I'll make sure there's no way it can spark any kind of protest. Although a little controversy might not be a bad thing for drawing attention to our cause ..." She trailed off, a little alarmingly. But then she turned to Faris and started dictating our PR statement, and, thankfully, she was right about her writing skills—she made the Latte Rebellion's intentions clear and unmistakable while also managing to make us sound like peaceful do-gooders who spent our spare time saving bunnies and kittens. By the time the meeting was over, I was mostly reassured, but the seesawing tension level left me exhausted.

Then, when I got home and pulled a sheaf of envelopes out of our mailbox, I found that two of them were thin missives addressed to me. From colleges. Small envelopes from colleges are *never, ever* a good thing.

I opened them with a sigh. Stanford and Harvard were now definitively out of the running for Future Home of Asha Jamison. I was obviously not destined for an Ivy-League education. Too bad; Cambridge sounded like a great place to live, and Palo Alto would have been pretty close to home. Plus, Stanford had a Social Policy program that sounded really cool. Something else I'd learned about from Thad.

I stood numbly in the front doorway for a few minutes, the screen door swinging in the breeze, trying to wrap my mind around the fact that I'd gotten my first official rejections. It seemed impossible. I'd worked so hard the past couple of months, and it was completely unfair and *wrong* that one semester of grades out of my entire high school career could ruin everything. Not when I'd done everything else right.

My eyes stung. I went straight to my room, closed the door, shut the blinds against the spitefully gorgeous spring day, crawled under the covers, and cried until my throat was raw. Sure, I was disappointed, but I also felt ashamed and humiliated because I knew I could have done better, should have done better. I'd always taken it for granted that I was a good, even an outstanding, student. It was simply a fact, part of my identity. I'd been ranked third or fourth in my class ever since starting high school, and I never really had to worry about staying there.

That's because you never had a life *before*, said the nasty little voice in my head, back with a vengeance now that I didn't have a cheering crowd to drown it out.

Was the choice really between having a life and having scholastic success? I didn't want to believe that. My academic cred was as solid as a rock regardless of what else I was doing. Or it had been. Now, it felt like the slightest tremor could bring the whole thing crashing down.

Part of me wanted to call Thad, to ask him whether he thought that was any kind of a choice. But the other part of me won out—the part that wanted to pretend today had never happened. Because then (a) I wouldn't have to think about it anymore, and (b) my parents would never find out. I'd just have to wait until I got an acceptance somewhere else, and pretend like that was the only one that had ever mattered to me. Pretend my ass off, until I believed it myself.

After a little while I fell asleep, tears drying on my face and throat aching. I had fitful dreams about running, stumbling up a steep slope, trying to get to the top of a mountain because I knew something horrible would happen if I didn't. Only I could never get there. The earth kept quaking underneath me. I was wearing a really ugly swimsuit and a paper bag on my head, and I kept falling and skinning my knees. When I fell, the bag came off, and, as it hit the ground in front of me, it turned into a towel.

I woke suddenly to the sound of the garage door opening and my parents' voices in the hallway. I sat straight up and the whole day came flooding back in an instant. I also got a pretty intense headrush, but I shook it off and threw the covers back, swinging my legs over the edge of the bed. In the process, the rejection letters went fluttering to the floor, so papery-thin and innocuous but holding my fate in their pages. I hurriedly gathered them up, envelopes and all, and stood in the middle of the room, undecided. The dirty clothes hamper? No, I might forget they were there and throw them into the washing machine, though "accidental" destruction was certainly one way to hide the evidence. My underwear drawer? No. Too shallow and easily emptied. I started to panic.

"Asha! Come help me put away groceries," I heard my mom call from the kitchen.

"Coming!" Frantically, I hauled up my top mattress, practically wrenching my right arm out of the socket in the process, and shoved the rejection letters as far as possible toward the center. I let the top mattress drop and pulled up the blankets so it didn't look quite as disheveled. There was *no* way my parents were allowed to know about this. No way.

———

Later that night, Carey called me. Before I could vent to her about my horrible afternoon and how difficult it was to maintain a stoic, normal façade in front of my parents—before I could even say *anything*, in fact—Carey let out a completely unintelligible string of half-screamed words that sounded like "ohmigodicanbleveigottin!"

"Can you slow *down*? What did you do, take a No-Doz?"

"Asha!" she said breathlessly. "Today I got my Berkeley letter! My *acceptance letter*! They said I'm being considered for an alumni leadership scholarship! I *can't believe it*!"

"I can believe it," I said, my heart sinking despite the fact that I knew I should be happy for her. "I knew you'd get in. Colleges will be falling all over themselves to get you to go there."

"That's not all! Stanford said yes, too, but I don't know yet about their scholarships." She sounded slightly muffled, like she was bouncing up and down.

"Are you *dancing around*?"

"Um ... sort of," she said. I could *hear* her grinning. "This means your acceptance letters should be here any day now, too, you know."

My heart sank a little further. I hadn't gotten anything from Robbins or Berkeley yet, but if Carey had already gotten her Berkeley acceptance ... that wasn't a good sign. I bet they waited longer to send out rejection letters. It surely wasn't their top priority to correspond promptly with the unwashed, unaccepted, intellectually inferior masses.

"Well," I said, knowing it was the right thing to say, "we'll have to celebrate this weekend. Wanna go into the

Bay Area and do something?" I felt like I was forcing the words out; I wasn't in much of a mood for celebrating.

"*You* just want to go visit Thad," she teased.

"I was thinking no such thing," I said, virtuously. "Besides, we're just friends. We connect *intellectually*." I cracked a smile; I couldn't help it.

"And I'm sure that when you kiss for the first time, it'll be a real *intellectual* experience," she said, laughing.

"I don't know if that's ever going to happen," I said, but I kind of hoped it would. *Kind of? Definitely*, I thought, picturing those intense blue eyes and his lean frame. Then my heart sank, and all the tension of earlier that day came flooding back into my brain. I didn't have a chance. I'd been rejected by Stanford and Harvard, and Berkeley was probably going to reject me, too. And Thad? Sure we'd talked a few times, but he was a college student. Why would he ever be interested in dating *me* when he had all those intimidating, smart Berkeley students to choose from, like some kind of brainy buffet? No, I was destined for some knee-socks-wearing, dorky, shrimpy engineer wanna-be, or perhaps I was doomed never to date at all. I'd be single and a virgin forever—a junior-high-school librarian, or a scientist hunched over the microscope that was my only friend in the world.

"I know what you're thinking," Carey said, into the long silence I'd just left. "You're thinking about how you're going to end up an old maid, alone in your science lab or whatever, married to your Bunsen burner."

"I'm about to graduate from high school and I've only

ever really dated *one person*, and that was a disaster," I said. My voice sounded hoarse.

"That was Ben Alonzo, and we were sophomores," Carey pointed out. "Bowling and cheese fries at the Park Place Lanes hardly counts as a date, don't worry."

"That's the *problem.*" I sighed. "That's the entire sad story of my dating life." I felt a stabbing pang of loss, the loss of something I'd never had in the first place. And if I was perfectly honest with myself, this wasn't really just about Thad, or relationships. It was about my whole life, about what I had and hadn't managed to accomplish. It was about lost potential, embodied by those stupid rejection letters.

Carey paused. "Asha. What did I tell you when you were crying all over yourself, right after Ben said he 'accidentally' kissed Andrea Wilson?"

"You said I was way too awesome for him." I let out a sound that was halfway between a laugh and a sob. "You said I was an unstoppable force of nature."

I felt like my heart was breaking, saying that, because I felt as far from a force of nature as it was possible to get. It seemed that all of my high hopes were unrealistic, unscalable mountains. My voice echoed dully across the phone line. "Carey. I…" I wanted to tell her about the letters. But then I thought of her overjoyed dance around the kitchen, and I couldn't.

"Asha, I promise it'll be *fine*. You will not be an old maid. In London, I bet all the cute English boys will fall all over themselves to talk to you. And then you'll get to college and all those smart, articulate hotties will *converge* on your dorm room. I swear." Carey sounded just a tiny bit annoyed. I knew I'd rained on her parade.

"Okay," I said, just so we could put an end to this conversation. "Thanks, Care. At lunch tomorrow we can talk more about celebrating, 'kay? Congratulations. You *rock*."

"Thanks!... But you're okay, right?"

"Fine, fine," I said, dismissively, glad she couldn't see me wiping my eyes.

"Well, good. That's great! I, uh... I guess I'll call Miranda now." She sounded like she couldn't wait to get off the phone. I knew Miranda would be a much more receptive audience, so I let Carey go.

I wasn't much of a friend myself, because all I could think about after she talked about the hotties converging on my college dorm room was the fact that Thad could never possibly be interested in me. Not only that, two of my four college possibilities were now nonexistent. Officially, I was now halfway to failure.

After wallowing in my misery for a while, I decided to turn on my laptop and try to console myself by looking at our T-shirt sales numbers. I went to the Latte Rebellion site first, just to see what was going on, and signed into the forum as an anonymous guest.

When the page loaded, I swallowed hard.

It was hard to believe how *big* this had gotten. Each of the different chapters of the Rebellion that Maria and Miranda had talked about had its own section of the forum, with names like "Lansing Heights Rebellion Chapter" and "Portland Friends of the Latte."

I clicked into one of the topics in the main forum, "Vive la Resistance," and found a long post by Sergeant Echo about disassociating ourselves from any violent activity. I felt a surge of relief. Despite Maria's comments about a little controversy being good for the cause, they weren't going to do anything drastic. I quickly hit "reply to post" and added my two cents, not that a post by "A. Nonymous" was going to really matter anyway.

"Bravo, Sergeant E. et al, for standing up for the Rebellion's core principles and not getting sidetracked," I typed. "We want to make people think, we want to stand up and speak out for what we believe in, but we don't want to be associated with violence and mayhem. Kudos to you for furthering the real mission. A."

I logged off, feeling reassured. At least something in my life was going according to plan. More or less.

The following April:
Ashmont Unified School District Board Room

It was eerie, but it seemed like almost every person in the boardroom was seated, and waiting quietly, even before the disciplinary hearing officer called the session back to order. There were rustlings of paper and the slight sounds of people shifting in their seats; there was an occasional whisper and, from time to time, the flash of the newspaper reporter's camera. But on the whole, it was so silent that I was holding my body stiff, tensing my muscles into rigidity so I wouldn't draw any attention to myself. My can of soda sat on the wooden table in front of me, untouched and dripping condensation.

I jumped when the hearing officer's voice boomed into the microphone. "Will the board secretary please note that the hearing reconvened at ten forty-five." Sheesh. He must have found a cough drop somewhere.

"Let's continue quickly." He consulted his notes. "Next we have Ms. Maria McNally. Come up here, please." Of course, Maria was already halfway out of her seat. She looked prim and proper in her granny glasses, a button-down white shirt, and a plaid skirt, with her two long braids coiled up in Princess Leia buns on either side of her head.

"Ms. McNally, it says here that you're a junior at University Park. Is that correct?"

She nodded, a little spastically.

"And I'm to understand that you're the one responsible for the school Latte Rebellion group, despite its failure to gain approval from the Inter-Club Council?"

"That's right, sir. I'm the president of the Latte Rebellion, University Park High chapter." She stood straight and proud in front of him, seeming to feed off the incredulous stares of the audience. Out of the corner of my eye, I could see my dad narrow his gaze at her. He was probably trying to construct an elaborate scenario in his head where she was the instigator and I was an innocent bystander who got sucked in against my will.

"From your standpoint, Ms. McNally, I'd like to hear more about Ms. Jamison's role in the events that led to this hearing. Of course," the hearing officer said dryly, "*your* rule-breaking is hardly in question, but that's been dealt with." He shot a sidelong glance at Vice Principal Malone, who nodded.

Maria frowned. "Asha was only involved to the extent that we asked her to give a brief speech. Which she did. End of story."

"Obviously it isn't nearly that simple," one of the school board members said, rubbing her temples tiredly. I flushed with guilt, even though there was no way they could read my mind, no way they could know about everything I'd done behind the scenes.

"Sir, she may have come up with some of the original ideas behind the Latte Rebellion, but the responsibility for the incident last week lies entirely in the hands of the individuals who broke school rules by bringing—"

"And what about the school rules *you* broke," he interrupted, frowning, "and Ms. Jamison? That's what we're focusing on here. The rules about Latte Rebellion materials on campus, which you violated both in letter and in spirit."

"With all due respect, the letter and spirit of those rules are *wrong*," Maria said passionately. Noisy whispers broke out among the school board panelists, and the audience fidgeted. I clenched my jaw. It was getting harder and harder to sit there quietly while everyone else had their say.

"The rules, Ms. McNally, are there to protect the school population and maintain a safe educational environment. Your enthusiasm for your 'cause,' however, is duly noted." It sounded like the hearing officer was trying not to roll his eyes. I could feel my frustration building slowly like kindling catching fire. What gave him the right to be dismissive?

"What I still want to know, however, is specifics, which you seem to be refusing to provide. Specifics about how Ms. Jamison's actions resulted in flagrant violation of school rules and dangerous behavior." He glared at me, then Maria. "Well?"

Maria seemed to shrink a little under his scrutiny. I swallowed, my throat dry.

"I've said all I have to say," she said finally. There was a very long silence.

"Fine," the hearing officer said, sounding aggrieved. "We need to move on. We still have witnesses to hear from. And we all want to leave on time, I'm sure." He shared a condescending smile with one of the hearing panel members, a white-haired woman in a purple suit.

More witnesses? Who could possibly be left?

Inflammatory materials distributed on school property. Two copies attached.

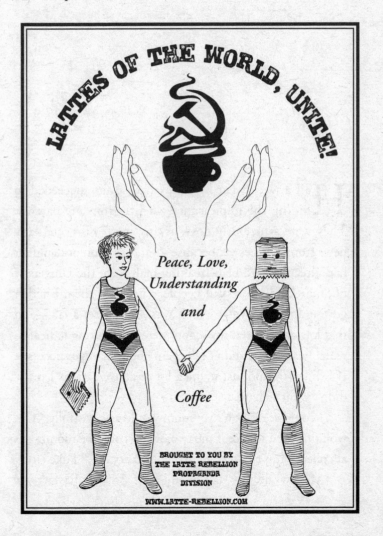

10

Half a week went by, and I had so far succeeded in hiding the unpleasant evidence from my parents. They were atrociously nosy, asking me if I'd gotten any news from colleges yet because so-and-so's son or daughter had already heard blah-freaking-blah from the University of Smart and Successful People. I just told them I hadn't gotten anything yet—which was, of course, a fib—and that lots of people at my school were still waiting to hear—which was true. I didn't tell them about Carey's successes. If I did, it would just invite a lot of conversations I really didn't want to have.

I could see it now. My mom would say, wistfully, "Oh, wouldn't it be so nice if the two of you could be roommates at college? You could study together every day." Puke city.

Meanwhile, my dad would say, "So why haven't *you*

heard anything? I knew those grades from last semester would come back and bite you in the ass. You're lucky we were so proactive or you might have to be taking summer school instead of going on that vacation you think you deserve. Speaking of which, ha ha."

It was such a hideous vision of things to come that I completely threw myself into school activities, mindless busywork, *anything* to keep my mind off the confrontation that would hopefully never happen. In the meantime, I got a letter that I was on the waiting list for Berkeley, which wasn't so bad, but wasn't so good, either. I hid that under my mattress, too. The only school I still had to hear from was the one that had also, over the past few months, become my top choice—Robbins College. I started to get a recurring stomachache trying not to think about it.

I did continue going to the Mocha Loco Rebellion meetings—always as myself now. Even Carey made the occasional appearance; despite what she said about being "too busy" for the Rebellion, she was still pseudo-dating Leonard, and she and I were on better terms since we'd mutually decided to avoid the topic of colleges. There were a lot of other people from our school going to the meetings, too; in fact, to my smirking satisfaction, I recognized a few of Roger Yee's Asian American Club groupies.

I hadn't worn my paper bag hat in ages, and it was a relief not to have to hide or worry about being recognized. It was freeing. I felt like I could sit back and watch everything unfold. And I couldn't help feeling a little proud. Sometimes I even found myself having to hold back a little, when some of the college students started to wonder why a random high school student was so knowledgeable about the Rebellion.

Of course, I wouldn't be a high school student for much longer, even if college was still out of reach. When the time finally came that I no longer had to endure the sweaty-feet-and-diluted-bleach smell in the hallways, I would cavort in celebration.

In the meantime, I started looking online for deals on airline tickets. I sent a bunch of web links to Carey, who kept promising to look at them and then forgetting. It was frustrating, but typical. She was probably still dancing celebratory jigs about Stanford and Berkeley.

About a week after she told me about her college acceptances, I called Thad, willing myself not to be a downer like I'd been with Carey. I was sure he didn't want to hear me spazzing about getting rejected.

"Hi," I said uncertainly, fiddling with the water glass on my nightstand, watching the accumulated bubbles disappear as I tipped the liquid to one side.

"Oh, hey, Asha," he said. He sounded happy that I'd called. "What's up?"

"Not much." Part of me felt like spilling my guts about everything—the rejections, my crappy winter report card, even the Rebellion. It was like a volcano building pressure until one day it would have to blow. But I settled for "How's school?"

"Well, I've got a term paper due in Dr. Malik's class in a few weeks."

I couldn't help laughing a little. "You could write about the Latte Rebellion."

"Actually, I was sort of thinking about doing that," Thad said.

I almost spilled my water all over myself. "That would be hilarious." Well, kind of.

"I'm serious," Thad insisted. "We're supposed to write on the topic of race and social change. You know, like the Black Panthers, that kind of thing."

"But the Latte Rebellion isn't really..." I trailed off. "We haven't *changed* anything. I mean, I doubt the people in charge think it's, like, historically significant."

I had to think about it for a second, though. We *did* want to see social change, even if it took place on a small, personal scale. But... seriously, the *Black Panthers?*

"Oh, it's pretty major," he said. "I've been doing some research, and I'm blown away by how quickly the numbers have been growing and the philosophy itself has been spreading." Thad sounded effusive, excited. "You know, whoever originally thought of the idea was probably very intelligent and most definitely very, very lucky to be in the right place at the right time in history for something like this to catch on."

"Really," I said, neutrally. "Yeah, I'd say 'lucky' sounds about right."

"I mean, you have to wonder whether this Agent Alpha and Captain Charlie, or whoever put up the original website, were incredibly skilled at judging public readiness for this sort of thing, or if they did serious research first, or what."

Or what, I thought, but I kept quiet. My mind was spinning. Why was he telling all this stuff to *me*? Sure, he was all into his term paper topic, but what if he suspected something, especially after my conveniently late entrance at the rally? I mean, my identity swap was about as subtle as changing my clothes in a phone booth. But if he did suspect, why wasn't he saying anything?

"Penny for your thoughts," Thad said. "That's a whole dollar adjusted for inflation."

"I'm not sure my thoughts are worth a *whole dollar*," I said teasingly, trying to think of something nonincriminating to tell him.

"Lots more than that, I'm sure," he said.

I swallowed nervously. He *had* to know. But I wasn't going to tell him. Not yet. I wasn't ready for that. Our relationship—or long-distance friendship, or occasional flirtatious conversation, or whatever—had not yet reached that level.

"I guess…" I hesitated. "I guess I was just wondering how these kinds of things get started. I wonder if people can ever really *know* how things are going to turn out. Like the Latte Rebellion Organizers. What if they thought it was just something local? I don't know if they ever realized it would be *relevant* anywhere else."

"On the contrary, I think that's how all these things get started." Thad sounded passionate now, excited again. "One or two people have an idea, they start small, and then they hope that someone else, some*place* else, will take up the reins. It's like Greg and me. If we start a clinic in, say, the 'hood in Oakland, and someone in Africa or China or New Orleans decides they want to try the same thing…It's so powerful, the spread of ideas, Asha. It can make the world a better place."

"As long as nobody misinterprets those ideas, it's all fine and dandy," I said in a low voice. "Like that hostage guy. Who knows *what* he thought we were about."

"He was probably against the whole philosophy. You'd be surprised how many people still think that mixed-race relationships are doomed to fail, that people are just 'too different.'" Thad paused for a moment. "I mean, there used to be laws against it. It's a sore topic for a lot of people. No wonder the ideas of the Latte Rebellion have been sparking so much dialogue."

There was a longer silence, but an easier one.

"You know, this conversation really got me thinking," he said. "I'm still going to write about the Rebellion, but you brought up a lot of points I might have missed otherwise."

I beamed. *I* had helped *Thad*. With a college assignment, no less.

Harvard doesn't know what they're missing, I thought recklessly.

———

"Okay," Maria McNally said, impatiently tapping a purple dry-erase marker against Mrs. Carville's whiteboard. "Any more ideas for upcoming events?"

"I still think we can come up with something better than another poetry slam," I said, rolling my eyes. Miranda smirked, and at the front of the classroom, Maria nodded, crossing it off the list she'd written on the whiteboard. The rest of the people attending the meeting murmured, some disgruntled, some in agreement. I sighed. I hadn't planned to be here, but Maria had guilt-tripped me into it, claiming my "expertise" was needed.

I glanced at the clock. We had about fifteen minutes until the bell rang, which meant we should be out of here in five if we didn't want to run into Mrs. Carville or any over-eager sophomore history nerds coming early to fifth period. After all, the Latte Rebellion technically didn't exist—at least, not at University Park High School.

Suddenly, someone opened the classroom door in a rush, slamming it against the wall with a loud bang. I jumped, whacking my knee painfully against the desk. As I rubbed it, wincing, three people crowded into the doorway, scuffling and laughing in a tone I didn't like. All three were wearing paper bags over their heads. That had to be deliberate, and I felt hot anger rise in my throat. A male voice, the one in front, said, "You better stay in here where nobody can see you, or you'll be some sorry-ass mutts."

"Hey," I said loudly, but that was all I was able to get out.

One of the intruders threw something that was smoking into the middle of the floor. It exploded with a bang, billowing noxious yellow smoke, and several people screamed and practically leaped out of their desks. The three intruders laughed and ran out, slamming the door behind them. Those of us left in the room started coughing and gagging on the rotten-egg stench. Angrily, I rushed to the door and opened it, scanning the hallway on either side of the classroom, but I didn't see anybody. Of course, my stinging eyes weren't helping much. Echoing footsteps were disappearing rapidly, and I couldn't tell where they were coming from. They could have turned down any one of the maze of hallways.

I slumped and walked back into the room, shaking my head when everyone looked at me expectantly. "I didn't see who they were."

I helped Maria open the few windows that could be opened, replaying the scene again in my mind. Obviously there were a lot of people—Roger, Kaelyn, the vice principal, even my parents—who thought the Latte Rebellion was trouble. But who would hate us enough to want to throw a smoke bomb?

I wasn't able to speculate any further due to a sudden, earsplittingly shrill beeping noise echoing around my skull. The fire alarm. I looked around helplessly; everyone was either plugging their ears or fleeing the room. Soon it was nearly empty except for Maria, her lap dog Faris, Miranda, and me, grabbing our stuff and getting ready to evacuate to the football field. The room still smelled like sulfur, but what other choice did we have?

First, though, Miranda carefully picked up the still-smoking firecracker, using her paper lunch bag. "I'm going to save this as evidence that we're doing the right thing, if people are pissed enough to firebomb our meetings," she said grimly. I nodded in agreement. Just then, I saw Mrs. Carville standing in the doorway.

Oh, *crap*.

Behind her was Vice Principal Malone, looming over her shoulder with a grim expression on his mustached face.

Double crap. Double crap on a cracker.

———

We were so incredibly lucky to get off without detention. Fortunately, all four of us were honors students—Maria was even a front office assistant—which meant we got the benefit of the doubt when we said *we* hadn't had anything to do with the firecracker.

But then there was the list on Mrs. Carville's whiteboard that we hadn't had a chance to erase—the list unmistakably titled *Ideas for Future Rebellion Activities*. The administration was already all too aware of the Latte Rebellion, as I'd discovered back when Ms. Allison asked me her nosy questions. Under pressure and in the face of obvious incriminating evidence, we were forced to confess that, yes, we'd been holding "discussions" for people interested in the Latte Rebellion, since we had been denied the opportunity to form an official club.

Ominously, all Malone said to that was, "hmm." Then he dismissed us from his office. I was so relieved not to be blamed for the incident that I didn't even care that I was walking straight back to a French test.

But then, after school, I came home to find this.

Office of Admissions
Ellis Robbins College

Dear Ms. Jamison,

This year has been one of the most exciting ever for us as we choose the entering freshman class from a pool of thousands of prospective applicants. Although we receive applications from many talented students, we are unable to admit all of our promising high school seniors for the fall semester.

Although we are not at this time able to offer you admission to the School of Social Welfare at Ellis Robbins College, we feel that your academic records and extracurricular activities show accomplishment and dedication. You have therefore been placed on a waiting list for admission, and we will contact you should a space become available in our entering freshman class.

Best of luck on your studies as you finish a stellar senior year!

"'...Sincerely, Jerkface D. Buttmunch, Assistant Director of Admissions,'" I concluded miserably, throwing the letter down on Carey's kitchen table and wiping my swollen eyes with an already-soggy paper napkin.

"Oh, Ash," Carey said, shaking her head. "This isn't necessarily a terrible thing. Where else did you say you got in? What about UCLA? That's still an option, right? What about your backup schools?"

I paused and took a deep breath, trying to calm down enough to talk again.

"Carey," I said in a hushed voice, "you can't tell *any-one*, but I didn't apply to UCLA. Or any backup schools. And I was wait-listed at Berkeley, too. I applied to a special public policy major in a really small program and they put me on a waiting list!"

"*What?* I can't believe that," Carey said. "You're still ranked at least fifth in the class, even after last semester, because you're taking all Honors and AP classes. And there's the Key Club, and your Social Justice thing…"

"I haven't gone to Students for Social Justice in ages," I said. "Anyway, even if I had applied to UCLA, I still wouldn't want to go. I wouldn't want to leave Northern California."

"Not since you met *Thaaad*." She smiled, but I could tell it took effort.

"It's not just that! I want to be able to see *you*, too. And Miranda. If she gets into that art school in San Francisco, then we could still hang out. Robbins was my last hope for that. I didn't get into Stanford," I croaked. "Harvard either."

Carey was quiet for a minute, and tears started streaming down my face again. Finally, she said simply, "I'm sorry, Asha. I don't know what to tell you. But you never know if a spot might open up later at Berkeley or Robbins. They're both really impacted schools, you know that. Tons of people apply and not everyone can get in, even if they deserve to." She put her hand on my arm.

"Yeah, whatever," I said, a sob making me almost incoherent. "You're right, and I'm stupid. And I probably wouldn't have even gotten wait-listed if you hadn't kept reminding me to study. Face it; I didn't deserve to get in." *You made your bed, now lie in it*, was what my dad would probably say if he knew.

"You know that's not true," she said, vehemently, but I couldn't quite believe it.

———————

The next day, Sunday, I woke up with my eyes crusty from crying myself to sleep, my throat raw and dry. I didn't want to leave my room, but around ten I got up and took a long shower, letting the hot water scald my skin for as long as I could stand it. What was wrong with me? I'd spent most of my high school career as the perfect student, or nearly so. Carey and I had studied diligently; we'd gone to countless club meetings; and I'd even spent a few years with her on the soccer team. We'd done everything right.

Then somehow, things had gone wrong. And I was afraid the blame lay squarely with me. The Latte Rebellion had been my idea to start with. I convinced Carey that our plan was brilliant and foolproof. Then I'd gotten totally caught up in the hype, conveniently forgetting that we actually had high school to finish. Of course Carey hadn't forgotten—she'd stayed on top of everything, including the senior class.

And here I was. I was left with two waiting list spots and no backup schools. And there was no way I could tell anyone, no way I would go crawling to my mom and dad on hands and knees to admit what had happened and ask for forgiveness. I couldn't even explain this to Nani, because she didn't know what a major mess I'd made of things.

I was screwed if I didn't make it off one of the waiting lists. But I didn't hold very high hopes of that. Who would actually turn down an admission offer from Robbins, so that a slot would open up for me?

I stepped onto the worn blue bath mat and dried myself off in the now extra-steamy bathroom, opening the window a crack. What a crappy year. I'd thought that senior year would be the apex of our high school careers, because we were on our way out of here. I'd assumed I would have my pick of the schools I applied to. I'd started thinking that Carey and I could go off to college together, and be roommates in a big, airy apartment in Berkeley, covered with indie band posters and hanging plants.

Wake up, Asha. I'd probably never even get to move out. I started having horrible visions of living at home at the age of thirty, single and working in a gas station, my room adorned not with posters but with dashboard hula dancers and bobble-head wiener dogs from the gas station's mini mart.

"What are you doing in there?" My mom knocked on

the bathroom door, her voice muffled but unmistakably testy. "Hurry up."

"I just got out of the shower," I said, hoping I sounded suitably meek.

"I need to get in there so I can get ready for the teacher appreciation brunch."

Great. *Everybody* was successful but me.

"I'm done," I said, wrapping my towel around me, brushing past my exasperated mother, and stomping off to my room. I shut my bedroom door, not waiting for a reply. It felt like the world was against me and all I could do was keep sabotaging myself. No more. It was time to be proactive. I angrily yanked on a pair of argyle socks. If I couldn't get into Robbins now, then I'd damn well go to junior college and transfer after a year. People did that all the time, right?

Maybe I'd ask Thad what he thought. I wouldn't tell him about the whole parents-who-would-have-major-cow-upon-finding-rejection-letters thing. I'd just ask him what he thought about transferring to Robbins. Since he'd transferred to Berkeley, he'd be sure to have some suggestions.

I had about two months left in my senior year. That was plenty of time to rearrange my life. I'd managed to rearrange it for the Latte Rebellion; this couldn't be that different.

I pulled on a pair of jeans and a random T-shirt and sat on the edge of my bed, phone in hand. But the minute Thad picked up, I was suddenly all freaked out again.

"So, how have you been?" I ventured, debating whether to tell him anything at all.

"Not bad," he said. "I'm almost done with that paper for Dr. Malik's class." He hesitated. "Would you mind looking it over sometime before I turn it in? Since you ... were a part of the Rebellion early on."

"Um, okay." I wasn't sure what I could add that would be of any help. I wasn't even sure I *could* add anything without incriminating myself.

"Thanks," he said sincerely. "So, to what do I owe the pleasure of your phone call?"

"Do I need a reason?" I said, trying to sound coy rather than defensive.

"Nope," he said, and I relaxed a little. But I knew I should get to the point and ask him about transferring from junior colleges. He knew about the process firsthand, and as an added bonus, there was zero chance he'd talk to my parents about it. *Come ON, Asha. Just do it.*

As I opened my mouth, he said, "So how's it going? Heard anything about where you might be going to college in the fall?"

Cripes, is he a mind reader? "Uh ... nothing worth sharing, really," I said, a little morosely.

"Well, then tell me what isn't worth sharing."

I sighed. "I've been wait-listed at Berkeley and Robbins College. I don't understand it," I said, frustrated. "I'm ranked fifth in my class, I have extracurricular activities out the wazoo. My AP scores were good last year. What did I do wrong?"

"I'm sure you didn't *do* anything wrong," he said reassuringly. "Berkeley has to turn down tons of people; it's just too crowded. There are so many reasons why a college might or might not admit someone. I read an article about it online back when I was applying to transfer—there's this whole list of criteria you'd never even think about. "

"Like what?" I said, curious despite myself.

"Oh, jeez, like if you're an athlete on a sports team they're trying to develop, or if your parents donated money to the campus, they might flag your file. Or if you're an underrepresented minority, like Native American."

"Are you serious?" I said, incredulously. "That's not fair. And who's to say what an underrepresented minority is? I mean, on most of those applications I get to check *one box* and if I'm lucky it says 'mixed ethnicity' and if I'm unlucky it says 'other.' I shouldn't have to play a guessing game just to fit into their system." I was on a roll now. "I shouldn't have to worry that I didn't pick the right check box, and now they'll reject me for being, say, too Asian, or not Asian enough. Or the wrong kind of Asian."

Should I have joined the Asian American Club? Or even the Chicano Club? Neither of those had really seemed appropriate. I mean, Roger was in the former. As for the other . . . well, I was only a quarter Mexican. I just hadn't felt like I belonged. Not anywhere. At the same time, I didn't see why I *had* to belong to any particular group.

"Funny, I know just how you feel," Thad said, irony in his voice. "The thing is, the system's just not built to handle the increasing complexity of the racial landscape."

"Racial *landscape*?"

"Sorry," he said, sounding amused. "These are the amazing vocabulary words you learn in college, especially in Dr. Malik's class."

"Great," I said. "You know, Carey *did* get into Berkeley. Obviously being at the very top of the class holds some weight."

"It always does," Thad said.

After a pause, I asked, "Do you think if I go to junior college for a year, I could try to re-apply and transfer to Robbins? Is it difficult?"

"Well, there are some hoops you have to jump through. But you got wait-listed, right? Have you thought about writing a letter of appeal?"

"What's that?" I rolled over onto my back, the bedsprings creaking, and stared up at the Van Gogh sunflowers poster on my bedroom ceiling.

"If you didn't get accepted, you can usually write a letter of appeal to the Admissions Office arguing your case and telling them why you should be admitted. And in a lot of cases, if you make a good enough appeal and your application was strong in the first place, they'll let you in. I bet you could do it."

"I'll ... have to think about it," I said, reeling. I actually still had a chance. This was almost too much to take in.

"You should," Thad said. "I'll help you if you want. It's only fair, if you're willing to read my long-ass American Cultures paper."

"Hey, you never said it was 'long-ass' before," I accused him.

"If I had, would you have said no?" he asked innocently.

"Hmm." I pretended to think about it.

"Aw, come on," he said. "Is this the thanks I get for helping with your appeal?"

"Well, okay, I guess I owe you one." I was glad he couldn't see me blushing.

"Then it's settled. I mean, your friend Carey wouldn't be the only one who'd be happy if you moved to Berkeley."

I blushed harder, warm all over, and grinned until my face hurt.

Exhibit A.11:
MATERIALS VIOLATING
BOARD POLICY SECTION 418.III.M, 418.III.N

Evidence submitted by Ms. Jamison's parents of possible involvement in disruptive activities. Two copies attached.

(excerpt from "The Latte Rebellion: A Case Study in Mixed-Race Viral Ideology" by Thad Sakai)

... therefore it is clear that in modern, technologically savvy movements of social change, the ease of idea transfer grows exponentially. In this way, the Latte Rebellion can be seen as an *ideological epidemic*, as defined by Forsell in *Contagious Culture:*

> Ideological epidemics can occur under the guise of any form of human communication, from fads in slang terms to viral Internet videos to popular songs. Even the clothes we wear are a form of communication and therefore fashion is vulnerable to cultural contagion. And, like a biological epidemic of viruses or bacteria, an ideological epidemic will tend to jump from person to person through conscious or unconscious imitation (101).

Though Forsell goes on to say that "many ideological epidemics have a tendency to spread quickly but burn themselves out with intense rapidity," I do not believe that the Latte Rebellion is such a flash-in-the-pan phenomenon (102). Just as the gene pool of those of mixed race is strengthened and enhanced by the addition of a variety of genes—rather than stagnating and self-destructing—the viral spread of the Latte Rebellion is enhanced by the gathering together of components (i.e., supporters) from a myriad of backgrounds, ages, and geographic locales.

11

When I emailed Thad the next day, I came really close to telling him that it had been Carey and me all along, that we were Agent Alpha and Captain Charlie and we'd started the Latte Rebellion almost as a joke. Also that, what with the smoke bomb and constantly getting roped into meetings and "roundtables" and agenda-setting, I was starting to feel a bit exhausted. But Thad was so *into* the idea of the Rebellion being a viral notion spreading like wildfire because of the Internet. I was afraid that if I told him how it started, he would be disappointed. Disappointed in the Rebellion, and disappointed in me.

The truth was, I was incredibly intimidated by reading Thad's paper on the Rebellion. He made it sound so much more *momentous* than it had ever been in my mind, even after I realized it was about more than just Carey and

I making a buck. But now that there were chapters all over the country, now that we'd made the news...I was starting to be convinced that the Latte Rebellion really was something significant—something I had frighteningly little control over.

So I didn't say anything. I just told him how great the paper was, how insightful, and that he would definitely get an A+ with whipped cream on top if I were teaching the class. That seemed to make him happy. He also said he wanted to see me again. When he said that, I knew I'd made the right choice by keeping my mouth shut about Agent Alpha—for once, my crazy ideas were *not* going to get me into more trouble.

Later that night I called Carey and told her about my latest conversations with Thad. Unlike how she was with Leonard, I wasn't interested in keeping this hush-hush.

"So are you going to introduce me to him?" She sounded indignant.

"Possibly. If you ask me very very nicely." I smiled, feeling a little vindicated given how annoying she'd been about Leonard when she'd first gotten together with him.

"This is totally unfair. Miranda got to meet him. Multiple times."

"If you'd come to the rally, you would have," I blurted out, even though I really didn't want to rehash that painful discussion from February. "*He* made it to my speech."

"We covered this, Asha," Carey said. There was an awkward pause, and I heard static as she sighed into the phone. "I had soccer practice."

"I know, I know. I'm just saying."

"Well, quit saying it. I'm glad I didn't go. I'm sure they would have roped me into appearing in my paper bag hat like you had to."

"It wasn't that bad," I said. Not entirely true, but I still wished she'd been there. "You could at least come to the Rebellion meeting at school this Wednesday. That won't require you to miss class, work, tutoring, *or* baby-brother-sitting. We'll just hang out."

"Huh. I don't know," she said skeptically. "I have to say, Asha, I'm surprised you guys still want to hold meetings at school after you were practically assaulted."

"That's why this is important." I tried to keep the impatience out of my voice.

"Yeah, well, what about Malone? 'You're not U.S. citizens, you're high school students,'" she mimicked. "What if he finds out you're still—"

"He won't find out," I said. "We moved the meetings to Mr. Rosenquist's room. Anyway, if you don't want to go, just say so." I was getting exasperated with this conversation.

"We already talked about this," she said impatiently. "How many times do we have to go over it? I'm sorry, Asha."

"That's fine," I forced out, even though it wasn't fine. I'd support *her* if the Key Club got trashed by disgruntled Interact Club malcontents. But I had to admit that was unlikely, and this was different. It was agitation on a scale neither of us were used to.

"Attention, students." Principal Philips paused and cleared his throat; I could hear papers rustling in the background. Everyone was blinking back sleep during homeroom period, which for me was history class, and half-listening to the morning announcements over the PA system.

"Due to an incident on campus last week, as well as some unsettling news coverage prior to that, it has come to the notice of the administration that a group known as the Latte Rebellion may be involved in gang activity or other disruptive goings-on."

A bunch of people giggled. I stiffened. *Gang* activity? Was he joking?

"This group is not officially sanctioned by the school administration or the Inter-Club Council, and some of their, uh, philosophies may in fact be inflammatory. Therefore, to minimize disruption to your high school experience, Latte Rebellion flyers, T-shirts, and any other materials have been banned from the University Park campus. As of tomorrow, anybody caught reading Latte Rebellion printed matter or wearing shirts or other paraphernalia will be given detention. Repeated offenses may result in on-campus suspension.

"In addition, all students will be required to attend an assembly this afternoon to review disciplinary regulations and the dangers of gangs in our community.

"Thank you, and have a productive school day."

There were murmurs throughout the classroom—lots

of "oh, my God, can you believe it?" or "did you hear the Latte Rebellion's a *gang*?"; one audible "*what* Rebellion?" and some fairly unanimous groaning about the assembly. I turned around to Carey, sitting behind me.

"This is *so typical*," I whispered loudly.

"Well, you have to admit they have a point," Carey whispered back. "They're scared things will get out of hand." She frowned. "To be honest, they kind of have."

"How can you say that? We've accomplished a lot." I was hurt. Even after everything that had happened, this felt like a new wound. I knew she wanted out of the Rebellion, but it felt like she was siding against me. Against what used to be *us*.

"*Shhh*," Carey said, as Mr. Velez walked past our desks to the front of the room. He told everyone to quiet down, and started talking about our next unit on the Vietnam War. I could hardly sit still, but figuring out how to do Rebellion damage control would have to wait until later. And so would the heart-to-heart I needed to have with Carey.

———

At lunchtime, in my car in the school parking lot, we held an emergency meeting of the Latte Rebellion—at least, Miranda and I did, munching baby carrots and chili cheese Fritos and trying not to freak out. Carey was mostly just eating the Fritos and making a poor attempt to put up with us.

"This is ridiculous," I said, with a frustrated sigh. "Just

because it happened to be *our* meeting that got targeted, the administrators have to get all authoritarian on *us*."

"They always do this," Miranda said, leaning forward from the back seat to grab the chip bag. "Like freshman year, when they thought everyone wearing a Raiders football jacket was in a gang, so they banned any clothing with the Raiders logo."

"Except this is worse," I pointed out, "because we're actually doing something worthwhile."

"If it was so worthwhile, maybe the Inter-Club Council would have accepted your petition, and you wouldn't be in this mess!" Carey said, staring out the side window, her hands clenched in her lap.

"*My* petition?" My head ached. I wanted to tell her to butt out, but I settled for a martyred sigh, leaning back against the headrest.

"Oh, come on, guys, are you kidding? This is *awesome*," Miranda said excitedly. "You know that the minute people with authority say something's banned, it immediately makes people a million times more interested."

"I don't know," I said. "I think most of the people interested in the Rebellion are already in it anyway, and most of them go to U-NorCal and won't care what some high school principal is saying."

"No way. Are you forgetting how many people at this school already have our shirts? I wonder what they're going to do with them now." Miranda fished the last Frito out of the bag. "I'm going to wear mine outside of school every chance I get. I might even wear it to class under my sweater and unveil it the second I get off school property, just to annoy Mr. Philips."

"You guys," Carey said tensely, "come on. I totally don't need your angst right now—I'm stressing about that English paper due next month, plus we have a soccer game against St. Elizabeth's on Saturday, and I have to work an extra shift on Sunday."

I was starting to get tired of Carey's constant more-studious-than-thou attitude. I was fully aware she had to work; I had witnessed her single-minded determination to get a scholarship. I felt a stab of guilt for being angry at her, because I knew how much she wanted to move out of the house, but now that she'd actually gotten accepted to her top choices? You'd think she'd be a little less wound up.

"Carey," I finally said. "You'll be *fine*. You're the smart-est person I know. Seriously."

"Oh please," she said, but with a tiny smile.

I was still peeved, though. She *knew* there were extenu-ating circumstances to our club petition not getting passed. But then again, our failure to establish an official club was yet another critical incident in the history of the Latte Rebellion that she had decided to miss. Of course, that was before she'd decided to bail on the whole thing. I didn't even like thinking about it. And now I was afraid she was bailing on our friendship. That was the last thing I wanted, even if I *was* angry at her.

———

The following Friday, I was eating lunch with Carey and Miranda at our usual table when Maria McNally rushed over, granny glasses askew.

"Oh my God, you guys! You will *not believe* what I just heard! Somebody sent a message out to the Latte Rebellion mailing list—"

"Wait, there's a *mailing list?*" I shook my head. Every time I turned around, there were some new shenanigans connected to the Rebellion. It was dizzying.

"News to me," Carey said, unsurprisingly.

"*Anyway,*" Maria continued breathlessly, straightening her glasses, "there's going to be a nationwide sit-in at every school and college around the country where there's a Latte Rebellion chapter!"

I almost choked on my sandwich.

"Whoa," Miranda said, her eyebrows raised. "What does *that* entail?"

Maria seemed disappointed at our failure to immediately keel over in shock at her announcement. Her shrill voice calmed down a little, and she frowned.

"I'll forward you the email. Apparently someone made an anonymous post on the discussion board about how Principal Philips has banned Rebellion paraphernalia, and then a few people from other high schools said they'd had their club charters revoked even earlier, after the news about that gunman. And then all these people chimed in, saying we should 'stay positive' and 'hang in there' … and then suddenly someone planned a sit-in. I don't know who. I guess it's like a flash mob kind of thing."

"So what exactly *is* the plan?" Miranda sounded interested. Meanwhile, I was reeling. Thad was right—this *was* an epidemic.

"We're supposed to get everyone involved that we can, like get them to sign up or pledge support," Maria continued excitedly. "Then, on April 18th at noon, everyone is supposed to gather at a central conspicuous location and hold, like, a mini-rally. People from the club can talk about their experiences and it'll raise awareness of the Latte Rebellion cause. You guys are in, right?"

"Yeah, right." Carey rolled her eyes. "There's a study session that day for the AP French test."

"I think it rules," Miranda put in. "It's about time we took a few risks. Otherwise nobody who isn't already involved is ever going to care."

"Exactly," Maria said.

I nodded, slowly. "But Malone already has his eye on us."

"Oh, but this is way more important than Mr. Malone. How else are we going to get him and everyone else to understand? And, Asha, you *have* to be a speaker," Maria gushed, her brown ponytail bobbing. "You and Miranda. You have the connections with the U-NorCal people. And," she said more quietly, "if Agent Alpha just happened to show up..."

"I'm not sure I have time to prepare anything." I frowned. "It's only a week away."

"Asha, this is *important*." Maria's voice was whiny now.

How she could go from shrill to excited to whiny in a matter of minutes was truly amazing to behold.

"I'll get back to you," I said firmly, and took a huge bite of turkey sandwich, effectively ending the conversation. I was still getting used to the idea of a sit-in, and I *really* didn't know if it was a good idea to resurrect Agent Alpha, especially if there was a chance I could get caught.

"I'll work on her," Miranda said, and I glared at her. "I'll speak at the sit-in," Miranda continued, "and I'll talk to some teachers. I can think of one or two who might be sympathetic. It would definitely help in case anyone decides we're breaking the rules."

"But they never told us we couldn't *talk* about the Latte Rebellion. They just said we couldn't have the shirts or the propaganda materials," Maria said with a tiny smile.

"The girl makes a good point." Miranda grinned. "But what if we *did* wear the shirts? That would really make a point."

"You guys are so going to get in trouble." Carey shook her head. "Philips said that anyone wearing the shirts would get put in on-campus suspension."

"He said they *might* get put in on-campus suspension," Miranda corrected her. "But I can't help thinking that if we *all* do it, he can't put, like, fifty people in OCS, can he? And if we get teachers who will vouch for this being a peaceful protest..."

"It could totally work," Maria said. "Let me think about that."

"Don't just think about it," Miranda said. "If we want

it to work, *everyone* will have to go along, or nearly everyone. Otherwise the administration will definitely pick on the one or two people who wear the shirts."

"I'll bring it up at the meeting on Saturday," Maria said. "Mocha Loco. You guys better come. Oh, and Asha, I want to know what the Rebellion Organizers have to say about the sit-in they're holding at U-NorCal. Despite Faris being our liaison, you're the one with the direct pipeline to Echo and Foxtrot. I want to know what they're planning behind the scenes."

She blathered to Carey and Miranda for a few more minutes about whether she could have Faris be appointed an official Sympathizer, but I couldn't pay attention. I was more worried about who was behind this "sit-in." Was it the same people who'd put together the unauthorized Latte Rebellion site? Or was it one of the myriad of people who'd founded chapters at their own schools?

"I wonder if this is going to make the news," I said suddenly. "I mean, if people all over the country are doing this all at the same time, then it might get, like, media attention." Would my identity come out then? And could I really afford that?

"It might," Carey said, frowning. "If people actually do it."

"True." I sighed. I couldn't help but envision twenty-five, fifty, even a hundred University Park students sitting on the grass in the quad, everyone else gathered around in awe and support as kids of mixed ethnicity told their stories. The administrators would realize how wrong they'd been in thinking the Latte Rebellion was a gang, and the teachers would be astonished at our articulateness and organizational skills. The local newspaper would send a reporter to interview us, and we would talk about how it would never have been possible without each individual's efforts— just as different ethnicities form inseparable parts of a whole mixed-race person, the entire success of the Rebellion was like a seamless integration of all its individual parts.

I pushed aside that little doubting voice that pointed out how random our success really was, and how we weren't exactly a unified movement. That didn't matter. What mattered was that people believed in the Rebellion, and if enough people believed, then we, like Thad and Greg with their clinic, might actually be able to change the world.

———

School was strange during the week preceding the sit-in. It felt like the air was charged with anticipation, like particles of static electricity were jumping from person to person ... or like Thad's "contagious" ideas, spreading like germs. Maria carried her sign-up clipboard wherever she went, asking likely sympathizers (with a small "s") to pledge their support for our sit-in, and either participate or just show up. I had to admire her persistence—not everyone was willing to risk being associated with the Latte Rebellion. Some people were downright hostile.

Like Kaelyn Vander Sar. I could have told Maria it would be pointless to try to talk to her. But no.

"Oh, hey, Kaelyn!" Maria bounded up to her between classes. I just happened to be walking a few feet behind them, so I overheard what happened next.

Kaelyn looked down her perfect snub nose as if Maria were something gross stuck to her shoe. "Hey, what?"

"Oh! So have you heard about the sit-in next Wednesday? It's going to be really fun. Supporters of people of mixed race or multiple ethnicity are going to be holding, like, a mini-rally on the quad." She brandished her clipboard.

"So?" Kaelyn said, snapping her piece of green chewing gum.

"Well, you should come," Maria said valiantly. "We've already got twenty-three people signed up."

"What, so you can take them all hostage like that guy in Indiana? No thanks. Anyway, I have a cheerleading meeting," Kaelyn said, rudely. "No annoying Latte-whatevers allowed." Then she turned and glared at me, as if she'd known the whole time that I was listening.

"Fine," Maria said, "but when everybody else in the school is out on the quad on the 18th, you can't say I didn't invite you."

"Fantastic." Kaelyn surged ahead, away from Maria and what she no doubt thought were contagious nerd pathogens.

I shook my head in disgust. I couldn't stand that Kaelyn would even put us in the same sentence as that hostage situation. She was obviously just parroting what Principal Philips said. But the odd thing was that she seemed so hostile about it. Carey would probably theorize that she was jealous of my Mexican J.Lo curves, but I didn't think so.

I *did* think that maybe, just maybe, she was scared. Scared that if the cheerleaders got involved they'd get in trouble and have their pom-poms taken away or something.

Either way, she was missing the point.

Still, she wasn't the only one to be rude to poor Maria. For every person Maria got signed up, she'd get five total no-gos. By the end of the week, she'd been laughed at by jocks, insulted by emo kids, ignored by stoners, and given the brush-off by fellow nerdlings. When she arrived at the Latte Rebellion meeting Friday lunch, she was practically in tears—a stark contrast to her usual crisp and confident self. I raised my voice above the fray.

"I had no idea people at our school would be like this," I said. "I mean, we live in *Northern California*. We're supposed to be progressive, right? And care about issues?"

"I don't know; that's what I thought, too," Maria said miserably. There was a chorus of outraged comments from the fifteen or so people at the meeting, especially Matt Lee, who was part of the Save the Environment club, and the two representatives sent by the Gay-Straight Alliance. Obviously *they* cared about issues. Was this sort of thing happening at other schools? From the activity on the website, you'd think there was this growing wave of support, but maybe it was all bluster and wishful thinking from a few enthusiastic individuals—a scenario that sounded embarrassingly familiar.

We started to discuss what we'd do at the sit-in, including having Maria relate her experiences of trying to sign people up. I was scribbling notes for my own speech, and Miranda was up at Mr. Rosenquist's whiteboard making a schedule, when she suddenly turned and said, "Guys, this is going to be the most memorable thing that has ever happened at this school."

For a moment, the room was silent. More than a few people were looking at me expectantly, as if I somehow had the final say.

I thought about the screams and the looks of fear when the smoke bomb had detonated, and I got out of my chair decisively and moved to stand next to Miranda.

"Right on," I said. "Let's do this." Miranda grinned and we did a fist-bump.

There were a few whoops and everyone clapped, including me. It was funny—even though Carey and I had started this, Miranda had really helped give it ... well, *meaning*. And now that Carey had wimped out, I was glad Miranda had my back ... because, to be honest, this was a little crazy, even for me.

———

The weekend brought me back down to earth a little. After a really uncomfortable lunch on Saturday during which I had to listen to my parents talking about various acquaintances' children and how they'd gotten into X or Y school, I finally caved and told them that Harvard was a no-go. I was still waiting to hear from other places, I said vaguely, hopefully. Lots of people at my school were still finding out where they'd gotten in, I said convincingly. I held out a lot of hope for schools closer to home, I said quasi-truthfully.

By the end of the conversation, they were at least nodding. And they'd quit talking about the accomplishments of other people's genius offspring, which was a relief.

"Asha," my mother said, "all we want is for you to be happy. We're sorry about the bad news, but we have faith in you." She reached over and put a hand gently on mine, where I was gripping the edge of the kitchen table tensely.

"Well, Harvard was kind of a long shot anyway," I said. "I don't know anyone who got in." I debated telling them about the article I'd read about admissions criteria, the one Thad had tipped me off to, but I didn't want to ruin the moment.

"You'll be successful wherever you end up," my dad added.

I nodded, not meeting his eyes. I knew he meant to be encouraging, but it sounded ominous.

"And no matter where you decide to go, we'll support your decision. It's your choice. All the schools you applied to are very reputable." I wasn't sure if my mom would be quite so understanding if she knew the real story. Oh, it wasn't like she would yell or anything, but she'd get her disappointed look, and Dad would frown, his eyebrows beetling down into a hard line. They'd tell me it was fine, but then they'd stay up late in their bedroom, talking quietly into the night, no doubt about my inevitable future career in the fast food industry.

No, I'd just have to hope that my letter of appeal was going to work and that I would get into Robbins College after all, so I wouldn't ever have to tell them what had happened. I'd just tell them I'd decided on Robbins, and lie about the other applications. Then everything would be perfectly peachy, right? Right. Maybe.

———————

"You know what you need to do? You need to talk about this at the sit-in at your school. I've totally heard about this kind of thing," Darla said. I was at the Mocha Loco Rebellion meeting, and I'd just related what Thad had told me about how being the "right" underrepresented ethnicity could affect your college admission. I'd even, albeit reluctantly, told them I'd been wait-listed at Berkeley and Robbins.

"Yeah," Leonard agreed. "This is *exactly* the kind of thing the Latte Rebellion should be targeting in our agenda of positive social change." There was a small chorus of agreement from the rest of the group. I flushed, sweating at being the center of attention for about forty people, and had the sudden urge to laugh hysterically.

"I don't know. I wasn't sure about speaking at the sit-in. I'm going, of course," I added hurriedly. "But I'm ... nervous in front of crowds," I said. And how.

"Are you kidding?" Darla said. "You—"

"*No*, I'm *not kidding*," I said, rushing to cover whatever she was about to blurt out about my secret identity.

Darla shut up, smiling conspiratorially and making a "zip the lip" gesture. Then Maria jumped in.

"But, Asha, this is *exactly* the kind of thing I was thinking of when I asked you about this before." She tapped her pencil against her notepad. "You really should think about it."

I did think about it. I drank the rest of my latte straight down and thought that maybe it was time to take control of my own life. My letter of appeal was just the beginning. If I was going to protest being wait-listed at Robbins, then I might as well go whole hog on the issue and speak out.

"Okay, I'll do it," I told Maria. "As long as it's not a huge crowd."

"Oh, come *on*. It wouldn't be like talking in front of a big crowd. It would just be the kids at our school. You'd know everybody."

"That's what I'm afraid of," I muttered.

Nevertheless, on Sunday, I spent two hours making notes of what I was planning to say at the sit-in—and then went over them again, and again, and again. I even copied everything onto index cards and practiced in front of Carey and Miranda, hoping that would make me less nervous. But it didn't, not really. For my presentation, I created a "college professor" look—I would put my hair in a bun, wear glasses instead of contacts, and dress up in my most serious, going-on-college-scholarship-interview outfit (a skirt-suit I'd barely gotten to use). Then, at the end, I'd whip off the dark-green blazer to reveal my Latte Rebellion T-shirt. Carey and Miranda clapped wildly when I rehearsed this, and even Carey had promised to at least be in the background of the sit-in for moral support. I was still petrified.

The thing they didn't understand was how terrifying it was to go up in front of everyone and *not* be safe under my paper bag hat. How panic-inducing it was to think that someone might realize that *I* was Agent Alpha. And how important it still was to me to get into Robbins College, even though I had to write an appeal.

But this really did mean something to me, even if I was scared.

At lunch on Tuesday, Miranda, Carey and I were sitting at a round table in the corner of the library, having a top-secret meeting about Miranda's speech. The whole event was only half an hour, and there were seven speakers including the two of us, so there wasn't a lot of time for each person.

"Point number one," Miranda said. "The Ignorance of the World at Large."

"Nice," Carey said. "Just don't denounce your potential supporters. The goal is to get the undecided people on your side, not against you."

"Good point." Miranda scribbled that down in her black spiral notebook. "Point number two: Ethnic Mutts Are Everywhere. Point number three: Ethnic Mutts Are the Future, So Why Malign Us? Leading finally to the climactic point, The Smoke Bomb, Or, It Could Happen To You."

"Nice," I echoed. "I like your use of 'mutts.' Way to reclaim the enemy's verbiage."

"Yeah, speech class really worked out for you, didn't it," Carey said teasingly.

Miranda grinned. "Speaking of things working out, I have something to tell you guys."

There was a long, expectant pause. She was doing this on purpose.

"So tell us," Carey said. "Don't leave us in suspense."

"Well..." Miranda took a deep breath. Her expression was carefully neutral, but then she broke into a huge smile. "I got into the Institute! I get to move to San Francisco!" She was practically bouncing up and down in her chair.

"Woo hoo!" Carey burst out, before remembering we were in the library. Ms. Yates gave us an exasperated look. "That is *awesome* news!" she added, more quietly.

Then they both looked at me and sobered, seeming almost embarrassed. I wanted to cringe at the way they were treating me, like I might burst into tears on them.

"Hey," I said, a little annoyed. "I think it's great you got into art school. Don't not-talk about colleges on my account." There was an awkward pause. "Speaking of which, Care, what about you? Have you decided where to go yet?" I was determined to keep this positive.

"Well," she said, carefully, "I'm trying to decide between Berkeley and Stanford."

"If you go to Berkeley and I go to Robbins, we could get an apartment together." I smiled.

"I know." Carey didn't meet my eyes.

"What?" I felt a sinking feeling in my stomach. "What aren't you telling me?" Miranda looked from one to the other of us with a worried frown.

"Asha … I think I might want to go to Stanford. I'm sorry—it's got nothing to do with you. I just think they have a better program for what I want to major in."

"Since when do you know what you want to major in?" I looked at her, flabbergasted.

"Um … since talking to Leonard about pre-med programs." She still wasn't looking at me, just doodling little squares on her notebook. Her bangs fell over her face so I couldn't see her expression.

"What does *he* know about pre-med? Isn't he a philosophy major?"

"Philosophy and pre-law. And his roommate is a pre-med major. I talked to him for a while about med schools, and I asked some of my dad's doctor friends."

"Well, I've been doing research too," I said defensively, "and I think I still have a good chance at getting into Robbins. I'm writing a letter of appeal. And I'm going to major in"—I thought quickly—"sociology and public policy."

Carey looked up at me in surprise. So did Miranda. I let myself feel a little triumphant, looking at their expressions.

"Yep," I said. "Just watch me. And I'm going to speak about it at the sit-in. I already wrote the letter of appeal." I reached into my backpack, where I had a copy of it stashed.

I'd been planning to show it to them, though not necessarily under these circumstances. But I felt almost feverish, desperate. I was *not* going to be left behind. I cleared my throat and read:

> *Dear Mr. Blake,*
>
> *When I read your letter informing me that I was on the waiting list to enter Robbins College, my first reaction was amazement. What had I done wrong? I'd submitted my application on time, my grades were nearly perfect, and my record of extracurricular activities was long and varied.*
>
> *Then I realized something. I realized that school admissions policies sometimes don't consider the individual student as much as they should. Sometimes the emphasis is on placing students in desirable categories. These categories might be racial, or they might consider other factors such as community service or overcoming hardship. In any case, these policies are well-intentioned. But they leave out those individuals who are difficult to categorize, who might fit in multiple places, or not quite fit in any place.*
>
> *I am an individual of mixed ethnicity. I indicated this on my college applications, not realizing that this, like the plethora of activities elsewhere in my application, would simply "water down" the evaluators' ability to put me in a category like everyone else, to boil me down to a single factor*

such as "socioeconomic disadvantage" or "athletic ability." Though I do not intend to imply that this was the sole factor in my failure to be admitted to the freshman class, I feel it is a symptom of something bigger, of something wrong in our society at large which tends to group people according to perceived identity, and ignore or dismiss or mislabel those people whom it cannot easily construe.

This was a primary factor in my choice to start a movement to address these types of issues. I did not see a support system in our school or our society that specifically focused on students of mixed ethnicity or diverse backgrounds. Therefore, two friends and I turned what was essentially a T-shirt brand we had created at home as a small business into an identifiable symbol of these issues, of the struggle to get them addressed and empower those who support the cause.

The Latte Rebellion ultimately became much more than the brainstorming of a few high school seniors. It grew far beyond our small community and gained a life of its own. I see this as proof of the need for such a movement in our society, of the receptivity of our society to issues important to the growing mixed-ethnicity population. As I became more involved in pinpointing vital issues to address, I realized that many of these very issues could be found in my own life. At first I was sad to realize that my inability to be recognized by college admissions

judges was another symptom of the institutionalized
bias against not-easily-categorized citizens. But
then I became elated at the opportunity to have my
individual voice be heard by writing a personal letter
of appeal. This was my chance to speak, not only for
myself, but for others in similar situations.

My goal as a college student is to study sociology
and public policy, in order to better equip myself
to address the healing of these injustices—in the
workplace, in our society, and throughout the
world. If any place is receptive to these ideas, and
sympathetic to the cause, I think Robbins is that
place. Please reconsider my application to your
undergraduate program. Thank you for your time.

"Sincerely, Asha S. Jamison," I concluded.

Carey goggled at me. "You can't do that! You're telling them *everything*."

"Give me one good reason why I can't," I said, thinking of at least five on the spot.

"Oh, *Ash,* don't play dumb. Aren't you worried people might find out about us? I can't afford that." She fiddled with her pen, flipping it over and around her fingers.

"Someone's a little paranoid." Miranda laughed. "I think the letter's killer."

"I'm serious!" Carey sounded miffed.

"I'm not using you guys' names," I said. "I'm not even saying definitively that I was Agent Alpha or anything. I'm just telling them that we came up with this idea ... *spear-*

headed this idea, and because of my creativity and leadership skills I ought to be let into their freshman class after all." I smiled tentatively.

"I think it could definitely work," Miranda said, flipping her long braids over one shoulder.

"It's a gamble," Carey said.

"And of course, *you* would *never* gamble," I said mercilessly, grinning; I was feeling a little better now that I'd told them what I was planning.

"You have to admit, it's not the kind of thing I would do." Carey smiled at me.

It's not the kind of thing you'd ever need *to do*, I thought.

"But," she continued, "it's the kind of thing *you* would do."

"What is *that* supposed to mean?" It was my turn to stare at her in surprise.

"Nothing," she said, levelly. "Just that you take more risks than I would."

"Huh," I said, letting the subject drop. It wasn't worth getting in another fight with Carey. But I left the library for our fifth-period class feeling odd, and kind of left out. And when I thought about Carey going away to Stanford without me, and Miranda moving off to San Francisco while I was stuck here, my mood plummeted, despite my best efforts.

That night at dinner, I was so nervous I could barely have a normal conversation with my parents. I only ate about half my dinner before pushing the plate of partly-massacred chicken and rice away.

"Don't you feel well?" My mother looked at me in concern.

"I'm fine, Mom. I, uh, have a test tomorrow. I'm kind of nervous." It wasn't exactly a lie. Telling my secret shame in front of all those people would be a test of sorts.

"Well," my dad said, "I'm sure you'll do well as long as you studied. We're very proud of how you've gotten serious and really buckled down, Asha. I'm sure it's going to show in your final grades. You might still have a chance at salutatorian."

"Maybe," I said. "I was ranked fifth after the third quarter grade report."

"That's an improvement," Dad said grudgingly. "You were down at eighth after that disappointing fall semester."

I ground my teeth and forced out, "Gee, thanks." I divided my remaining rice into three even little piles, still not looking up. I wanted to ask him why grades mattered so much to him. Whether he cared if I was even happy. But I really didn't want to start any arguments, not tonight of all nights.

"May I be excused? I want to study a while longer before bed." I tried not to sound sarcastic, but it was hard.

"Are you sure you're feeling all right? Do you want me to bring you some ginger tea?" Mom pulled away my half-finished plate and put her hand on my forehead.

"No, Mom, I'm fine." I shrugged out from under her hand and got up. "Really, I'm feeling okay. Like I said, I'm just nervous about my oral report."

"I thought you said it was a test." My dad frowned.

"Yeah, um … it is," I said, feeling sweat breaking out under my arms. "There's a part where we have to give an oral report to the class on one of the essay topics he handed out."

"Sounds challenging," Dad said. "What class is this for?"

"AP History," I said quickly, and hurried off to my room before he could ask me any more questions, before I could blow my cover story even more. I'd made him suspicious, I could tell. He still hadn't quite forgiven me for last semester's slipping grades. He was so attached to his vision of my rosy, successful future that he didn't have any room to see alternatives.

And my mom just went along with him. But then again, she'd never had *any* trouble in school whatsoever. She figured if it was easy for her, it would be easy for me due to good genes. Then, if I worked even harder, I wouldn't be stuck in the same situation she was, teaching grade school without any opportunity to "move up in the world." My good genes would magically mix with all that hard work and make me a prize-winning doctor or lawyer or whatever.

I sank down onto my bed, squeezing my eyes shut and trying to force back tears of frustration. My shoulders ached with tension. Maybe I was an anomaly, a black sheep—at my school, in my own house, and even with my friends.

Angrily, I shoved all my textbooks to the floor and pulled the rejection letters out from under my mattress, setting them in the middle of the cleared desk space. I sat in my desk chair, my head in my hands, and stared at them. Stupid pieces of paper. Stupid pieces of paper that had ruined my life, ruined my plan for cruising on to a good college and a stable, successful career.

But it wasn't the letters. I knew that. I just didn't want to think about how royally I'd screwed up by letting myself get so wrapped up in the Rebellion that I forgot about everything else. And I *really* didn't want to consider the idea that maybe, deep down, I didn't quite feel bad enough about it. That maybe I felt, in a way, that it had all been worth it.

———————

The next morning I could hardly eat, but I forced down a banana because my mom was hovering. Then, on the way to school, I stopped by the coffee counter in the grocery store to get a latte, hoping it would infuse me with the mojo necessary to get through today.

By the time I'd picked up Carey and driven to school, I felt jittery and on edge. After parking, we sat in the car as I made sure everything was ready to go as planned. My index cards were safely tucked into the pocket of my blazer, along with a few other key items. The front buttons were fastened securely and no part of my rule-breaking Latte Rebellion T-shirt was visible. I put my glasses on and checked my appearance in the rear view mirror, moving a lock of hair to cover a zit on my temple.

"Asha, you look *fine*," Carey said, exasperated. "Let's go! I have to stop at my locker and we only have five minutes."

I certainly looked like a schoolteacher, but that was a good thing. I took the glasses off and put my contacts in—I'd put the glasses back on right when we were dismissed from fourth period, at 11:50. People could think whatever they wanted to about my outfit.

And I did get a few stares as we walked down the hall to our lockers. David Castro whistled and said "Hey, baby, are you one of those naughty secretaries?"

I swatted him on the arm with my notebook. "You wish."

"Yeah," Carey said, "get your mind out of the gutter."

"Aw, but I *like* it there," he said, grinning impishly. I swatted him again, but he dodged and headed off down the hall, laughing. He was an ass, but I hoped he and Matt would be at the rally. After all, they were regulars at the Rebellion meetings. Maybe if I got too nervous I could just imagine him in his tighty-whities. I leaned over and whispered that to Carey, and she snickered. Then she put one arm around my shoulders.

"Asha, you can so do this. You're funny, and your speech is really going to kill."

I swallowed, still nervous despite the distracting and not altogether pleasant mental image of a skinny, half-naked David Castro. "Let's hope the crowd at lunch is as forgiving as you are. Or else I might get cafeteria food thrown at me."

———

When the bell rang at 11:50, I just about jumped out of my skin. Sweat seemed to spring from every pore, and to cover my sudden nervousness, I fumbled with my books and papers, sliding them into my backpack. I could hear whispers about the sit-in, and a few people looked at me sideways before resuming their whispering. I tried not to look at anyone, tried not to attract extra attention, but I could tell by the prickling at the back of my neck that people were staring at me.

I'd arranged to meet Carey and Miranda out on the quad after I took my contacts out. The girls' bathroom was an ordeal at the best of times; you always had to fight crowds putting on makeup at the mirror, and usually you had to endure the stench of various kinds of smoke. This time, I was unlucky enough to run into, of all people, Kaelyn.

"Oh, Asha. I can see why you usually wear contacts," she said in a syrupy voice when she saw the glasses in my hand. I could see her reflection in the mirror, smirking at me as she ran a brush through her already-glossy light-brown hair. "Those glasses are hideous."

I wasn't sure whether that was a compliment, a sympathetic observation, or a burn, but based on her tone, I was betting on the latter. I figured my best strategy was to be noncommittal. "Uh-huh," I said, trying to concentrate on not dropping my contact lens in the sink.

"But I guess it makes a good disguise, huh?"

Okay, that was weird. I tried to ignore her, and grimaced into the mirror as I took my other contact out.

"I mean, if you don't want people to recognize you. Like if you were afraid of getting into trouble."

I stopped, turned around, and stared at her.

"Is that a *threat*?" I paused. "Is this about the sit-in?"

She looked at me innocently, hair spray clutched in one perfectly manicured hand. "Why should I care what you do with your time? I'm just saying."

"If it's a threat, I'm not threatened. Anyway, you're one to talk, since you're not even going to show up. Talk about scared of getting in trouble." I smiled sweetly.

"Hey, I have a cheerleading meeting. Some people have *real* things to do with their time." She turned back toward the mirror and started spraying her bangs.

"Yeah, okay." I rolled my eyes.

I almost felt let down. Kaelyn's problem wasn't that she was scared of trouble. It wasn't that she was evil, or racist, or even that she was a mega-bitch (although she kind of was). It was just that she was completely and utterly self-centered. I was willing to bet it had been a long time since she'd done anything for another person, something purely out of the kindness of her heart, something that gave her that special feeling you get when you know you're doing the right thing. And I kind of felt bad for her.

She didn't know what she was missing.

———

The following April:
Ashmont Unified School District Board Room

"We've come to our final scheduled speaker," the hearing officer said, not bothering to hide his relief. There was some shuffling of paperwork from the hearing panel, and I caught the eye of Vice Principal Malone. He was the only one who didn't look relieved at all. In fact, he looked pained, and when the final official witness sauntered up to stand in front of the room, her perfect hair bouncing and her short skirt swishing, I found out why.

My mother nudged me. "That very pretty girl—she looks familiar. Is she your friend?"

I shook my head, mutely.

Of all the people in the whole damn school, why did it have to be Kaelyn?

Nobody warned me I'd have to deal with any hostile witnesses. But at least I had one final ace up my sleeve. All I had to do was get through the next few minutes.

Exhibit A.12:
MATERIALS VIOLATING
BOARD POLICY SECTION 418.III.M, 418.III.N

Web page encouraging participation in possible terrorist group. Two copies attached.

Latte Rebels, Now is the Time to Unite!

There is no time like the present,
and the present holds the key to our future!
All Latte Rebellion chapters are
urged to participate in our

Nationwide Sit-In!!!

It is time to raise awareness of mixed race
in every community!
Your school is the best place to start.
If you talk, your teachers and fellow students will listen.
The world will follow.

April 18 is the Time to March!

(flyer found in student's possession)

I, _____, DO SOLEMNLY
PLEDGE TO ATTEND THE LATTE
REBELLION SIT-IN ON WEDNESDAY,
APRIL 18, IN SUPPORT OF THE CAUSE
OF THOSE OF MIXED ETHNICITY, AND IN
PROTEST OF THEIR UNFAIR TREATMENT
BY THIS SCHOOL AND BUREAUCRACIES
EVERYWHERE.

I HEARD ABOUT THIS SIT-IN FROM:

_____

I HEARD ABOUT THE LATTE REBELLION
FROM: _____

COMMENTS: _____

_____

SIGNED: _____ DATE: _____

12

When I finally stepped out of the bathroom and left the building, I felt like I was in one of those ridiculous high school TV dramas, and this was the slow-motion moment of truth when the main character walks down the hall, her heart beating (or some crappy song playing) in her ears. If this were television, pretty soon I'd get shocked back into reality with some kind of contrived good news, somebody running up to me yelling "Asha, Asha, all the teachers in the entire school came to the sit-in! We're not going to get in trouble! There are news crews waiting in the quad to cover us on local TV! Anderson Cooper is on the phone! You have to come quick!"

And then I'd rush out and see all the teachers, including Principal Philips, linked arm-in-arm, beaming and wearing Latte Rebellion T-shirts. All the kids who'd ever made fun of us or not taken our cause seriously would be on the sidelines, grimacing and grumbling because they didn't get to be on TV. Kaelyn would have fallen on her butt in the mud, just because. It would end with Miranda, Carey, and me riding around on everybody's shoulders and "Don't You Forget About Me" playing in the background.

Then I snapped back to reality as if a rubber band had been shot at my head. This was University Park High School, not *The Breakfast Club*. I was no popular prom-queen Molly Ringwald. This was for real, and I was scared. I'd sweated through the armpits of my T-shirt, and as I stepped out of the building into the bright, breezy sun-light, I hoped nobody could tell I was shaking.

It was 11:56 now, according to the clock on my phone. As I made my way across campus to the quad, I watched people crowd into the food lines, yelling and joking and shoving, waiting for their helpings of soggy fries or High-lander-burgers or pizza. A few people were already eating their lunches at the rows of picnic tables under the awning next to the cafeteria and lunch carts. Was it my imagina-tion, or did the tables look a little emptier than usual? It seemed like there were spaces here and there where the chipping blue paint of the benches showed through, places where normally people would have staked out a spot at the very beginning of lunch.

I continued my slow-motion walk down the side of the lunch area, heading for the other side of the social sci-ence building. Again, I wondered if I was imagining it, but it seemed like people were drifting in from one side or another to join me as I walked toward the quad—a little band of marchers, of Latte Rebels. I didn't know if they were coming to join the sit-in, just to watch events unfold, or if it was complete chance that they were walking this way and they were really headed for the parking lot or something; but it felt momentous. I swallowed hard.

When I turned the corner, I could see people sitting on the grass, standing under the scattered trees, eating lunch at the two or three lone picnic tables. I couldn't quite take everything in all at once.

My gaze found Miranda, with Maria and a couple of other people from our school Rebellion meetings, standing by the big oak tree in the middle of the quad, which seemed to be the staging area. I was a little surprised to see Carey there, too, right out in the open as opposed to hiding behind a bush or something. I also couldn't help noticing that there were campus guards and teachers all over the place: the peach fuzz who patrolled the parking lot was at one end of the science building, talking into a walkie-talkie and leaning stiffly against the wall. Ms. Allison was innocently eating a wrap under a tree with Mr. Rosenquist. Vice Principal Malone, a.k.a. Herr Gestapo, was lurking in the doorway of one of the classrooms trying (and failing) to look inconspicuous. And one of the janitors was picking up trash very, very slowly, his beady eyes darting from one person to another as if he'd been told to keep an eye out for trouble.

And there were a lot of people to keep an eye on. I scanned the area. There had to be at least fifty here already, counting teachers and staff. To my eternal shock, I even saw Lou Pratt with a couple of his beefy football teammates. Who would have known? My stomach lurched, only partially from excitement.

I walked, now at normal speed, over to Carey and Miranda, trying to fixate on their faces. If I thought too hard about this, there was a chance I'd run screaming, which would ruin the atmosphere.

When I got to the tree, I could see a sleek laptop computer sitting on a table. A handful of people had gathered around it, jostling to try to get a better look at the screen.

"Wow, what *is* this?" I peered at the laptop apprehensively. I could see the unofficial Latte Rebellion site on one window, and another, smaller window showing grainy, fuzzy people moving about.

"Hey, Asha!" Maria was practically squealing with excitement. She grabbed me and pulled me into a prime spot in front of the screen. "Check this out! Leonard said a bunch of the Latte Rebellion chapters are going to film the sit-ins as they happen, using a webcam or digital cameras, and post the footage to one of the Rebellion sites. Isn't that *cool*?"

I gulped. It *was* cool, but it didn't help the acid roiling in my stomach.

"Yeah," Miranda said. "The goal is to make at least one of those dumb five-minute human-interest stories on a cable news channel."

My sense of amazement—and even pride—that we were doing this at all warred with my acid reflux at the thought of being on television, which (oh God, oh God)my parents might see. Momentarily, the reflux won.

"Nobody said I'd have to be on TV," I muttered.

"Asha, you're not going to be on TV, don't worry. Just the webcam," Miranda reassured me, as if appearing before the entire Internet public was any better. She put her arm around my shoulders and steered me away from the group a little. "I'm sorry, I know this is unexpected."

"I'm not a big fan of it either," Carey said, surprising nobody. "If that webcam even turns in my direction, I'm out of here." She gave me a pat on the shoulder and then made her way to an inconspicuous spot behind a tree.

"Lucky her," I said a little testily. "I wish you'd told me."

"It'll be *fine*," Miranda said, sounding a little aggravated at having to reassure me several thousand times. "I promise. You won't even have to look at the webcam. You're supposed to address the students *here*. Plus, the sound on Maria's laptop is awful anyway."

I let out my breath. At least the Internet public wouldn't hear much. They wouldn't even really get a good look at me, since I'd be facing the crowd. I wasn't quite ready to be world-famous even if we only ended up as a novelty video clip.

I turned slightly, to gauge what I was up against in terms of listeners. Again, my stomach flipped. At least ten additional people had shown up, and more were still trickling in with cafeteria lunches.

What had we done?

I turned away from the crowd as the first wave of total panic hit me. "Oh my God! Miranda, I have no idea what they want me to do! I—" I flapped my hands anxiously. According to my watch, it was 11:59.

"Chill, girl!" Miranda laughed sympathetically. "Think of it as a dry run for that salutatorian speech. You may yet be addressing our fellow lemmings at graduation."

"So you keep saying, but it's not helpful," I said plaintively.

"Listen—after we make the introductory remarks, just sit over here with me, and when Maria tells you to go up there, you go up there and say your thing, the shirts are unveiled, and then you come back. That's it. Easy." Miranda tucked a stray lock of hair back into my bun. "The speakers are hardly going to mention the Latte Rebellion, anyway; not at first. They don't want to get shut down before they have a chance to make their point."

I wasn't so sure about that. I wasn't so sure about anything at the moment. I could feel parts of my body that had never sweated before break out in nervous droplets.

In total contrast to my waffling, Maria marched briskly up in front of the oak tree, her chestnut-colored ponytail bobbing. She looked like a demented Brady Bunch sister in her plaid skirt and button-down shirt. Miranda followed, calm as usual, with a small, enigmatic smile.

I swallowed bile, remembering the group of jerk-wads—whoever they were—who'd tossed the smoke bomb into the classroom a few weeks ago. What if it hadn't been just an empty threat? But the quad was swarming with teachers. Teachers who suddenly snapped to attention as I took my spot at the tree with Maria and Miranda.

This was it. And now I had to face whatever was coming next.

"Welcome, and thank you for joining our event today," I said, a little shakily.

"Ladies and Gentlemen," Maria said, her loud, irritating voice perfectly suited to this type of thing. "Some of you know exactly why we're here. Many of you don't, but we're glad you joined us. Nice to see you, Ms. Allison, Mr. Rosenquist, Mr. Malone."

She nodded at each of them in turn, her eyes meeting theirs defiantly. I had to admire her cojones. Somewhere along the way, this had turned into her pet project, and she wasn't going to let it fade into obscurity.

"All we ask is half an hour of your time, to listen to your fellow students," I put in. "Then, if you choose to join in our declaration of solidarity, we welcome you."

Some people just looked confused, but there were some unruly cheers and a few Sympathizers smiled knowingly. David Castro, with a total lack of subtlety, thumped his fist to his chest in a mock salute.

"First, though, I would like to take a moment to explain why we're here." I was warming to my topic just a little, buoyed by the fact that when I looked out at my audience, I saw so many faces that were paying rapt attention and grinning encouragingly. "We are here because each of us has an interest in letting the world know that people of mixed race, of mixed ethnicity, are everywhere. That we are part of society, that we contribute to society, and that we're not willing to be pigeonholed into traditional categories. We're not going to put up with prejudice, and we're not going to be pushed aside!"

A handful of people, here and there around the quad, applauded, and there were more cheers. Everyone else just kind of gaped openmouthed at the audience members who were cheering. I even gaped a little myself, because one of the people applauding was Mr. Rosenquist, the psychology teacher and our would-be club advisor. Guess he really had wanted our proposal to succeed.

Then Miranda took over. As usual, she attracted a lot of attention with her cascade of braids and her tall, willowy frame, so all eyes were on her as she began to speak.

"We only have half an hour, but we have an exciting program in store for you," she began. "We have no fewer than six speakers who will briefly tell you about themselves and their experiences as people of mixed ethnicity. Then there will be a short break for a group photo—the speakers and the audience all together, showing solidarity. As some of you know, this is a nationwide sit-in, so it's also being held at other schools. Like some of them, we are webcasting online right at this moment."

There were some "ooohs" and more shouts of support. Mr. Malone made as if to stalk up to the tree, but my tenth grade U.S. History teacher, Mrs. Cho, put a hand on his arm and whispered something. He stopped, crossing his arms and leaning against the wall with a frown. I'd have paid good money to know what she said to him.

"After the group photo, we'll have a few minutes of open floor for those who want to add their comments. Again, we thank you all for coming." Miranda stepped backward and sat down on the picnic bench behind the webcam. I followed her, yielding the floor to Maria.

I was to be the last speaker. I was supposed to lead everyone in revealing their Latte Rebellion T-shirts for the webcast. That was really going to make Mr. Malone have a cow, if anything was. If we weren't all already on his detention list.

"First," Maria said, going back to her usual bossy, nasal tone, "we have Ayesha Jones, senior class president." Everybody clapped as Ayesha got up from a nearby bench and walked up to the front. Like Maria and Miranda and myself, she was dressed as respectably as possible, in a suit jacket and pants that she'd probably worn to some leadership conference. The cream-colored fabric set off her brown skin, which could have been deliberate. She took off her sunglasses and beamed presidentially.

"Hello, everyone." There were loud cheers and more clapping. Class presidents were elected in a popularity contest and we all knew it, but you couldn't help but like bubbly Ayesha, who was nice to everybody. "Thank you," she continued. "Now, I only have a few minutes to tell you about my experiences, so I'll start by playing a little game."

Miranda and I looked at each other. A few people whooped sarcastically.

"I'd like you to raise your hands if you think you can guess what my ethnicity is. The only hint I'll give you is this: There are seven. That's seven chances to get the answer right, people! Each person I call on gets one guess. If you're correct, I'll give you a prize. All right?" She grinned.

There was even more unruly noise as people heard the word "prize." Little did they know they would be getting official Latte Rebellion T-shirts.

"Okay! Who's first?" A few hands waved in the air. "You." Ayesha pointed at David Castro.

"Black," he said.

"Correct. African American is one." David easily caught the bundled T-shirt thrown his way and looked smugly at his friends sitting on either side of him. Then Carey waved her hand, barely visible from behind her tree. I was shocked.

"Welsh," she said. A bunch of people looked up in surprise.

"Right on," Ayesha said. "How did you know?"

"A lot of Welsh people have Jones as a surname." Carey smiled proudly. Carey, College Bowl trivia champion, who also happened to have a Welsh great-grandmother. Carey, who hadn't even wanted to be associated with this event. I frowned. I'd given her ample opportunities to be part of this with me, and *now* she decided to speak up?

By the end, Ayesha was revealed to also be part Cherokee, part Irish, part French, part German, and part Salvadorian, and an excited group had crowded closer to the podium-tree. A few people started unwrapping their prizes and I saw Mr. Malone stand a little straighter.

"My point," Ayesha said, "is that if you judge a book by its cover, you might easily be wrong. I've been in so many situations where people make racist comments about

Spanish speakers without knowing I have a Latino grand-father. And it makes me feel like they didn't bother to get to know *me*. Let alone different cultures. Thank you."

There were cheers and whoops as Ayesha went back to her seat.

Maria was next. She talked about being 50 percent Mexican, 50 percent Scottish, and 100 percent misunder-stood. Hers and the next speech went by in a blur. I hardly remembered who spoke or what they said, I was starting to get so nervous about my upcoming moment in the spot-light. By now, the crowd was excited and loud, and we'd attracted even more students who'd wandered in, wonder-ing what the fuss was about. The picnic tables had people standing on them in order to see better, and I saw Mr. Malone shake his head sharply at a guy who made as if to climb a tree. I twisted my hands behind my back to keep them from trembling.

The speaker right before me was Shay Saintmarie—the one cheerleader who seemed to be at all interested in what we were about. I was shocked to see her there. I figured that by now, Kaelyn would have talked her out of what-ever interest she'd once had in the Rebellion, or threatened to have the Bimbocracy blackball her or something. When Shay got up from her picnic bench to go up to the front, I saw Kaelyn and Roger Yee slouched in the back of the quad, glaring. Why they'd even bothered to show up was anybody's guess.

"Hi, guys!" Shay was wearing her cheerleading uniform and her boyfriend Darnell's varsity track jacket. There were wolf whistles from some of the guys in the crowd and she did a little twirl, showing off the fake lacy panties under her cheer skirt.

"God, this is *not* a strip-tease," I muttered to nobody in particular. "Somebody save her from herself."

"I just wanted to say that my sisters on the pep squad are *so great* because we're all shapes, colors, and sizes! *Woo!*"

Miranda rolled her eyes. A few people snickered.

"In some places, like on this one episode of *Orange Coast*, you wouldn't even be able to get on the squad if you weren't white and blond. And some people don't think it's right if you marry someone who isn't the same color or race," she told the crowd. "When we lived in Arkansas, some kids threw mud at me because they said that's what color I was, mud, and that's what happens when you mixed dirt and water."

My jaw dropped. So did Miranda's. The crowd was silent now, staring. Even the cranky janitor looked outraged.

"Well, my name is not *mud*," she continued. "It's *Shay*. And I have just as much right to exist and be proud as anybody else. Thank you." She did a little curtsy, flashing her lacy panties at everyone standing behind her—including the webcam—and flounced to the back of the crowd. It looked like Kaelyn and Roger were already gone. Still reeling from that bizarre experience, I tried to gather my thoughts, but there was no time. Maria was already back in front of the group announcing…me.

"Asha has been special to us from the beginning, as many of you know, and she has something shocking to

share with you. Please give her your attention and respect."
Maria flung one arm out and I got up on cue, walking to
the tree.

I looked at the crowd but I couldn't single out any
faces. It was all a blur now. I could tell that people had
taken out their cell phones, ready to take pictures or film
clips, so there went my last shreds of hope for anonymity.
Still, I knew that Miranda and Carey were behind me, and
that was all that mattered.

My nerves had kicked into high gear, and all I could
focus on was what I was about to do. I took out my index
cards, patting my pocket to make sure the other item I'd
brought was still in place. I took a deep breath. The air
smelled like scorched hamburgers from the cafeteria, which
didn't help my nausea any.

"Okay, people," I said, glancing at my notes. "I know
you've been standing here for a long time, listening to
people talking, so I'll make this short." As I expected, that
earned a small chorus of shouts.

"My name is Asha Jamison. Some of you might remember me all the way from sixth grade, when I was the spelling
bee champion. Some of you might even remember when I
was on the soccer team. You might think of me as an athlete, a nerd, a 'shrimpy Asian'"—I briefly looked up and
gave Lou Pratt a significant glance, and his football buddies
laughed and thumped him on the back—"or, if you're more
open-minded, something in between. Reality is always
more complicated than black and white, right?

"Like many of you, I have my ups and downs when it

comes to grades, and I've always been lucky to have more ups than downs. I'm still hoping to be able to speak in front of you at graduation, right next to my best friend and future valedictorian, Carey Wong." I waved at Carey, who tried to hide behind her tree. Some best friend. David Castro, in the front row, whistled.

"Despite all of that, the college application process threw me a curve ball. I thought I did everything right. But some schools still rejected me. A few of them were incredibly competitive, so that, I understand. But for two schools right here in Northern California, I was placed on the waiting list—schools which supposedly admit their freshman classes based mostly on academic merit and extracurricular activities." I took a deep breath.

"Well, as it turns out, I heard from a reliable source that if you don't meet *other* standards for admission—such as overcoming hardships, or even being part of a particular social group or ethnic minority—then you might not be as competitive as other students. If you're a good candidate but you don't fit into the college's categories ... then maybe you're at a disadvantage. Maybe, like me, you just won't quite get in." There were gasps, which was the reaction I was hoping for. I felt a momentary surge of adrenaline.

"Now, I want to finish up by saying that maybe ethnicity isn't the cause here. But I think that because we, as individuals of mixed race, don't easily fit into check-box categories, I think that we are being overlooked and underestimated. I think we are underestimating *ourselves*.

"Well, I'm not doing it anymore. I won't be overlooked, and I won't let anyone underestimate me. Last night I wrote a letter of appeal to my top choice college, where I was wait-listed, telling them how I *deserve* to be a student at their school!"

There was a rousing round of clapping and a few cheers from Miranda and Carey. But I still had one more task, possibly the most nerve-wracking of all. As I concluded my speech, I noticed that somehow, imperceptibly, more teachers had gathered and were "stationed"—if that was the right word ... if it was deliberate—at various points around the quad. I wondered if someone had blabbed about our plans. Or if the teachers had been keeping tabs on the Rebellion forum.

"Oh, and one last thing, before our group declaration of solidarity," I said to the crowd. Here was the part that nobody knew about, the part I had agonized over during the early morning hours when I couldn't sleep. I reached into my pocket, drew out the folded object inside, and opened it up.

Slowly, deliberately, I put the paper bag over my head. By hiding my face, there was a good chance I'd be *revealing* my identity as Agent Alpha. But things had changed. I'd changed.

I couldn't see very well now—my peripheral vision was pretty much shot—but I heard a quickly spreading murmur.

"Now, before we gather in front of the webcam so the world can see what a great turnout we had, I would like those of you who agreed to participate in our T-shirt-wearing event to please reveal those T-shirts!"

I knew that Miranda and Maria were coming up behind me, ready to be the ones that the webcam saw up close, though it wasn't really necessary now that my face was covered. Mouth dry, I unbuttoned my suit jacket and tossed it aside, revealing my Latte Rebellion T-shirt. Dozens of other people had done the same, and I could see a whole rainbow of Latte-related shirts—from Mutts Rule! to Fear the Latte! A few people besides me were even wearing paper bags on their heads. It took me a moment to realize that part of the swirling feeling in my chest was pride.

There was one moment of utter silence. Then sheer pandemonium broke loose.

Suddenly, right in front of me, there was a series of loud cracks and smoke began pouring from another smoke bomb. Multicolored sparks flew into the air as the firecracker next to it detonated. I jumped back, falling on my butt. Miranda and Carey rushed over and crouched next to me, pulling me up and back toward the table, all of us coughing from the noxious stench.

In the shelter of the picnic table, I tore off my paper bag hat and straightened my glasses so I could see what was happening. There were screams and some students started running from the area, and the loitering teachers had snapped to attention. Mr. Malone and Mr. Rosenquist started toward the scene of the melee.

As the nasty, sulfurous smoke cleared, I could see David Castro wrestling with someone whose paper bag had half-fallen off. It was Roger Yee. In retrospect, I shouldn't have been surprised that he'd been behind the firecracker incidents. At the time, though, all I could do was stand there between Carey and Miranda, trying to make sense of what I was seeing and shaking the ringing out of my ears. An even bigger shock was that David—immature, goofy, always-mellow David—was so angry. I couldn't quite hear what he was growling at Roger, but it sounded like "you goddamn hypocrites have nothing better to do."

I heard Roger breathlessly grunt something about us being wannabes who had nothing better to do than steal membership from other people's legitimate organizations. Incongruously, I wanted to laugh. Was that really his problem?

David didn't seem to find it funny. He wrestled Roger underneath him and was about to throw a punch, his face red, when Mr. Rosenquist grabbed his arm and yanked him back. Meanwhile, Mr. Malone was practically sitting on top of Roger to keep him from going after David.

"That has to be uncomfortable," Miranda said under her breath—Mr. Malone was about six feet five and very muscular. I nodded, and coughed again. I really didn't feel bad for Roger, though. It was David I was worried about, because he'd obviously come to our defense, or at least tried to do the right thing. I was afraid that now he'd be blamed for something he didn't do, that his actions would be misinterpreted and Roger Yee, Mr. School Aristocracy, would get off scot-free.

By now, a ring of people had gathered around the erstwhile combatants. But before Mr. Malone could make one of his dictatorial pronouncements, there were shouts from across the grassy area. A girl screamed shrilly. Somebody else was fighting, over between the social science and English buildings. It was hard to see because people had rushed over there too, crowding around and gawking. It seemed like there were a couple of fights going on in different parts of the quad. Carey and I stood there in shock, immobilized. Miranda had the presence of mind to grab the computer, and she kept the webcam on, pointing it at the fray. With all the cell phones already out, she wasn't the only one filming.

After a few minutes, the melee calmed down. The fights were stopped, and a number of people, including David Castro and Roger Yee, had already been hauled to the office. I wasn't sure where the principal was going to fit them all.

I felt horrible, and not just because I'd been scared half to death by the firecracker going off right in front of me. I felt responsible for all this. What if, by putting on my paper bag and showing my Latte Rebellion shirt, I'd dropped the straw that broke the camel's back, making Roger and his unknown cronies do their thing?

Holding hands, Carey, Miranda, and I sort of half-crawled behind the picnic table.

"You!" Vice Principal Malone barked. "You three! Stay right there." He was surveying the aftermath of the whole mess, watching as students huddled together in small groups talking excitedly, or gathered their books together, frantically talking on the phone.

The three of us froze and got up slowly, as if held at gunpoint by a policeman. My heart sank. We weren't going to get out of this without a trip to the principal's office. I hoped against hope that they wouldn't call my parents, but I was pretty sure it was inevitable. Mr. Malone talked to the campus guard, nodded, and then walked over to us.

"We need to talk to you girls in the office." He waited a fraction of a second while we gathered our bookbags. "Good. Now, come with me."

As we were escorted away, I was horrified to see actual police—wearing face shields, with batons at their waists— taking up positions throughout the quad.

"Who decided we needed the riot squad?" Miranda whispered to me.

I shook my head.

When we walked into the office, it was like fighting a crowd at a concert. There were all sorts of unfamiliar adults in suits conferring with school administrators; there were a few more of the people in riot gear; and there were at least ten other students in varying states of disarray and injury, a couple with Latte Rebellion T-shirts. There was even a kid sitting outside the nurse's office, cradling an obviously broken arm and wincing while the nurse prodded at him gingerly.

And then there were parents.

"My daughter called me and told me there was a *riot at school*, and you're telling me I can't pull her out of *class*?" one tiny woman was shrieking. "This is outrageous!"

"Can't I at least talk to him? You have to admit these are extreme circumstances. I just want to know my son is safe," said a tall dark-skinned man in a gray suit holding a cell phone, who looked like he'd just come from work.

"Please," the receptionist said loudly over the din, his voice harried. "Everyone stay calm and I'll take care of you one at a time. *Please.*"

There was also someone who looked like a newspaper reporter, followed by a cameraman, trying to get the receptionist to give him permission to interview students and go into classrooms. It was complete chaos, and Mr. Malone had to politely move a few people aside as he escorted us into his office, signaling to one of the secretaries to join us. On the way in, I saw David Castro sitting mutely in a chair just outside. He had a black eye and a cut lip, his dark hair was disheveled, and his expression was murderous. But when he looked up at us, he grinned wolfishly.

Mr. Malone closed the door and the uproar in the outer office was abruptly cut to a dull roar. Slowly and deliberately, he walked around his large wooden desk to his chair and sat down. He leaned forward, elbows on the desk, and steepled his fingers together, looking from one of us to another. The secretary sat in a folding chair to one side, pen poised over a notepad. By now I'd just about convinced myself I was going to hurl. Carey looked equally nauseated, and even Miranda looked worried.

"Well, girls," Mr. Malone said in a sigh of a voice. "I'm very disappointed to see you in here like this. All three of you are model students; you all have excellent grades." He paused, then cleared his throat uncomfortably. "Ms. Levin, Ms. Jamison; after I spoke with you before, I was hoping that I wouldn't have to see you in here again. You assured me that your account of the smoke bomb incident was true, that it was a fluke and you had nothing to do with it. I had no reason at all to disbelieve you.

"Now, I'm going to ask what the three of you were doing on the quad today, and I want you to be truthful. I need to assess your involvement in today's incidents, and whether we will need to take any further disciplinary action. Ms. Dominguez will take notes."

"Further disciplinary action?" I blurted out, horrified. I knew he'd have to call my parents, but ... I didn't have even a single detention on my record.

"Yes," Mr. Malone said, calmly. "Everyone involved in the fights, and everyone who we know was involved in the 'sit-in' that precipitated the violence, has been suspended for the remainder of the school day. Essentially, this is a precaution that will enable us to determine what happened."

"Suspended? I can't be suspended!" Carey cried. "My parents will kill me!"

Miranda inhaled sharply. I knew she'd had detention a couple of times, but I also knew her parents were strict; they wouldn't be very happy about this. Carey's parents would, of course, completely flip. Carey was the perfect daughter; they'd never understand how this happened.

Which was why I said what I did, despite everything that had happened between Carey and me.

"Mr. Malone," I said. "This had nothing to do with Carey. I think you should let her go back to class. She was just there because I asked her to come see my speech. The same with Miranda."

"Ms. Jamison, I was there. I know Miranda gave her own speech, and it was just as provocative as yours, if not more so. I don't want you to cover for your friends. I want you to tell me exactly what happened. This Latte Rebellion... we've always thought it had the potential to cause trouble. I *will* find out the truth, whether from the three of you or from somebody else, and a full report will be made to the district as well as the police." Mr. Malone said this quietly, stroking his mustache, but it struck fear into my heart. I was even more determined to make sure Carey did not take the fall for this.

"Mr. Malone, I promise to tell the whole truth and nothing but the truth," I began. He flashed me a dangerous look. "The Latte Rebellion... it's just a club. One that talked about issues that were really important to me. Even if school administrators thought it was a gang, it's not! We—I went to meetings at U-NorCal and everything. Lots of people at school went, too. Carey never had anything to do with it; it was me. I asked her to come today. I promise." Tears started to fall from my eyes, involuntarily. I wasn't even sure what I was crying about; I wasn't sure if I was nervous, or angry, or both.

"I only wanted to be part of something important. I finally felt like this was a club that really *meant* something to me. And the Inter-Club Council didn't deem it worthy of existing, so we did what we thought we had to.

I'm sorry." I looked down at my lap. If I hadn't been half-sobbing, I'd have held my breath, wondering what Mr. Malone would say now. If he even believed me. Was he enough of a callous jerkface to accuse me of lying?

I heard him exhale, a long breath. When I looked up, he fixed me with a piercing stare. I bit the inside of my lip and willed myself not to look away. Without breaking his gaze, he said, "Miranda, I'd like to hear your version of the events, if you don't mind. Again, this is no time to cover for your friends." His frown, somehow, got even frownier, as if he didn't like what he was hearing. As if he was determined that someone was going to take the fall.

"Well, we got involved in the club," Miranda began. She looked at me for a half second, her face unreadable. "Asha and I." I held in a sigh of relief. Carey just kept staring down at the desk disconsolately.

"After our proposal for a club charter was unfairly dismissed, we went to a couple of meetings with the U-Nor-Cal chapter, and so did some other people from school. We all thought it was a good idea to continue meeting here at school, despite not being an official club," Miranda said defiantly. "There's a Black Student Union and an Asian Student Association and the Chicano Club, but there isn't anything, Mr. Malone, for kids of mixed race." She stared at him, her chin held high, as if daring him to dispute that fact.

"You're free to join any club you want, Ms. Levin. I don't see why you couldn't have just participated in whichever club was the most…relevant." He scratched his mustache, glowering. "If you're mostly Hispanic, for example, you could go to the Chicano Club."

All three of us looked up in outrage at that, even Carey.

"I'm sorry, sir," Miranda said icily. "I don't subscribe to the one-drop rule."

"You are being unfair and out of line, young lady." There was a long, *very* painful silence, during which Miranda and Mr. Malone had a staring contest and Carey and I tried to pretend we weren't there. For a minute, all we could hear was the scratching of Ms. Dominguez's pen. Finally, after Miranda showed no sign of crumpling under his Stare of Death, Mr. Malone looked away.

"Well, since you seem to know so much, perhaps instead you can tell me about how this…*sit-in*…got so out of hand." Mr. Malone's voice was just as icy as Miranda's had been a moment before.

"I don't know how it got out of hand. I know there are troublemakers here who don't like what we're doing, for some reason. All I can tell you is, the sit-in wasn't our idea. It was a nationwide event at schools and colleges all around the country. Our chapter decided to participate."

"And I presume you thought that was a good idea, too," Mr. Malone said, sarcastically.

"Yes, I did," Miranda said. She sounded calm, but she was clenching her hands in her lap. I couldn't take it anymore; my mouth opened, ready to defend her.

"Miranda, you don't have to—"

"I *do* have to," she interrupted, staring at me hard. I

knew what she was trying to do, and I hated it. At the same time, I loved her for it.

"Ms. Levin, I'm going to have to ask you to please go to the secretary and someone will escort you to on-campus suspension," Mr. Malone said, impatient now. "I don't have time to debate philosophy with you."

"Fine," she said, getting up gracefully, letting all of her five feet ten inches tower over the vice principal's desk for a moment before she glided out of the room.

Unfortunately, the moment she left, the room felt heavy, stifling. I could feel my impending doom echoing in my brain like the heavy breathing of a phone pervert about to say something disgusting.

"Ms. Jamison, you might think I have no idea what goes on here, but I assure you I'm not clueless." Mr. Malone leaned back into his chair and folded his hands behind his head with false casualness. "I know that other students look to your leadership and creativity, and I'm very disappointed to see a promising student such as yourself involved in this kind of rabble-rousing.

"Next year, when you're in college, you'll have plenty of chances to go to rallies and parades and what-have-you, but this is a high school. There just isn't room for this kind of behavior, and the less mature students clearly can't handle it. I have to be able to rely on more mature students, such as yourself, to be a model for good citizenship. And people have to see that discipline is carried out fairly." Was that a pleading note I detected in his voice? I hoped that meant I wasn't completely screwed. He hadn't seemed to even want to deal with Miranda; maybe I'd get lucky, too.

Or maybe Miranda would be facing a harsher penalty later, after today was over. I fidgeted in my seat.

"This is why I'm sorry to tell you that we're going to have to call your parents. I'd like them to take you home for the rest of the afternoon, and I do not look forward to having to explain all this to them." He rubbed his temples for a moment and closed his eyes. I really didn't envy him; he was going to be deluged with parental freak-outs for the foreseeable future. However, I was much more concerned with my own future.

"When you say discipline will be carried out fairly," I said, my voice trembling, "what's going to happen to Roger and the people who set off the firecrackers? If we're getting suspended just for wearing T-shirts?"

"Well, they'll be dealt with appropriately, no question about that," he said matter-of-factly, opening his eyes and pinning me with a curious stare. "Bringing explosives onto campus is a violation of rules, and a crime."

"What about me?" Carey asked in a tiny, sulky voice. "I wasn't even part of the event."

"Oh," he said, looking at her as if he'd forgotten she was there. "Ms. Wong." He sighed. "It doesn't appear that you had any central role in today's incident. Given your outstanding academic and disciplinary record, I'm inclined to believe your friends. You're free to go back to class, or if you prefer you may call your parents to pick you up."

We both looked at Mr. Malone in surprise.

"Contrary to popular belief, I do not enjoy sending students to OCS," he said dryly. "Frankly, it gives me a headache."

Carey giggled obligingly and scampered for the door, patting me sympathetically on the shoulder on her way out. I was relieved for her, sure, but I felt a little gross about the whole thing. Maybe she *had* been the smart one, trying to stay uninvolved, but I still couldn't think about that without feeling disappointed. Crushed, even. And now it was time for me to face the music. Alone.

Mr. Malone looked back at me and his eyes narrowed. "Now that your friends aren't here to distract you, why don't you tell me one more time what happened."

I bit my lip, and my heart sank. There was no way I could repeat what I'd just told him and be absolutely positive my story was consistent. As we stared at each other, I knew he was fully aware of that. But I had to try. I opened my mouth to start, but before I got so much as a word out Mr. Malone looked at his watch and said, "On second thought, why don't we wait until your parents get here. I'm sure they'll want to hear your explanation just as much as I do."

I blanched. How bad was this going to get?

"Ms. Dominguez," he said. "You may go until Ms. Jamison's parents arrive. Should be about fifteen minutes." His secretary scuttled out and I was alone in the room with Mr. Malone, the old clock with its yellowing plastic face ticking away loudly above his desk, my butt starting to go numb from sitting in the hard, uncomfortable chair. And then I knew things could, and probably would, get much, much worse.

Exhibit A.13:
SUPPLEMENTARY EVIDENCE

(excerpted from The Ashmont Herald, "Violence Erupts at Local High School")

When a peaceful sit-in at University Park High School yesterday was disrupted by violence, it left students terrified, teachers shocked, and parents outraged.

"After I saw all those people fighting, I got so scared I called my dad to come pick me up," said freshman Lisa Hughes. Her father, local attorney Jason Hughes, was appalled.

"It's outrageous that something like this could be allowed to happen in our public schools," he said. "Free speech does not constitute a free pass for violent behavior."

The students involved in the sit-in saw things a little bit differently.

"This was a peaceful rally to promote awareness of mixed-race individuals," said junior Maria McNally, representative of the Latte Rebellion unofficial campus group. "It's not fair to blame the organizers for a hate crime perpetrated by a few troublemakers who were not part of our group."

Wednesday's sit-in was only one of dozens of similar events that took place nationwide and were broadcast on the Internet via webcam. The Latte Rebellion is a growing underground student movement that began locally here in the Bay Area, and gained some media attention earlier this year when Latte Rebellion materials were found in the possession of Blue Sky College gunman Raymond Gretch.

The Latte Rebellion club, though popular with students, has long been suspected by faculty and administrators of fomenting turbulence in the UPHS student body...

13

When I was in third grade, I got sent to the principal's office for pulling Amy Federman's hair after she grabbed my notebook and wouldn't give it back. Sitting there on the little orange chair, waiting for tall, scary Principal Kim to come out of her office, had been the longest ten minutes of my life.

Now, waiting in Mr. Malone's office for my parents to pick me up, I wished I could enter that kind of time warp and linger there forever. I would rather have stayed in the administration building listening to parents haranguing the receptionist and the school nurse tut-tutting over David Castro's split lip than face my parents and explain to them why I'd gotten suspended. But after what seemed like mere seconds of me fidgeting in the hard plastic chair and sweating, my mom knocked on the door of the office.

The look on her face was angrier than I'd ever seen, and I could hardly look her in the eye as she sat down stiffly in the chair to my left.

And just when I thought I couldn't feel any worse, my dad walked in, brisk and businesslike in a dress shirt and crisp black jeans. More like stormed in, really. He set down his briefcase and sat in the chair to my right. I felt like I was sweating gallons, but there was no way I was taking off my jacket. The Latte Rebellion shirt was under there, and I didn't want to provide any more ammunition for the impending siege.

There were a few terse handshakes and introductions, and then it began.

"Now," Mr. Malone said, very quietly, with exaggerated patience. "I'm sure your parents are just as eager as I am to hear what happened."

I felt sick, but there was no point in keeping anything secret anymore. If I didn't come clean now, my parents would just hear some sort of ridiculous hyperbole or lies from the school—or worse, from other parents. And I realized I didn't really care what Mr. Malone thought. I just didn't want Carey or Miranda to take the fall.

And, when it came down to it, I *wanted* my parents to hear the story. I wanted them to know what we'd gone through, how far we'd come from our original lemonade-stand idea, and how proud I'd been of what we'd accomplished. Even though the situation was completely different now and I wasn't entirely sure I wanted to continue being a part of it.

So I knotted my fingers together in my lap, stared at a spot on the wall just above Mr. Malone's left shoulder, and started at the beginning. I told them about how Carey and I got the idea for the Latte Rebellion, that our plan was to earn money for a vacation before college; I talked about Miranda's logo and the shirts, about Bridget and Leonard and how everything got out of hand. Nobody interrupted me, which was frightening. I kept waiting for the cross-examination to start, but they just sat in silence, Mr. Malone with his eyebrows slightly raised as if he were interested despite himself. By the time I got to the end, and told them about the firecrackers and how scared we all were, I had tears running down my face yet again. My mother's face softened and she moved her chair a little closer to mine, putting one of her hands on mine.

"I didn't know . . . people could be so *hateful*," I choked out. "And I didn't know that any of this would end up mattering so much. But it matters to me."

My mother squeezed my hand, then let go, frowning again. There was a slight sheen of anxious sweat on her forehead and she brushed it away absently. "I know it does. I know you wanted to help people. But you have to understand, Asha, it's important to maintain balance. You have to stay focused on your own welfare, too."

"There are other ways of helping people than disrupting the school day," my father said, still sounding majorly peeved. Out of the corner of my eye, I could see him crossing and uncrossing his legs, a sign that he was trying to control his temper. Mr. Malone just watched, silently, but

I could tell he had something more to say and was just waiting for us to finish.

"The sit-in was only supposed to be a lunch thing," I said, my voice muffled. I sat up again and wiped my eyes with my sleeve. "I wasn't even really involved. I didn't organize this. I just gave a speech, that's *all*."

"The point is, you shouldn't have been involved, period," my dad said, glaring at me. He took a deep breath and I knew that a lecture was coming. "Didn't you say the Rebellion or whatever it is was banned by the school? What made you think it was okay to defy the rules? You're almost done with high school, and you pull a stunt like this—for *attention*, as far as I can tell—well, let me just say that I think the vice principal was right to suspend everyone who was involved."

"Now, wait a minute," Mr. Malone began, putting his hands up in a placating gesture, but I couldn't let him finish.

I looked up, flashing each of them an angry glance in turn. "I didn't *do* anything, I had *nothing* to do with the firecrackers or the fighting, and I did *not* do this for attention! Not because *I* wanted attention, anyway. I—we— think this is an important issue, but maybe you wouldn't understand." My voice got louder, and I could feel my face get hot. I turned to my dad again. "I thought for sure you'd understand because you're half-and-half, too, but I guess you're really just..."

I trailed off at the look on my father's face. It was dangerous, angry. "I'm really just what?" he said quietly.

My brain froze, and for a second I almost let something

truly awful slip out of my mouth. Part of me wanted to. But instead I hung my head and said, "Nothing."

"Listen," Mr. Malone said placatingly. "I know this is difficult, and I don't want to make this any more complicated than it already is. But there is a prior warning on Asha's record, so my hands are tied. I'm sure you understand that because violent events did occur, and your daughter was present … and because the fact remains that specific school rules about explosives were flagrantly disregarded … it's district policy to consider whether a disciplinary hearing is warranted. We have a zero tolerance rule. I'm sorry."

"*What?*" My father sat forward in his chair. "I don't know anything about a prior warning. And now you're saying we have to go straight to a disciplinary hearing? We can handle Asha's discipline at home."

Uh-oh. I wasn't sure which was worse, a school board hearing or the idea of my dad choosing my punishment.

"Mr. Jamison, I'm sure you understand that due to the nature of the incident, we need to take all possible precautions." Mr. Malone stared steadily back at my dad, his hands folded calmly in front of him. "We are trying to ensure the safety of your daughter as well as the rest of the student body. We suggest that Asha remain at home in off-campus suspension until the district decides whether a hearing is appropriate. You should find out within a day or two."

"Now, wait a minute," my mother said, frowning. "What is supposed to be the ultimate outcome of this hearing?"

Mr. Malone stood up, a clear hint that our time in his office was finally, at long last, over. "Mrs. Jamison, the hearing will determine whether or not Asha should be expelled."

My heart pounded and I felt like I might pass out. Me? *Expelled?*

My mom paled. Then her lips tightened with anger and she gestured with her chin toward the door of the office, without a word. I followed, meekly, and my dad brought up the rear after shaking hands with Mr. Malone. Without a word to me, he told Mom, "I'll see you at home," and stalked out the glass doors of the administration building.

Mom's expression was cool and businesslike as she signed me out with the receptionist, but I could tell: she was steamed. Steamed like rice in a rice cooker. When she was done processing my paperwork, she took me by one arm and yanked me out the door, her dark, arched eyebrows pulling together in a thunderous frown.

On the drive, she was completely silent, not speaking to me at all, even when I said meekly, "Mom? I'm really, really sorry." She just shot me a look full of disappointment and turned her eyes back to the road. I clamped my jaw shut, grinding my teeth. There had to be something I could say to make things better, but I couldn't think of anything. I couldn't think at all. The only thing that crossed my mind was ... my car. I'd have to come back to get my car. Or maybe Carey could bring it back for me. I clung to those thoughts instead of worrying about what was probably my imminent and untimely demise.

After driving in silence for a few minutes, she finally spoke.

"I had to call a substitute teacher so I could come here, you know. And Dad had to take time off work. If you're having disciplinary problems at school... let's just say this is too serious to be solved by a simple 'I'm sorry, Mom.'" She clenched her hands tightly around the steering wheel, precisely at ten and two, as always.

"Asha, if I'd had any idea... I've been feeling for a while that this Latte business isn't a wise use of your time, especially after that horrible news story, but I was hoping I was wrong. It's the kind of thing that can influence you in ways you don't even realize. I wish you could be just a little more like Carey, working hard all the time and not making trouble. When you get to college..." She trailed off with a sigh. I could tell what she was thinking—that I'd probably ruined my chances at college.

"And what are we going to tell your Nani?" she continued, a new note of aggravation making her voice harsh. "If you get expelled... she's probably going to blame it on me 'not teaching you enough culture' or some other mumbo-jumbo."

I looked out the window, a couple of angry tears rolling down my flushed cheeks. I was tired of people thinking I was just an impressionable vessel for whatever random ideas might float my way. This was the most I'd thought for myself in a long time, maybe in my whole life. I sighed with frustration. My whole family wanted me to live up to an ideal I couldn't attain. Even before all this happened, my mother knew I wasn't a perfect paragon of success. Yet the expectations still hovered over me, my mom and dad both setting standards that seemed impossibly high. I couldn't win.

Meanwhile, Roger Yee was probably at home celebrating with Kaelyn about his starring role in the downfall of the Latte Rebellion. As exasperated as I was with my parents and Mr. Malone, my rage at Roger was so towering that it could only be adequately expressed by exaggerated cartoon violence. If I had an iota of Miranda's drawing talent, I'd be thrashing him in effigy in panel after panel.

When we got home, I trudged inside. Mom gestured sharply toward the living-room couch, so I sat down obediently and leaned back against one of the plush, wine-colored throw pillows. It was funny; all those other kids at school who called their parents were able to cry on their shoulders and get patted on the head and told everything would be okay. Meanwhile, I was shaking, not just with dread of the upcoming shout-fest but with fear at how close we'd all been to the exploding firecrackers, to the fighting. For the first time, it hit me how close I'd come to getting seriously injured. I clamped my hands together to try to keep them from trembling.

I hoped Roger would get expelled for this. Of all people! He was Asian American, too. He should *get* it, what we were doing. But apparently he just wanted to impress his friends with who had the biggest club membership, and get into Kaelyn's short little cheerleading skirt.

People like Roger, or Kaelyn—they always talked a

clever game, but in reality they all seemed to be self-centered, or ignorant, or indifferent to anything that really mattered. Or scared.

Especially me—I was the biggest coward of them all. I couldn't even tell my parents the truth about not getting into Stanford, about getting wait-listed at Berkeley and Robbins. My jaw ached, I was clenching it so hard.

I was only sitting on the couch for a minute or two before my dad got home and started in on a lecture so long that by the end of it, my head was spinning and I could hardly think straight. My mom just sat there in stony silence watching my dad pace back and forth, wearing a little path into the tan carpet and saying, "what were you *thinking*?" about a million different ways until he finally ran out of steam. Then Mom said, "Asha. Did you ever once even *think* you might get carried away by all this? Did you think about the consequences at all? Expulsion, Asha. I don't agree that it's called for, but that's beside the point."

Of *course* I never thought I'd get carried away. That was obvious. I sat there, unsure what she wanted to hear.

"Well," my dad said. "If you don't have anything to say about that, then maybe you can explain these." He brandished a wad of crumpled papers. "It looks like the Latte Rebellion isn't the only thing you haven't been forthcoming about. Why didn't you tell us about these rejection letters?"

"You were searching my *room*?" My mouth dropped open.

"What were we supposed to think, when we got a call

from school saying you were being held in the front office after being involved in a disruptive incident?"

I turned to my mother, appealing to her for some kind of reasonableness, but I could barely form a coherent sentence. "When have I ever—I'm not some kind of drug addict, or—it's not like I'm sneaking around behind your back!"

"Isn't it?" My dad kept on, relentless. "I can think of one big thing you've been hiding; two if you count these letters. I found some other paperwork, too, that you probably thought was cleverly hidden. A pledge to participate in the sit-in? Honestly, Asha, do you think we're oblivious? You lied. You've broken our trust in you."

My mother sighed, exhaustedly. "We've been so worried about you ever since your grades slipped last fall ... and now ..."

"Mom, I really thought it was *important*." My voice was harsh and ragged, but I couldn't help it. I was just so angry. "I really thought that colleges would be interested in the fact that I was involved in something socially aware. And not just colleges. You even heard about it on the news. People are interested in this. I've actually helped create something that could change people's lives."

"I know," she said, softly. "But when that takes away from everything else, from who you are ..."

"It *is* who I am," I said, just as quietly. But I couldn't stop thinking about what she'd said.

————

Later that night, as I was lying in bed contemplating my punishment—which was essentially being grounded for the rest of eternity—I thought back to what I almost said to my dad in the vice principal's office, what I could have said. That my dad was brown on the outside and white on the inside. A coconut. An insult. One that we'd made light of and tried to reclaim in the Latte Rebellion Manifesto, but for my dad, it would have been deadly serious.

Grandma Bee and my Gramps had raised my dad to speak only English and taught him never to make a big deal out of his ethnicity—they were afraid it would attract the wrong kind of attention. Like when their house was vandalized back when they lived in Texas, before my dad was born. When I was little, I begged Grandma Bee to teach me Spanish, but she always claimed she'd forgotten everything. When I got older, I realized that couldn't be true. She just *wanted* to forget.

I pulled the pillow over my head and sighed. My dad had basically grown up a plain old mainstream American. And was I really that different? Sure, I probably ate a hell of a lot more curry than the average person. I had a small collection of nearly new *shalwar kameez* shoved to the back of my closet. I had a Nani and a Nana on my mother's side, and a Gramps and an Abuelita—who insisted on being called Grandma Bee—on the other. You'd never mistake my skin for white, although it wasn't all that dark brown, either. But what did any of that matter? All I'd thought about on a regular basis—before the Rebellion, anyway—was how many days were left until we could graduate and get out of here. What did that make me?

And then there was what my mother had said, about being so involved in something that I was losing myself. I didn't think that was true about me, but she had a point. I'd spent all this time feeling responsible for the Rebellion, feeling like it was somehow my fault that everything got out of hand (and my dad wasn't helping with that); my fault that Carey and Miranda were in various kinds of trouble—not to mention Maria McNally and David Castro—and that the school had briefly become a battle zone.

It *was* my fault that I'd gotten distracted and let my grades slip and blown off all those application essay workshops, which probably resulted in my rejection letters and waiting lists. But I'd done what I could about that; I'd gotten my grades back up, and I'd already sent in my letter of appeal. With that letter, hopefully Robbins College would realize what I already knew: that I was more than just the sum total of my grades, or the exact composition of my DNA. And nobody could take those accomplishments, that knowledge, away from me, no matter what happened at the disciplinary hearing.

The Latte Rebellion ... well, it *had* meant a lot to me, and it still did. But it was way bigger than me now; way beyond Carey, Miranda, or me; it truly did have a life of its own.

I threw the covers off and went to the window, sitting on the floor below the sill and staring out at the starry sky. Maybe it was time to finally let some of this go.

The next morning, a call came from the front office. My mom picked it up—she hadn't quite run out the door yet—and after a few terse "yes" and "no" answers, hung up and turned to where I was sitting at the kitchen table, eating a bowl of cornflakes.

"Well, the school has set your disciplinary hearing for next Monday," she said, putting on her sweater and picking up her car keys. I could tell she was still disappointed that they'd decided to consider expulsion. And I wouldn't be allowed back at school in the meantime. Suspended. I couldn't even conceive of it. I hardly ever even stayed home sick.

Oddly, though, the time passed quickly. All I did was eat, sleep, pick up my assignments from the front office, and do homework. Except for those quick trips to school, I was pretty much stuck at home, since my dad made a point of coming home for lunch and my parents took turns calling me on the home phone every hour or so to make sure I didn't go anywhere else. I had to get all my gossip via email.

Sunday, though, I was allowed a *very* brief study session with Carey and Miranda, who brought some extra worksheets from an AP prep workshop they'd attended. The first thing I found out—in whispers, when my parents had left the kitchen—was that there had been no Roger Yee at school, either. Thanks to the zero tolerance policy for violence, he'd been summarily expelled, but I didn't feel much satisfaction at the news. Well, maybe a little. But it was tempered by the fact that he'd already arranged to finish out the school year at Seward High across town, thanks to his dad knowing someone on the school board. Rumor also had it that he was being forced to do some kind of community service.

"Picking up trash," I suggested, flipping a page in my calculus book.

"Um … being a big brother to disadvantaged children," Miranda shot back.

"Disadvantaged *mixed-race* children," I added. We laughed. Carey looked up briefly from her Barron's AP European History and smiled distractedly.

I sobered. Carey had definitely been distant the past few days, throwing herself into studying extra hard after Wednesday's catastrophe, even though she didn't really have anything to worry about. She'd been let off the hook as far as the "riot" was concerned. So it wasn't like she needed to study *that* hard—she'd already gotten her scholarships.

As for me, I wasn't sure how I felt about my own prospects, but at least I knew that my friends were rooting for me—including Thad, though I hadn't been able to do more than email him since my parents had temporarily taken custody of my phone. "Unjustly imprisoned," I'd written. "Please send chocolate." And when he'd sent me a hollow chocolate Easter rabbit with a nail file inside, I had to laugh.

After the days of enforced lockdown, I was looking forward to—hopefully—going back to school, even though I got really weird looks when I showed up in the office to pick up my classwork. People had heard about my speech, about the firecrackers; some of them had even seen the footage online at the Latte Rebellion unofficial site. I didn't know what Kaelyn or the other gossipmongers might have said, or whether they were silently blaming me for what happened, but it put me on edge. When I ran into Ayesha Jones coming out of the front office that Friday, she gave me a sympathetic smile and a hug, but it didn't make me feel much better.

I still had my disciplinary hearing looming over my head, for one thing, even though Miranda was sneakily helping me prepare. She'd even brought me a handbook from the American Civil Liberties Union talking about my rights during the expulsion-hearing process, and insisted on making sure I wasn't being "taken unfair advantage of." I gave her a huge hug, but I wasn't sure how this was going to help me if the school board had already made up their minds, like my parents had.

Meanwhile, the Rebellion blog was brimming with comments and inflammatory rhetoric about how violent incidents only proved the importance of the Latte Rebellion mission, blah blah blah. It got so that I stopped visiting any of the Rebellion websites. Even when I visited the original page that we'd set up back in October, it felt like I was looking at something somebody else had invented, a long time ago.

Of course, I felt like it was important for people of mixed ethnicity to have a voice, an identity. There was no question about that. But I still wondered: was all this—

this chaos, this cacophony of voices—what a movement really was? Was that the only way for us to be heard?

I felt like my one lonely voice had been drowned out in all the shouting, and I didn't know what I was trying to say. I wished, more than anything, that I was in a place where *my* voice mattered.

14

There were murmurs throughout the boardroom as Kaelyn stood in front of the disciplinary hearing board in her short skirt and Roger Yee's letterman jacket, smiling slightly and not looking in the least nervous.

Unlike me.

"Well?" the hearing officer said impatiently. "You asked to make a statement."

"Yeah," Kaelyn said, in a speculative tone of voice I didn't much like. "I just thought the panel should be aware that Asha and her friends were probably planning this from the very beginning."

My mother inhaled sharply next to me, and I heard a brief burst of mumbles from the audience. The photographer's flash went off and I hoped he hadn't been taking a picture of me. I was livid.

"I knew they were responsible for this Latte Rebellion stuff ever since the Inter-Club Council pool party last summer," Kaelyn continued. I seriously doubted that part, since we hadn't even come up with the idea for the Latte Rebellion at that point. I half-stood, not caring if I was interrupting.

"What, are you psychic?" I said, scornfully. "If you knew all along, then why didn't you just blab to Mr. Malone before all of this happened?"

Kaelyn turned around. "Oh, I thought I'd let you girls have your fun." She winked at me slyly.

"Ms. Vander Sar," the hearing officer snapped. "You realize you could be in serious trouble, if you're determined to have been withholding information that could have prevented these events."

He had her there. And though I knew for a fact she was bluffing about her knowledge of the Latte Rebellion, I'd be willing to bet she'd been hiding something about Roger, about his intentions to get back at us.

Kaelyn was quiet for a moment, thinking.

"Well, it was more like a good guess, sir," she said innocently. "I really didn't *know*, and I never thought all *this* would happen. But I do know that Asha and her friends were the ones who instigated the whole feud, picking a fight with Roger at that pool party."

"Oh my," said one of the more elderly school board members, and the audience threatened to become unruly again. I shot up out of my seat, ready to give Kaelyn what for, but before I could say anything, the ace that I had up my sleeve sort of . . . slipped out a little early.

"That's a *lie!*"

I whirled around at the shout. David Castro was standing a few rows back, glowering. "They never did anything like that."

"Excuse me, Mr.—?" The hearing officer looked at him questioningly.

"David Castro," he said, standing a little taller.

"Mr. Castro, if you don't sit down, I'll have to ask you to leave the room."

"I'm sorry, sir, but I have to agree with David," said another voice, this one from the seats next to the door. It was Shay Saintmarie, dressed in a neat bead-trimmed suit jacket. "I was standing near them at the pool party, and I saw what happened. Roger made a stupid comment to Asha, and they all got into an argument. It was all just a misunderstanding. There is no 'feud.'"

Kaelyn whirled around and shot her an incredulous look.

"Yeah," David continued, though he hadn't even been there at the ICC pool party. I had to love him for leaping to our defense, though. It was the moment I'd been looking forward to the whole agonizing morning—the time when I actually got to tell my side of the story, and got the audience to put in their two cents, too. The room erupted in noise this time, and it took the hearing officer several minutes to quiet things down.

The panel couldn't ignore that, even if they tried.

"Is this true, Asha?" my mother asked, quietly. "About the argument?" I hadn't told my parents that part. I hadn't thought it mattered, but apparently now it was at the heart of everything.

"Mom, he called me a towel-head." The words tasted bitter in my mouth. "Carey threw iced coffee at him. We all got into an argument. Then he took off. It was stupid."

"That *boy* is stupid, if he thinks it's acceptable to call people offensive names," Mom said flatly. Suddenly I realized that the room was silent and everyone was listening to our conversation.

"Excuse me," the hearing officer barked into the sudden quiet. "I find all this very touching, but I'm not sure why it's relevant to whether Ms. Jamison should be expelled."

"Because she wasn't responsible for the fights at school, or the explosions," David said, frustrated.

"But we've clearly established that she not only founded the organization, she continued to be involved, even against school rules."

"Maybe Asha should get the chance to explain for herself," Shay suggested. In the ensuing chaos of clapping and voices, I heard Miranda let out a whoop of agreement.

"Now, I'm still the one in charge of the proceedings here," the hearing officer said hoarsely, above the din. Then it seemed like the whole audience was standing up, looking at me expectantly and shouting for me to tell my story. The school board members were shaking their heads, and the hearing officer looked ready to kill somebody. This was probably his worst nightmare.

It really *was* like a teen movie.

"Well," I began, hesitantly. "Like Shay said... it all started with the pool party."

———

The hearing officer declared another recess while the board took a break to discuss their final recommendations, but as I scuttled down the back hall to the least crowded bathroom, I was feeling surprisingly good. Not having to keep my role in the Rebellion a secret anymore... I felt like I'd been lugging around one of Nani's giant, hard-plastic India suitcases crammed full of gifts for every relative under the sun, and I'd finally been given leave to let it roll down the hill without me.

As I re-emerged into the momentarily empty back hallway, someone stepped in front of me and I stopped short.

It was Roger Yee.

"Who let *you* in here?" I said, and I'm not afraid to admit I was outraged. I drew myself up to my full height, which was still a few good inches shorter than Roger, and glared up at him and his stupid floppy hair. "Back for more punishment?"

"Yeah, whatever. You're the one who wanted an open hearing." He sneered at me but didn't meet my eyes. "You know, you have some serious ego issues. I have a follow-up appointment with the school board. I didn't come here to have a fight with you."

"Right, because last I heard, you eschew violence of

any kind. You're a veritable Mahatma Gandhi." I paused, then stepped backwards. "Oh, no, wait—that's right. You'd never be a Gandhi, because he's one of those towel-heads."

For a second I was afraid he *would* hit me, but then I asked myself if it really mattered. It was all over anyway. Just let him. I grinned mercilessly.

"Touché," he said, spreading his hands wide. "Jesus. Are you ever going to let that go?"

"Are you ever going to stop saying stupid shit?"

He sighed. "Maybe one day," he said, a little wryly. There was a long, awkward pause, during which I tried to figure out how to get the hell out of this excruciating conversation. I was amazed nobody had walked by yet.

"I have to say, what I can't figure out is why you guys didn't just join the damn Asian American Club," he finally said.

Not him, too. "You're the one who said I was 'barely Asian,'" I pointed out. "That didn't exactly make me *want* to join."

"I *know* you're Asian," Roger said, shifting agitatedly from foot to foot. He looked as uncomfortable as I felt. "Don't you want to, you know, represent?"

"Represent?" I echoed, incredulously. "Roger, tell me, what do I represent? Do you want me to choose a side? Is the Asian part of me somehow *better* than the other part?"

Roger goggled at me and opened his mouth, but I didn't let him interrupt me. "Let me tell you, I'm definitely not Indian enough to fit in with my Indian family. And I don't exactly fit in the mainstream either, now do I? So what am I supposed to represent? Who am I obligated to represent *to*? Not you, that's for sure." It seemed like my words were inadequate to what I was feeling. "I'm way more than just my genes, or my family, even. When is that ever the whole story? Can't you just let me be who I am without having to put a label on it?"

I remembered Carey telling him, *I don't call* you *Fu Manchu*. And I didn't know what else I could say to him.

So I walked away, back to the hearing room, leaving him standing there confused and scowling.

"…and here I am, basically on probation until they tell me I'm off the hook," I said, carefully chopping an onion, my eyes watering from more than just the pungent juices.

Nani glanced up at me. I tried not to meet her scrutinizing gaze, and after a moment, she turned back to the heavy wooden cutting board where she was cleaving a raw chicken into stew-sized pieces. "Suspended expulsion," she said, as if testing the sound of the words in her mouth. "So you could still be expelled, even after all this."

I sighed. This was the last thing I wanted to talk about. "Only if I violate school rules again. Which I'm not going to do," I concluded in a resentful mutter, wondering why I had to rehash a story she'd already heard from my parents.

"I'm quite sure you won't," she said. Her tone was light, but I still felt defensive.

"And if I'm a *model citizen*," I said through gritted teeth, no longer even pretending to chop the onion, "they'll strike the expulsion hearing from my record."

"Asha," Nani said, putting the chicken down and washing her hands at the sink. I cringed a little internally, waiting for whatever disappointed lecture was surely coming. Finally, she turned toward me and leaned back against the counter, tiredly, the lines around her dark-brown eyes seeming even more pronounced than usual. "*Beti*, listen to me. Nobody expects you to be perfect. Do you understand?" She smiled a little sadly. "I know it can be difficult to live up to what others expect of you. But remember that it's not always others' expectations that are the issue."

I wiped an oniony tear from my cheek and sighed. "That's the thing. *Nothing* turned out the way I expected."

"In some good ways too, though, am I right?" She moved closer and enfolded me in a soft hug. I hugged her back, smelling dish soap and spices. "That's always life. Don't be so hard on yourself."

"Yeah, that's Mom and Dad's job," I said sardonically, moving back to my station at the cutting board.

"*Whsht*—be respectful!" she said, but I could see that she was hiding a smile.

And I felt a little better. Even though I still couldn't cook for crap—I hadn't even managed to chop a whole onion—and even though I was almost-but-not-quite-expelled.

———

A few weeks after my probationary return to school, things had finally calmed down; people were done gawking at me, and everything went more or less back to the usual routine.

I was still technically grounded, but my parents had hardly criticized me in days. I was allowed to study with Miranda as long as we stayed in the kitchen where we could be under surveillance. I felt like life was almost back to normal—as long as I went into denial about everything that had happened over the past couple of months, and as long as I didn't think too hard about the fact that Carey wasn't a regular part of our study group anymore. We still ate together at school most of the time, but after her testimony at the hearing, I just wasn't ready to have things go back to the way they were. She'd done what she thought she had to do, but I won't lie—I was angry and hurt. And she knew it, and there was nothing more to say.

Then something happened that changed my life yet again.

It was a Friday. I was exhausted from a week of AP testing in English, Physics, and Calculus, and I pulled into the driveway with a huge sigh, almost looking forward to a weekend of being grounded because I'd get to stay inside and sleep. But the minute I slammed the car door shut, my mom came running out of the house, a barely suppressed smile on her face.

I was immediately filled with trepidation and had to force myself to be optimistic. I hadn't broken any regulations lately, so the school couldn't have called, could they?

If they did, it had to be something else, like maybe they'd miraculously decided to call off my suspended expulsion early. Or maybe Mom got that classroom materials grant she was all excited about. I tried to brace myself, but I wasn't prepared for her to suddenly grab me in a tight hug.

"What's this all about?" I gingerly hugged her back, then pulled away and made for the front door.

"There's...mail for you on the kitchen table," she said, a note of excitement in her voice.

"From where?" I threw my backpack down in the front hall and went into the kitchen, my stomach fluttering nervously.

"Just look," she said, following behind me. I shuffled through the pile of mail on the table. There was...a fat envelope. Not the junk mail kind, but the kind that meant you'd definitely gotten into a college. It was addressed to me.

From Robbins College.

I ripped it open, not caring that I destroyed the envelope in the process, and pulled out the cover letter. My mom leaned over my shoulder to read it for herself, too impatient to wait for me to tell her what it said.

Dear Ms. Jamison,

We have reviewed your letter of appeal thoroughly. Your unusual circumstances were intriguing, and it is clear that you have given careful consideration to your academic future and why it should include attendance here at Robbins College. We have also taken into account your present status on the waiting list.

Although we are unable to offer you a place for the fall semester, it is with great pleasure that we extend to you an offer of admission to Ellis Robbins College, School of Social Welfare, for the spring semester. We hope that you will want to join one of the most vibrant and stimulating intellectual communities in the world.

Congratulations!

Christopher Blake
Office of Admissions
Ellis Robbins College

As I read these words from the Office of Admissions, I experienced a mixture of emotions. At first, elation was all I felt—I'd gotten in. I'd gotten in! This big fat envelope was most definitely full of admission information, dormitory request forms, and all the other paperwork that would make it official that I was a Robbins student.

But after a minute, my spirits came back down to earth. In fact, they sank slightly below the earth's crust, to be specific about it. I wasn't admitted for fall after all. They were saying yes—but it was a deferred admission, for the spring semester.

My mother sighed and put a gentle hand on my shoulder, and I wondered if she was as disappointed as I was. I hadn't exactly *failed* her, but I sure hadn't lived up to my parents' original expectations. Or mine. And there was nothing more I could do about it. This was the best I'd been able to manage, and it still wasn't good enough.

What hurt even more than that, though, what made me want to hide in my room forever in abject humiliation, was the thought of telling Miranda and Carey that I wouldn't be moving out with them after all. After everything that had happened, after all the work I'd done to make up for getting distracted and slacking off, I was still going to be left here by myself—no Miranda, no Carey. And no Thad, either.

———

The weird thing was, even though this wasn't the ideal situation—getting into my dream school, but having to wait a semester to go—my parents ultimately seemed to be relieved. They released me from my punishment a week early, in honor of my eighteenth birthday on May 13th, and right after that they encouraged me to invite a few friends over to have pizza and watch movies. I didn't miss the gesture—they'd forgiven me for the sit-in incident and the near-expulsion, even if they weren't saying it explicitly, and even though they still wanted to keep an eye on me.

Part of their reason for relenting was the long heart-to-heart I'd had with them when we went out to dinner at the Thai Palace to celebrate my Robbins acceptance. They'd reacted to the situation more positively than I'd expected, telling me that in the long run, one semester wouldn't matter.

"Sometimes the right school is worth the wait," my mom said, smiling as she filled my plate with spicy green papaya salad.

I poked the papaya strips with my fork. "Yeah, but I should have been able to get in without writing the appeal."

"There's no point in dwelling on that now. You should think of this as an opportunity rather than a setback," my dad insisted, between mouthfuls of peanut-crunchy pad thai. "You can get some real work experience, and by the time you get settled in at Robbins, you'll be much more mature and focused than all those other students who went in straight out of high school."

My dad had had to enter college late himself, working tough hours at the same time that he was taking classes for his A.A. degree. He'd been the first in his family to even *go* to college. So I tried not to be offended by the implication: that I wasn't mature enough right now; that I'd wasted time on pointless moneymaking schemes when I could have been valedictorian and working at some mindnumbing grunt job for minimum wage and "life experience." Like Carey, who was Mother Teresa as far as my dad was concerned, even after everything that had happened.

But in the end, I felt like I *had* matured, like I'd learned something about myself at least. It was hard to explain that to my parents, because they couldn't get past the fact that I'd kept it all a secret from them. And maybe I could have been honest about the college letters, if nothing else…

But there was no sense in "brooding," as my mother referred to it. And she was right in this case. The whole saga was over, as my parents reminded me a few nights later when I asked them if I could go out to meet Thad sometime.

"That is," I said meekly, "if it's okay with you guys. If my fun allotment for the rest of the school year has been severely curtailed, I'd understand."

My dad turned down the TV and both of them looked at me with that weird, unique parental mixture of pride and sympathy. Since I wasn't letting the Rebellion rule my life anymore, they said, they had no reason not to trust me to make the right decisions.

I'd faced the consequences, and I'd been punished enough.

"Asha, we want you to know you can always talk to us if things in your life are getting out of hand, or if you need help figuring things out." My dad's voice was uncharacteristically gentle. "There's no need to suffer in silence. We're here to help."

"I know, Dad," I said, a little choked up.

"So go call your friend," he said. "Just make sure I get to meet him before you decide to get too serious."

Paradoxically, the minute they said I would always have them to fall back on, I realized this: I wouldn't always be able to—or even want to—rely on them to bail me out of every catastrophe. And they knew that, and it was okay. If I could handle the Latte Rebellion on my own, I could handle whatever came next. It's just the way life is.

I did have one more big argument with my parents, though, when I told them that I still wanted to use my share of the T-shirt earnings to take a trip to London this summer. They almost had a fit around the breakfast table. It was like they'd forgotten about the monetary side of the Latte Rebellion (to be honest, I had too, for a while), and so my mom was arguing that I should give the money to a worthy cause like the tutoring organization I used to work for, and my dad was saying I should invest it in an IRA or put it in the bank for college.

"It's never too early to save for retirement," he said, between bites of English muffin. "Believe me, I know. If I'd started putting money away when I was your age—"

I dropped my cereal spoon into my empty bowl with a loud clink.

"I'm eighteen," I said pointedly, in the silence that followed. "And it's not like I'm blowing the money I saved up from my job last summer. This isn't going to affect my plans for college. It might," I said to my dad, "even make me a little more 'mature and focused' than I would be otherwise."

"I frankly just don't know if you're ready for something like that," my mom said, tilting her head and looking at me with a cool, assessing stare.

We went back and forth a little bit, my dad protesting that I didn't know what I was getting into, yet again, and me pointing out that European kids did this kind of thing all the time, spending years backpacking through the mountains before going to college, which may have been a teensy exaggeration; but ultimately, his protests were half-hearted. My mom sat quietly for the rest of the debate, but I could tell she still had reservations, too. She was just better at not saying anything.

At one point, though, she asked me, "Carey's still going with you, right?"

That stopped me short. If I admitted the truth to myself, I realized I didn't know the answer to that question. Given everything that had happened over the past school year, Carey probably wouldn't want to go anymore; but I couldn't picture the trip without her. I gave my mom a noncommittal answer, but I knew that I needed to talk to Carey. I just couldn't seem to work up the courage to ask her about it.

———

A week and a half after I stopped being grounded—and only a few weeks before graduation—I finally saw Thad again. I'd only spoken to him once since I'd ceased being monitored by the Powers That Be. I hadn't even said much about the hearing; just the outcome, though I made sure to tell him that my letter of appeal to Robbins had been successful. But because we hadn't seen each other since the rally, I'd started having this horrible sinking feeling about ever getting to see him again. Such a promising meeting of the minds, dashed before it ever had the possibility to grow into something more.

Then, one Saturday morning he called me while I was still sitting in my PJs on the couch, lazily watching reruns of some insipid 1950s sitcom with a perfect Barbie wife and 2.5 clean-cut kids. The late-May sun was shining in, making me warm and sleepy. I heard my cell phone ring distantly from where I'd left it somewhere in the kitchen.

After a moment, my mom walked in and said, "It's Thad." She smiled and handed me the still-ringing phone. I quickly downed a swig of orange juice to try to clear the cobwebs out of my brain. I couldn't help feeling excitement in the pit of my stomach.

"Hey," he said when I picked up, rushing back to my room for some privacy. Was that eagerness in his voice, or was it just wishful thinking?

"So what's up?" I toyed with a still-unbrushed tangle of hair, glad he couldn't see me in my ratty shorts and Powerpuff Girls T-shirt.

"Sort of depends on whether you're ungrounded yet."

"I'm ungrounded," I said, flushing with embarrassment but grinning at the same time. "Ungrounded, unsuspended, and not-expelled."

"Good," he said. I could hear the smile in his voice. "The thing is, I'm going to see a speaker at U-NorCal this afternoon and I was wondering if you wanted to grab coffee afterwards. Know anywhere good in your neck of the woods?"

"Sure!" I winced at my chipper tone of voice and tried for nonchalant. "Yeah, that sounds great."

We settled on four o'clock at Mocha Loco. I didn't really want to go there—I wasn't sure I was quite ready yet to face Leonard, in case he wanted to talk about the Rebellion—but it was the closest place to campus. When I pulled up and parked my car across the street, I could see Thad sitting at one of the outside tables in the shade under the awning, his shock of black hair as out-of-control as I remembered it. A quick thrill sent goose bumps up my arms. I couldn't suppress a wave of relief at seeing him actually there, smiling as I approached.

"Hey, how was the lecture?" I walked up to his table and stood in front of him, shifting a little from foot to foot. This was the first time we'd seen each other in person since the rally.

"Great," he said, beaming. He got up and pulled me into a hug, and my entire body buzzed with the pleasure of actually touching him, in public, like it was meant to be after all. I put my arms around him, a little belatedly, and realized I'd trapped him into a longer hug than was probably normal. Reluctantly—and a little sheepishly—I let him go. He took a step back, but he was still smiling.

"Yeah, the lecture was pretty good. Not as much fun as the Latte Rebellion rally, though," he added with a mischievous wink. I rolled my eyes. "Have a seat—want me to grab you a coffee or something?"

"Sure." I sat gingerly in the plastic patio chair, which was hot from soaking in sunlight, my hands fidgeting nervously in my lap.

"Let me guess—a latte?"

I looked up at him sharply, then noticed the cheerful crinkle at the corners of his eyes and realized he probably didn't mean anything by it. It wasn't *his* fault I was sick of the whole thing.

"Actually, an iced tea would be great," I said. "I'm kind of over the latte thing." He raised his eyebrows, but went inside the crowded café to order, and I tried to relax enough that I wouldn't sound like an idiot when he got back. I was just reapplying my lip shimmer when a familiar voice said, "Hey, Asha."

I looked up. It was Carey; she was just coming out of Mocha Loco. I hadn't seen her outside of school for a week at least, and we'd only had one quick phone conversation about physics homework.

"Hi," I said, a little uncomfortably. I wiped a sudden prickling of sweat off the back of my neck. "Um ... how'd you do on the lab?"

"I did okay," she said, which probably meant she got an A-minus.

"Here to visit Leonard?" I'm happy to say I asked this without a trace of sarcasm.

"Yup, I was taking a study break," she said, not looking directly at me but instead making a show of cleaning her sunglasses. "What about you?"

"Meeting Thad," I said, a little proudly. "He's in town for a lecture on campus."

"Oh, was that him walking in? Finally, I get to see this alleged college man." We grinned at each other, and for a second it was like things were okay again. Then I had to go and ruin it with my big mouth.

"So I wanted to ask you," I started, nervously. "I'm

thinking that July might be a good time to go to London."
I could hardly breathe, waiting to hear her response.

"Yeah," she said, sounding reluctant, and then it was like I knew what she was going to say. "You know, about this summer...I'm not sure I'm going to be able to take any time off. I agreed to take full-time hours at Book Planet. I want to be able to afford a car, even if it's a crappy one, before I leave for Stanford. Then I can come home on weekends and help my parents out."

I just looked at her, feeling the bottom drop out of the plans we'd worked so hard for. I wasn't exactly surprised, but I'd still been hoping for...something.

She turned her head and stared out at the traffic on Oak Street for a minute, then turned back toward me and met my gaze with a sad little smile that felt like an ending. "I'm sorry, Asha. I know we had this vacation idea, but...things change."

Things change. It was like everything in my life was summed up by that one simple statement. The only thing that hadn't really changed was that both of us were eventually going to end up in the Bay Area after all, but I knew even *that* would be different than what I'd expected. Things weren't the same between us anymore.

"Well, I'll send you a postcard," I said. "I'm still going to go."

"Good for you," she said, and then there was a long and painful silence. "Well, I'd better get moving. I have to baby-sit my brothers tonight. Talk to you at school on

Monday?" I couldn't help noticing it was a question rather than an assumption.

"Sure," I said. I didn't want us to ignore each other for the rest of the year.

When Thad came back with my iced tea and his iced coffee, I had my head resting in one hand, staring blankly at the graffiti-carved tree in the sidewalk in front of our table.

"So, you're over the latte thing, huh?" he asked, startling me out of my thoughts.

"Oh," I said. "Yeah. I guess I am, kind of." I tried to keep the angst from showing on my face, but failed miserably—emphasis on the miserable.

"What's up?" He looked at me searchingly. "Was that a friend of yours, just now? Did something happen?"

"Um..." I just sat there for a minute with the words frozen in my mouth. I had no idea what to say, where to start. "That was Carey," I finally began, lamely. "We were best friends." It just slipped out that way, in past tense, but the second I said it I realized that it was true, and that I'd known it for a long time now. We were still friends but we weren't close—not like we'd been before.

Thad just looked at me steadily with those blue eyes, then took hold of my hand in a firm, warm grip. And then, unbelievably, everything spilled out. Like a floodgate that had burst open, I was telling him the whole story, from that very first afternoon last summer when Carey and I thought of the Latte Rebellion, to the fear I felt when violence broke out at the school sit-in, to the latest blow—

Carey not wanting to go to London anymore. I felt like I wanted to cry, but I clenched my jaw instead. The whole time, Thad just listened sympathetically, nodding every now and then, or asking a question, like how we got the idea for the manifesto or when we first realized the Rebellion was catching on as a real movement. He didn't seem shocked, but he was definitely interested.

"I have to admit," he said, smiling, "I sort of knew from the beginning that you were involved in some way."

"Well, I was there at the rally and everything," I pointed out. "Of course I was involved."

"I know, but there was something about the way you talked about the Rebellion ... I could tell it meant something to you. I could tell you had a personal investment. I didn't know you were *the* Agent Alpha, though," he said teasingly. "I should make you autograph my term paper."

"I won't! But you can acknowledge me as a primary source." I smiled weakly. He'd suspected all this time but hadn't said anything. He'd waited for me to tell him myself. I wasn't sure what that meant.

"So what are you going to do now?" he asked, still holding my hand lightly in the middle of the table. His thumb stroked mine gently for a moment and I couldn't help a slight shiver. "Do you have any idea what you want to do in London?"

"I'm not really sure, to tell you the truth." I sighed. "Since Carey's not going. I mean, it was supposed to be our big blowout before college starts. I feel a little aimless ... I have this whole semester to kill after I get back, too, and I'll have to look for a job. And I still don't know what I want to major in. I told them Sociology and Public Policy, but I'm not really sure..." I gave him a half-shrug and an embarrassed smile.

"I know the feeling," Thad said. "My work-study job is only good for this year. I'm hoping to find a professor in Econ or Public Health who needs a research assistant. Or a slave."

"I'm sure any professor would be glad to have you as an assistant," I said, cementing my dork status for eternity, if it had ever been in doubt.

"Thanks." He grinned at me and squeezed my hand. Then he sobered. "I'm just extra stressed because I'm also trying to get a foot in the door at that clinic that Greg and I want to work with and maybe model our ideas after."

Then his face brightened. "Hey, maybe you can drop by there while you're in London. It would help if we could send someone to talk to them personally, and I know neither of us will be able to get to England until at least next summer, even if we get a grant."

"Mm-hm," I said hesitantly. Something was taking nebulous form in the back of my head, something I didn't quite understand yet. But Thad's idea of sending me to the community clinic... it had just planted the seed of an idea in my mind, an idea that was melding and hybridizing with everything that had happened over the past year.

"You can be, like, our representative," he wheedled, folding his hands together mock-pleadingly. "Tell you what; I'll buy you another iced tea."

"I can't say no to you," I said finally—a little flirtatiously, too, I might add, but it was starting to feel more natural. I relaxed back into the chair and let the sun's warmth soak into me. "I mean, look at that face."

"This face?" He gestured at himself. "This totally mixed-up face? I look like a Japanese gangster crossed with an English soccer hooligan and a Dutch...something. I'm Japanetherlish." He looked at me mournfully. "American as apple pie, right?"

"Well, hey, I'm..." I thought about it for a second, then laughed. "I'm Mexindirish."

"Or Irindican," he said, after a pause.

"Either way you slice it, that's one weird pie," I said.

He grinned at me and grabbed my hand again. "Apple pie is overrated."

———

Monday, June 15

Hayley McGill, Executive Director
Whitechapel Community Health Centre
12-16 Asquith Lane
London E1 1BU
United Kingdom

Dear Ms. McGill,

My name is Asha S. Jamison and I will be a student at Ellis Robbins College of Social Welfare beginning in January, intending to double major in Ethnic Studies and Public Policy with an emphasis on Social Justice. I am also a colleague of Thad Sakai and Greg Androvich, students at UC Berkeley, with whom you have been in contact regarding the practicalities of establishing and funding community clinics.

Later this summer I will be traveling to London and, at the request of Mr. Sakai, would like to meet with you in person to obtain valuable suggestions for starting his first clinic in rural Central California, and perhaps also discuss opportunities for a mutually beneficial partnership.

I would also like to herewith apply for your advertised student internship. It would be of immense value to me to work with your clinic, and I can offer excellent interpersonal skills as well as typing and organizational abilities. I am also extremely enthusiastic about working with different ethnic groups in the community, as I am of mixed ethnicity myself. It would be an honor to help you in your mission of educating the public about their health.

Thank you for your time.

Regards,
Asha S. Jamison

Epilogue

The July sun is shining warmly down as I walk across Westminster Bridge, so I take off my sweater and let my hair hang loosely down my back, feeling the welcome heat soak into my bare arms. Traffic roars past to my left, everything from big black cabs to ridiculously tiny minis. I stop halfway across and stare around me. The Houses of Parliament and Big Ben are golden Victorian monoliths just ahead; the Thames river winds sluggishly away below; and everywhere there are crowds of people. A passing car belches out a greasy smell, but it doesn't bother me. The city itself is vibrant and alive.

The fourteen days I've spent walking around London have been some of the most incredible of my life. Scary (even though my mom's cousin helped me find a spare room in a college dorm), but more exciting than the rest of my life put together. I've ordered pints of cider in the nearby pub with a Brazilian girl who's staying in the room next door to me; I've spent hours with the treasures in the British Museum; I've walked aimlessly for blocks, from Bloomsbury Square to Trafalgar Square and everywhere in between, just watching the melting pot of people.

And, in a few short days, I'll be part of that melting pot. I start my internship on Monday at the Whitechapel Community Health Centre. I'll mostly be filing and typing letters and helping set up the conference room for seminars, but it feels like I'm going to be part of something important, like I'm going to be helping people in a way that's so much more tangible and long-lasting than clubs or rallies or T-shirts. And I'll get to do some serious research for Thad.

Speaking of Thad, he was practically bouncing up and down when we kissed goodbye before I left (and I was, too, but possibly for different reasons)—he's really looking forward to what I'll be able to tell them about the clinic. He's already planning a cross-campus independent study with Greg and me for the spring semester, when I'm at Robbins. I'll be living in North Berkeley; Thad still lives with Greg and another guy a handful of blocks south of the Berkeley campus. Close enough that I can realistically hope for a repeat of that kiss.

It all seems far away now, though. I feel like my life is taking place in the middle of a wide-open road, with high school and the Latte Rebellion far off in one direction, out of sight, and college and my future hidden off in the other direction.

I start walking back toward the Tube station so I can ride the subway back to the dorm. My small but cozy room is on the third floor, overlooking a tree-lined square full of rosebushes and wrought-iron benches. I feel lucky every time I look out the window.

Overheated, I buy an iced coffee from a cluttered and musty convenience store before taking a long stairway and an even longer escalator into the depths of the station. Waiting for the same Northern Line train as me, standing near the edge of the platform, is a young woman who looks about my age—maybe a little older. She's playing the guitar and singing in a raspy but heartfelt voice.

She reminds me a little of Miranda, in a way—she seems like a free spirit, someone who doesn't worry about how other people perceive her. She has skin almost the exact color of mine, only with more of an olive tint, and reddish-brown dreadlocks bound into a blue kerchief.

The train pulls up with an earsplitting whistle of brakes and a gust of warm wind. I follow the guitar player onto the train car. She sits in an open seat near the door, still playing soft chords. I sit next to her. Then, on a totally crazy impulse, I take the latte I just bought and hold it up in a friendly mock salute.

She looks up at me with startlingly green eyes, smiles, and hands me a photocopied flyer with a coffeehouse name and address.

Her band's name is Beyond House Blend. *Every Friday Night!* the flyer proclaims.

"I'm there," I say. And I mean it.

Acknowledgements

Without the input, help, and moral support of countless friends, family, and colleagues, *The Latte Rebellion* would never have come to be and would most likely still be a half-finished NaNoWriMo project drifting in the ether of my laptop's memory.

Thanks, Mom, for teaching me to read voraciously and for encouraging me to write. Thanks to Mike Wiley and Steven Horn at IGN.com for giving me the opportunity to make writing a part of my day job—and planting the seeds of a future career. Thank you to the MFA program at Mills College for giving a struggling visual artist a fancy degree in creative writing.

Thank you to National Novel Writing Month for providing the excuse—er, opportunity—to take a snippet of an idea and turn it into a full-fledged story, and thank you to Jeffrey Callison and the folks at Capital Public Radio's Insight for allowing me to read a passage of my embarrassingly horrible first draft on NPR.

Endless thanks to the inspiring (and brutally honest) members, past and present, of my critique group, WritingYA: Erin Blomstrand, Yat-Yee Chong, Tanita Davis, Kelly Herold, Meeta Kaur, Anne Levy, Jaime Lin-Yu, Katina Bishop, Jennifer March Soloway, JoNelle Toriseva, Mary Whitsell, and Sarah Zacharias. You all rock. Special thanks to Tanita Davis for pie, lemon curd, Finding Wonderland, dealing with my random freakouts, and being willing to read about eighty million different drafts of this novel without complaining.

Thanks to the far-flung yet closely connected kidlit blogging community—there are too many of you to name, but without your support buzzing through the intertubes, my day-to-day writing life wouldn't have been the same.

Thanks to Sheela Kinhal Shah for answering questions about Diwali, and Russell Irwin for providing insider info from a high school administrator's perspective. Thank you to my teen test audience Molly Souza, and to the myriad of friends and family who read my novel at different steps along the way—Rob, Mom, Don, Beth, Shin Yu, Cindy, Jay, Ross, Mike, and anyone else I might've forgotten (sorry, the Rebellion ate my brain cells).

Thanks to Lee Bailey for making me look like a normal human being in that beautiful, beautiful author photo.

Epic thanks to my editor, Brian Farrey, for insight, advice, and putting up with my occasional pestering; Lisa Novak, who created the incredible cover design; Sandy Sullivan, for her editorial eagle eyes; and everyone else at Flux for giving *The Latte Rebellion* a chance to see the light of day.

Thanks to my cats, Roxie and Zelda, for being awesome writing companions. Thanks to Mom, Dad, Gramp, Grandma, Dadi, and Dada for creating a complete ethnic mutt (i.e., me) and therefore making the idea for *The Latte Rebellion* possible in the first place. And thanks to Rob—fellow latte, partner in crime—for love every step of the way and giving me the time and space to make this a reality.

Lee R. Bailey

About the Author

Sarah Jamila Stevenson is a writer, artist, graphic designer, introvert, closet geek, enthusiastic eater, struggling blogger, lapsed piano player, household-chore ignorer, and occasional world traveler. Her previous lives include spelling bee nerd, suburban Southern California teenager, Berkeley art student, underappreciated temp, and humor columnist for a video game website. Throughout said lives, she has acquired numerous skills of questionable usefulness, like intaglio printmaking and the Welsh language. She lives in Northern California with her husband, who is also an artist, and two cats with astounding sleep-inducing powers. Visit her online at www.SarahJamilaStevenson.com.